Taxes, Death & Trouble

Taxes, Death & Trouble

An Audrey Wilson Mystery

C. M. Miller

Writers Club Press
San Jose New York Lincoln Shanghai

Taxes, Death & Trouble
An Audrey Wilson Mystery

Writers Club Press
an imprint of iUniverse.com, Inc.

For information address:
iUniverse.com, Inc.
5220 S 16th, Ste. 200
Lincoln, NE 68512
www.iuniverse.com

ISBN: 0-595-13684-2

Printed in the United States of America

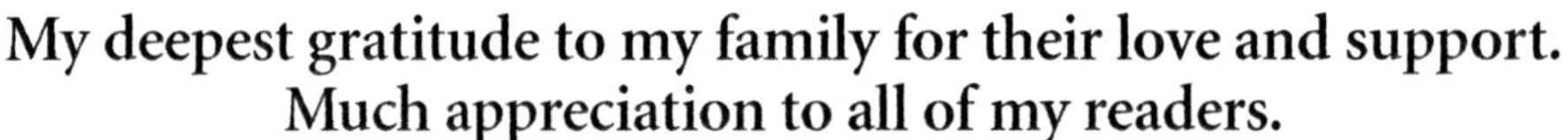

My deepest gratitude to my family for their love and support.
Much appreciation to all of my readers.

To Mommy. You continue to inspire.

Acknowledgements

To my editors, Karen White-Owens and Barbara Vinegar for reading between the lines. Donnetta Armstrong, Michelle Willis and Jan Toler. To Prentice, my loving husband. A little faith goes a long way.

I am grateful to everyone who reads this book and hope it brings you pleasure.

Prologue

Sunshine streamed through the classroom window, warmed Jackie Daniels' face, then danced onto the vacant desks. The students had been gone for a while but the room still held their spirits. Her hand quivered as she graded yesterday's homework assignments. She tried to concentrate on the task at hand. But it was hard. Everything distracted her.

She repositioned the pencil in her fingers. The wood, once smooth and yellow, now ugly and ragged from her teeth clamping down on it. She drummed it on the desk, then cursed in irritation at the marks she'd left behind.

Jackie kept telling herself to ignore the clock. The spindly hands on the apparatus clapped out every second, making it difficult to refrain from looking up with each beat. Where was her four o'clock appointment? It was quarter past and her nerves frayed as the seconds unwound.

What an idiot she had been for wanting to meet with someone who had every reason to hate her. It seemed stupid now, but recent events compelled her to take some kind of action. Now it seemed her rush to resolve a bad situation might have made things worse.

She had planned the meeting, hoping to make the transition as easy as possible. Thinking back on the telephone conversation, she should have listened to her first mind and not pursued this. She'd held the phone while the party on the other end berated her for calling. Jackie was patient, understanding and determined. Using every weapon in her socialite training, towards the end of the exchange Jackie felt they had reached a form of détente. They agreed to meet at four o'clock the next day.

By 4:30 it seemed apparent that the meeting would not take place. Her disappointment was peppered with relief that she wouldn't have to deal with this now. The pressure in her chest subsided as she started packing up her things. Remembering it was the Thursday before Easter, she began to look forward to the extended weekend.

The more she thought about her plan, the crazier it seemed. She'd been foolish to try bringing diplomacy to this volatile situation. She still hadn't told her boss what she was attempting. He would not be pleased.

She turned off the lights and closed her classroom door. The doors to the other rooms were closed. Their transoms showed no sign of light from within. She descended the stairs and entered the executive administrator's area. Her heels tapped on the polished wood floors leading to James Franklin's office.

The light was on and there were papers on his desk. The battered leather briefcase sat on the mahogany colored chair where he'd tossed it that morning. She breathed in the fragrance of his cologne and smiled. Thinking of his gentle nature, the tension she'd felt earlier melted away. No matter how bad things seemed, he would make everything all right. Suddenly craving the reassurance her mentor would give, she decided to look for him.

Not finding him in any of the classrooms or study halls, Jackie headed downstairs to the cafeteria. Fluorescent light flooded the dark hallway when she opened the heavy door leading into the dining area. The sleek tile floor and brilliant lighting caused her to blink. Potpourri scented cleaning fluid blended with the smell of grease lingering from the noon meal. She scanned the room. It was void of people. Its polished floors shown like glass. Chairs were turned upside down on long folding tables, their legs pointed upwards in the pose of dead insects.

Her shoulders fell dejectedly. Where could he be? The only place left to check was the supply room. She turned on the light in the outer room and saw no one. To her right was the small utility closet where the cleaning supplies were kept. The old knob jingled when she put her hand around it and turned. The rapid tapping of approaching footsteps made her heart lighten. She turned toward the sound.

"I've been looking all over for...what are you doing here?"

Chapter One

Audrey heard the ruckus the moment she drove up. As she approached the entrance to the animal shelter, the barking intensified. It was a gloriously sunny Thursday afternoon. D-Day, a day of celebration. The day her divorce was final. She was here to reward herself with a new mate. She'd already tried living with dogs. The seven years of marriage to one and prior to that, eighteen months betrothed to another. Bow Wow. Life sure can be Ruff. This time she'd try it with a cat.

She pulled open the door and nearly fainted from the stench of urine, feces, and ammonia.

"Good morning." A shriveled, poodle faced woman behind a counter yapped, pushing a clipboard in her direction.

"Have you ever visited us before?"

"No, I haven't."

"Please fill out the parent section of the application. If you find an animal that you're interested in adopting, complete the bottom portion of the card. We'll need a description and the number from the front of the cage. Afterwards, bring this back to me."

Audrey looked at the form and shook her head. Another example of our politically correct society gone amuck. The 'Parent Section' of the sheet was a sort of personality questionnaire the potential owner completes expressing why he wanted a pet. She wondered if the animals had to fill out similar paperwork. It seemed only fair.

Audrey thanked the woman and followed her nose and her ears to the holding area. She stepped gingerly around a section being mopped by a uniformed worker. The back of the man's white jumpsuit had the letters D O C, department of corrections, stenciled in blue. He mopped the floor trying hard to make himself invisible to visitors of the facility.

Audrey looked at him and spoke which seemed to surprise him. To her he was just another man at work. The D O C was the only employment agency that gave some brothers steady work in this part of the country. He returned the greeting and continued pushing the dirty mop along the floor.

Audrey walked past row upon row of yelping, growling, and barking dogs. Occasionally, a particularly pleasant looking cur would catch her attention, but she had been fooled by that before. The decision had been made before she'd arrived; no more dogs.

The cat room was located in the rear of the building. By the time she reached them, the odor was so strong she contemplated leaving. Or heaving. Instead, she fished around in her handbag for a tissue and put it to her nose as a filter.

"Pretty stinky, huh?" An elderly couple was on their way out of the cat room. Audrey nodded her head, agreeing with the woman's comment, then continued on her quest for the perfect pet.

Like all of the other relationships in her life, she felt the results of her expedition today would be based on how accurately she'd outlined her request before putting it into the universe. Audrey had been very specific when she'd determined that she was going to do this. She wanted a cat with just the right personality.

Her sister Renita told her that she was putting way too much time into this. 'It's a cat for Christ sakes. You're not looking for the father of your children.'

Renita didn't like cats.

Most of the cats snoozed lazily, either bored or already resigned to a life of incarceration. As soon as Audrey saw the orange tabby with the white beard, standing on spindly legs away from the rest of the pack, she was drawn to him. She walked over and put her hand inside the holding pit. The cat glared at her like she resembled the person who had left him on the side of the road. He hissed and turned his head.

The other cats, realizing they had company, began to do the Lazarus bit, suddenly lively and vying for Audrey's attention. The orange tabby looked on with disdain. This cat had obviously not just fallen off the tuna wagon. He refused to fall into that old 'Save me great human' routine. This little guy had principles. She felt an immediate connection and quickly penciled his information onto the clipboard.

Twenty minutes later, Audrey loaded the cardboard pet carrier into the back seat of her car. The cat screamed all the way home.

Audrey parked in front of the section of renovated rowhouses that the realtor called brownstones. She collected her packages from the back seat, balancing them so that she could make it to the front door in one trip.

She noticed all of the mail jammed inside her box and decided she'd deal with that later. She unlocked the door and set the packages in the foyer. By this time, the cat had gone hoarse. Raspy delivery not withstanding, he still let Audrey know just how undone he was about being cooped up in the box. He was determined to give her a piece of his feline mind.

The Humane Society had given her a list of pet supplies that would make the transition easier for her new arrival. She took the packages to the kitchen. Ignoring the rest of the instruction sheet, Audrey gathered the pet carrier from the hallway and brought it to the kitchen. When she opened the lid the cat thanked her by digging its claws into her hand.

"You son of a bitch!"

The cat ran down the hall towards Audrey's bedroom. She ran her bleeding hand underneath a stream of cold tap water before applying the gel of a sliced aloe vera leaf to the abrasions. The relationship had not gotten off to a good start.

Audrey picked up the pamphlet she'd gotten from the Humane Society. **Bringing Your Pet Home.** *Have your pet's food dish waiting. A full tummy takes the jitters out of any uncomfortable situation.*

"Who writes this stuff?" Audrey wondered as she tossed the brochure onto the counter. She dug the plastic bowl from the bag of supplies. She filled the dish with beef liver and was nearly run down as the cat ran from the back room, pouncing on the dark slimy meat, practically inhaling it before looking up for more.

"There's certainly nothing wrong with your sense of smell is there?" the cat wound himself around Audrey's legs, crying loudly. Audrey filled the dish a second time. The cat ate more slowly this time. After he'd finished, he went to the door and started using it as a scratching post. He stopped, turned to her. His expression said, "Well? You gonna let me out of here or what?" Audrey opened the door to get the mail and the cat darted out. He sat on the stoop, looking out at the street.

"Oh, I see where we stand we stand with each other. I feed you and you just go catting around, doing what you want to do. Well you'd better be careful crossing the street is all I gotta say." She gathered the mail and took it inside.

The one constant since being out on her own was the growing mound of bills. Audrey had helped establish her ex-husband's law practice, running the office and taking care of all business transactions while he did his lawyer thing. When she decided to leave him, he refused to give her a dime. He didn't see the work she did as anything more than her performing her wifely duties. She took his butt to court.

She quickly depleted the money from the settlement she was awarded when she opened her own financial consulting business. She had dreams of a thriving business filled with savvy clients who gave her unrestrained license to chart their financial futures. Ha! The only clients she had been able to secure were small businesses and individuals who needed someone to prepare their taxes.

Not only was the overhead more than she had anticipated, the revenues were substantially less than she'd ever thought possible. This wasn't what she had envisioned at all. She knew that if she didn't develop a plan to get some clients who had real finances soon, she'd have to make a career change. She might end up working at Kroger's asking that age-old question, 'Paper or Plastic?'.

But she was grateful to have a steady income. She had a new client who had big aspirations as well. He was thinking real estate, stock market, online trading. So what if he was a janitor at Rosemont Academy? The important thing was, he had been consistent in his saving, and he had the right frame of mind in terms of building a future. She and Ed Dixon would be meeting at six o'clock that evening to go over his retirement plan and some property purchases that he anticipated making in the near future.

Rosemont Academy was the only private school that was predominately African American in the region. Its' alumnae included local as well as nationally known leaders in all disciplines. She would cut her entrepreneurial teeth on this client and build from there. Though the money he was paying Audrey at this time was nominal, once Ed made a go of his businesses, they would both be in the money.

Chapter Two

Ed Dixon could tell by the way the morning started that it was not going to be a good day. He cleaned up the mess left by the filthy kids as they prepared for their long weekend. The only good thing about this day was that it was almost over. He hated his job as a janitor at the Academy. The only way to get through the monotonous work was to let his mind travel to any place other than the school and his work there. If he remained in the present, he would surely lose his mind. His thoughts drifted to the small room he rented and the way the day began.

Before the alarm sounded, he bolted upright in the hot, full-sized bed. Looking down at the sheets that twisted snake-like around him, he realized that he had been dreaming. It was the same dream that awakened him most mornings. Why did it scare him so?

He used to find the dream pleasant; an innocent fantasy that made his empty bed a place of comfort. But when the dreams changed he began to feel an overwhelming sense of discomfort whenever he closed his eyes to sleep. He could never get back to sleep afterwards. The dream had come to him for months. He had gotten to the point were he thought nothing of them. But when the dynamics of the dream changed, he became worried.

It was one thing dreaming about having sex with someone you barely knew, but when you dreamt about killing them, it was a different matter. He began to consider going to one of those sleep clinics. But those places seemed like scams. Who knows what kinda shit one of those quacks could put into your water when you weren't aware? Next thing you know you got cancer. Or the clap.

The dreams always began the same way. He'd be in the corridor of the school doing his work, mopping, sweeping. But he didn't have on any clothes. Suddenly the door would open and Jackie Daniels would appear. She seemed to float towards him, her clothing, diaphanous and flowing. Her skin was smooth, the color of pecans. Those green eyes fixed on him, freezing him, forbidding him to move. She hovered near him; her ethereal presence gave off an eerie light. Ed was transfixed.

They caressed. She would push him onto the floor, mount him and they'd have sex. He'd awaken with the haunting feeling of her touch still lingering. Their hot tongues and bare skins welded together leaving a forbidden aftertaste that wouldn't go away.

The sudden sound of a door closing brought Ed back to the present. He hated his job. Hated the fact that he was cleaning up after these spoiled rich kids who had no respect for him or anything else. They were gone now, but he could still hear the echo of their laughter, their loud radios and the kind of hot fast talk that used to result in a youngster ending up with a mouthful of soap. If he had anything to say about it, those days would return. The days when a child knew his bounds and stayed within them.

But nobody asked his opinion, or cared that he had one. They didn't even know that he existed until they wanted something cleaned up or lifted or toted. He was just the high school janitor. Ignored. Invisible.

He sighed as he headed towards the basement to collect the cleaning materials. How on earth had he ended up doing a job that he hated at a school that would never admit children of his was beyond him. The children who attended Rosemont Academy were the products of well-to-do families. Many were the aftermath of too much drink or stakes planted to ensure an equitable division of an inheritance or divorce decree. Their parents had deposited them there as one drops coins into a fare box, leaving their future to the lackadaisical coachman.

Their heirs repaid them by roaming through life with little concern for anything. The boys were loud, disrespectful and brash. The girls were fast, dressed tacky and cheap. They wore heavy make-up and short, tight fitting skirts. Dixon would watch them between classes, rubbing their breasts on the firm chests of the eager boys. The boys responded by rubbing them inside their sweaters and between their thighs.

He mostly ignored the students, as they did him. Ignoring the faculty presented a different matter. They constantly made inane requests, calling upon him to straighten or to clean the most trivial things. They were too ignorant to discriminate his position from that of the butlers and maids they struggled to employ in their homes. Most were new moneyed blacks, insecure about their societal station. They wanted desperately to distinguish themselves from their common working class counterparts, to sever the roots their sharecropping forefathers had deeply planted. For the most part, Dixon was able to shrug off their platitudes and snobbery. But then there was Jackie Daniels.

The other teachers there were middle aged, some close to retirement. Jackie Daniels was young, vibrant and fresh. The day she arrived the walls of the somber institution were filled with a kind of electricity far too intense to be contained by its tradition.

Her countenance was that of a polished courtesan. Her suits fit a little too snug. Her skirts barely met the criterion of what was considered a respectable length. The shirts and jackets were tight and cut to accentuate her full breasts. Her heels were never less than three inches high, making it difficult for her to walk without swinging her buttocks with a little too much rotation.

This local motion seemed to go into overdrive whenever she was around the pubescent boys who attended the school. She pretended not to notice the low whistles and expletives (GodDamn!) of approval as she passed them.

Ed hated a tease. She caught him watching her once. His eyes roamed her firm figure with a mixture of disgust and longing. She busted him. Made a big stink about it, too. It seemed to Ed she went out of her way after that to get a rise out of him.

The day she caught him, he had been mopping the floor, cleaning milk that one of the hooligans had spilled. He remembered looking down at the floor as the thick strands absorbed the filmy mess.

He had not brought the heavy mop bucket that he used for swabbing down the floors each evening before going home. Instead he'd used a lighter, five-gallon bucket to rinse the dirty mop.

Periodically, he'd bent down and wrung the mop head tightly with his huge hands. He hadn't been conscious of watching her. Hell, what did she expect? The tramp had raised her skirt to show her entire thigh while she straightened her stocking. He could still see the tiny manicured hands going slowly up her taut leg. Ed's eyes traveled the path cut by her long red nails as they invited him up and inside. He caught a glimpse of darkness between her legs and found himself straining to see if it was underwear or just Jackie.

The next thing he knew the red nailed fingers were stabbing at his face accusingly.

"What are you, some kind of pathetic pervert? I'm going to Mr. Franklin!"

The entire cafeteria was silent as everyone stopped what they were doing and focused on him. In the course of ten seconds, she had reduced him from a man of six foot four to a worm slightly an inch long.

Making matters worse, that bastard Franklin had actually called him into his office and reprimanded him. Dixon was outraged. But even that wasn't the end of it. Since that day all of the students called him 'Dicks On.'

It was around that time that his nightly dreams started to change. They began as always. He'd be doing his job without a stitch of clothing. Jackie Daniels would appear, but now she had with her a hoard of heckling students. They would stand around and make comments about his performance with Jackie, grading him on everything from his appearance to his technique. He responded by really trying to throw it on her. The crowd would chant, 'Dicks On! Dicks On! Dicks On!' while he pumped for all he was worth. But Jackie just laughed at him.

"Is that the best you can do, Dicks On? You're pathetic!" She'd mock, pushing him away. Suddenly everyone was pointing between his legs, laughing sardonically. Ed looked down and saw that his member had shriveled up like a raisin. He pleaded with them to leave him alone, to stop taunting him.

When they persisted, he grabbed them one at a time, sometimes two simultaneously and choked them with his broad callused hands until they were dead. Jackie was still laughing, taunting. She laughed until the grip of his fingers cut off her air supply and she was still. He watched her fall to the ground. The dream ended with him casually sweeping the bodies with the wide push-broom, pushing them down the corridor with the other detritus.

Ed didn't need a shrink to tell him his job was getting to him. He used each grueling minute he spent there as fuel to propel him away from his current situation and into a whole different way of living. He was too old for this petty bullshit. Ed Dixon had plans. If he could just stay focused on his goals; everything would be just fine. That was the only way he could continue to deal with this crap.

Sighing, he descended the stairs. The outer room, which housed buffers, strippers and other heavy equipment, was dark and slightly musty. He trudged to the small room to the right of the stairwell where the cleaning materials were stored. Fumbling for the light switch, he placed his labor hardened hand on the knob that lead to the utility closet and turned.

The door was locked. He never locked this door after lunch. In the afternoon the kids were too busy thinking about getting out of school for the day than to come down here. Keeping the door unlocked saved him the hassle of going through the huge key ring to find the one that fits this room.

Ed mumbled a couple of cuss words as he tried two keys before he found the one that fit. He expected the door to open with ease when he turned the knob, but there was something pressing against it which prevented him from going inside. He put his shoulder against the door and shoved his way in. Pushing up the switch that lighted the room, he waited while his eyes adjusted to the dull light in the windowless space.

The room was in complete disarray. There were cleaning supplies and boxes strewn about. Shelves had been half emptied, their contents left in a pile upon the floor.

"Fucking bastards! Why can't they leave things alone?" Ed grumbled. "The problem with kids today is that they don't care nothin' about nothin'". He reached down and started cleaning up the mess.

"Don't care about nothin' don't respect nothin'. They need to go somewhere and get some lessons in respect is what they need." He continued straightening the mess, mumbling all the while.

"R-E-S-P-E-C-T, find out what it means to me! Running around here all wild and crazy, cussin' and half nekked." He continued to straighten and put the supplies in their place. "Parents too busy makin' money and gettin' the fat sucked out they asses. They need to be home teachin' they kids some manners."

The plastic band that held a roll of fifty large towels had split, leaving the towels in a huge white mound in one corner of the room. Ed began picking them up, trying his best to put them back into some kind of order. He lifted another handful of the towels and almost dropped them when he saw what he had uncovered. As soon as he saw the expressionless green-eyed stare, he knew that Jackie Daniels was dead.

His eyes roamed the pretty young face that taunted him even now. He remembered all of those dreams that he'd had and her ratting on him to Franklin. He knelt before her lifeless form and touched her parted lips. With his rough hands he pulled the curly reddish brown hair away from her face. The brass buttons of her vest had been ripped away, leaving one breast fully exposed. His curiosity got the better of him and he moved the rest of her torn clothing away.

His hand inadvertently grazed her brown skin. It was like he was watching someone other than himself as he helped himself to a full view of her frontal anatomy. He hadn't been with a woman in, what, almost a year? The dreams came flooding back to him. How she had made love to him. His heart pounded. He felt the hardness in his pants rise until it released a warm stickiness inside his pants. A trickle of drool escaped his lips, splashing Jackie's chest before rolling underneath her.

"Oh shit!"

He felt an overwhelming feeling of shame as he realized what he had done. He stood and unzipped his pants and let them drop to the floor. Grabbing one of the towels, he mopped at the goo in his pants.

"What the hell are you doing?" he scolded himself. He bent down to pull up his trousers when he heard someone behind him.

"What's going on in here? What on earth are you doing, Dixon?"

Ed turned around. His pants were still halfway down, his penis semi erect. James Franklin looked at him like he was some kind of strange monster that had escaped and landed in his school. Then his eyes widened as he looked down and saw the partially clad body of the teacher, staring but seeing nothing.

"What in God's name? You stay right there! I'm calling the police!"

Ed grabbed at his pants while pushing past Franklin. As he made his way up the stairs he could hear Franklin calling for him to stop. He didn't know why he was running. He hadn't done anything wrong. He kept going until he reached the parking lot and his beat up old Monte Carlo. The Principal's voice rang in his head as he started up the old car and screeched out of the parking lot. He didn't know where he was going he just kept driving. When he reached the old cemetery at Cedar Glen, he parked inside an abandoned covered bridge. He needed time to think.

Chapter Three

It was after 5:00 when Rob Hollingsworth and his partner Jake Hurley arrived at Rosemont Academy. The school was already crawling with police. Once the identity of the victim was known, the Chief issued a restrictive order regarding the Jackie Daniels murder case. The decedent was the daughter of the district attorney for the city of Rosemont. This would be the most high profile case of Rob's career. He felt proud to be given the lead position in the case.

He walked around the yellow tape and stepped inside the small space, careful not to disturb the evidence markers that were already in place. The victim lay sprawled on the floor with an assortment of cleaning materials. She was African-American, mid twenties, attractive. She was found lying on her back, the buttons of her vest had been torn loose during the struggle. She hadn't been wearing a brassiere. Her skirt, panties, and stockings were still in place. Her shoes had been strewn in opposite sides of the room. To the right of the body was a white towel. Ignoring the marker, Rob touched it and drew back his hand in disgust. The towel was covered with a gooey substance that looked to be semen. The forensic technician shot Rob an irritated glare.

"Sorry, Al." He said. The man looked away.

He and Jake scribbled on note pads while being briefed by the uniformed officers. The Headmaster of the Academy had discovered the school custodian fleeing the scene. He'd returned to his office to await their arrival for a formal interview.

They walked through the scene to assess the crime for themselves. They briefly studied the condition of the body. There were scratches and red welts around her neck. The apparent cause of death was strangulation. The perpetrator had used his hands. The photographers arrived next and had everyone move out while they took pictures.

"Why don't we go see Mr. Franklin." Jake said and they headed up the stairs to the Principal's office.

James Franklin's many television appearances didn't come close to capturing the rugged good looks of the Academy Administrator. He was tall and slender. Though well into his fifties, the infrequent flecks of gray did little to belie his youthful appearance.

"The officers who answered the call reported that you saw the perpetrator at the scene."

"That's correct. Each Friday I personally take time out of my hectic day to check on the condition of the school before we break for the weekend. Since it's a holiday weekend, I was doing my walkthrough on Thursday instead of Friday this week. Anyway, I'm doing my walkthrough. I was downstairs and I see lights on in the supply area. Our man's usually gone by four, four-thirty. I'm thinking maybe he forgot to turn out the lights. I went to investigate and there he is naked as the day is long! He's standing over poor sweet Jackie like some kind of crazed animal. He was pulling on his trousers when I tried to stop him. Do you know that he almost knocked me down running out of here?"

"I tried to stop him but he's strong as a bull. He ran when he saw me. I hollered after him that I was calling the police. He knows he's in for it. I'll do anything that I can to help you apprehend this fellow. He's a bad one, he is. I just wish I had known he would be capable of something like this before it happened. Poor Jackie. She was a wonderful teacher and a beautiful person."

Franklin walked behind his desk and opened a drawer. He pulled out a manila folder and brought it with him as he made his way back to the detectives.

"This is Dixon's personnel file. I thought this might help you in your search. There's a picture of him in there too." His hand shook badly as he handed over the file.

"You okay Mr. Franklin?" Rob asked.

"It's all so shocking. Something like this happening to a popular teacher and by a member of our staff. You gentlemen are probably used to events of this nature. With all that's in the news lately, it's like murders at schools are becoming common place. We're not accustomed to this sort of thing at the Academy. Only the best and brightest students attend our school and we maintain high standards when selecting faculty members."

"What about non-faculty?"

"Well, you do the best you can with that sort of individual. Someone who cleans up after other people may not be the brightest star in the sky, but these people need our help. I try to make sure that our custodial staff, including the cooks and mess staff, recognize that we keep the bar at a certain level and we expect them to at least strive to become a degree or two better than the lot they have been dealt." Rob and Jake eyed each other. The principal either didn't get it, or didn't care. He just kept right on talking.

"You know this fellow and Jackie had a run-in a while back. She was very upset. Maybe he was still holding a grudge." Franklin shook his head. Remorse shrouded his face.

"If I had known he was capable of something like this, I would have fired him on the spot. You try your best to uplift society's cast-offs, you know, try to give these people the benefit of the doubt." He grimaced.

"Now look what happens. When you follow your heart instead of your head, you lose every time."

"Tell us about this run-in Dixon had with the decedent."

Franklin winced at Rob's description of his colleague. He seemed older and smaller now than when they'd arrived. He walked over behind his desk, exhaustion weighing on his shoulders, pulling them inward. He dropped himself into the chair and looked up at them, his eyes searched theirs for an explanation. His face bore a perpetual frown.

"Jackie came to my office one day. She was very upset. She said that Dixon had been watching her."

"Watching her?"

"That's right. Well, it might not sound like much to a couple of guys like you, but this was a delicate young girl. Dixon is a big monster of a man. He's enough to scare anyone. She said that he was looking at her in an improper way."

"Mr. Franklin be straight with us. We don't have time to play games. What was Dixon doing?" Jake Hurley's jaw tightened. He was running out of patience. He probably had a date, Rob surmised, as Jake checked his watch, and was sick of dealing with this pompous guy.

"Dixon was looking up her skirt. Can you imagine?" Franklin asked. "In an institution such as ours to find a member of our staff carrying on like that."

"What did Dixon say about it?" Rob checked his watch. The more time he spent with James Franklin, the less he liked him. Like Jake, he was ready to make a wrap of this meeting.

"Oh, of course, he denied it. But several students corroborated the story. I warned him that if he didn't know how to control himself around our students that he needed to seek employment elsewhere." Franklin pounded his fist on the desk with such force it caused the officers to jump.

"The last thing we need is to develop a reputation that we allow things like that to go on here. I told him he was being given a second chance," He pointed his finger in emphasis, "if he blew it, he'd be out of here faster than he could blink."

"You'd fire the guy for looking up a woman's skirt?" Rob laughed to himself when he heard Jake's question. His partner would never learn. He'd been reprimanded by the department on more than one occasion for minor misconduct infractions. He didn't seem to care. Some of the comments he made to civilians were down right unprofessional. Though he wouldn't admit it, something had happened to take the fire out of him. He was doing barely enough to get by, waiting for his retirement.

Jake had made comments to him on the way to meet with the principal in reference to Jackie Daniels that it was a shame for "all that" to go to waste. If Jake worked at the school he would have been doing more up her dress than just looking.

"Detective Hurley this is a very serious matter. Some very wealthy and powerful people send their children to our school. I know many of them personally and consider them friends. If anything happened to one of their children at this school this place would be shut down and turned into a parking lot before you could eat a doughnut."

"We get your drift, Mr. Franklin." Rob's insult threshold had been reached. He didn't like this prick at all. "Can you tell us anything about Ms. Daniels personal life?"

"Not very much I'm afraid. She was a fine young teacher, very responsive to her students. Her peers admired her. Her parents are A.J. and Amanda Daniels. A.J. and I are very good friends. This news will devastate him."

"The Daniels' have been contacted. We're keeping this thing under wraps for now. The media will have a field day when they find out so we'd appreciate it if you wouldn't speak to anyone about this just yet."

"Oh, of course." Franklin shook his head ruefully.

"Dr. Franklin?"

"Yes?"

"We'll need a listing of all of the faculty and a list of her students."

"What for? You already know who did this. You need to be out there looking for Dixon. He's probably halfway out of the country by now."

"We need the list Dr. Franklin. We could get a court order..."

"I'll get the information for you right away."

* * *

A.J. Daniels left work early that day. After spending the afternoon with his mistress, Madison Tate, he was still basking in the glow of their time spent together.

He whistled along with strains of Brahms that filled the black Mercedes as it rolled up the interstate. Caught up in the music and reliving his time spent with Madison, he was startled by the ringing telephone. He pushed the button on the console and listened as Amanda's frantic voice clashed with *Elvira Madigan's Theme.*

"Are you on your way home?"

"You sound upset Amanda. What's wrong?"

"The police called. They're on their way over here to speak with us. They wouldn't tell me what it was about."

"I'll be there in about twenty minutes."

A.J. pushed the button, ending the call. What the hell could the police be bothering them about? Amanda said they wanted to talk to both of them. He couldn't imagine why.

He and Amanda had been married almost thirty years. She knew about Madison and all the others as well. He knew she was long past caring what he did with his leisure time. What she did care about was being married to a powerful man, living in a sprawling mansion and being able to shop whenever the feeling moved her.

The love had been sucked from their relationship years before. They started out young, idealistic, in love and excited about all that a life together would bring. But after many years, and countless affairs on both parts, theirs was a union of convenience.

They each came from poor backgrounds. But Andrew Jackson came up hard. He and his brothers were raised in the slums of Detroit where they lived with their mother Connie, and a series of "uncles." Clyde, their abusive father, stayed away on drunken binges, leaving their alcoholic mother to deal with them the best that she could. While neither of them would ever have won parent of the year, the boys were grateful that their mother never left them, unless one counted the periods when she blacked out from drinking too much.

The three brothers had to fight often. Most of the other kids had some of the same problems as the Daniels. They were dirt poor, lived in the slums, and suffered through abuse by an alcoholic parent. What made A.J. and his brothers different was that both their parents were drunks. They'd get into loud brawls in the street using broken liquor bottles and knives as exclamation points. The neighborhood kids derived little pleasure in this activity. It cut a little too close. Many of them had fathers who came home drunk and acted a fool, sending their mothers bare foot or bare assed into the street. The main reason the brothers were ridiculed was because of their names.

A.J.'s two older brothers, George Washington and Abraham Lincoln Daniels, grew thick skins as a result of all of the constant ribbing about their names. They'd fight at the drop of a hat and spent as much time in detention centers as they did home.

A.J. was a fighter as well, but he always hated it. He never saw it as a viable way of resolving problems. Even when he'd win the fights, the kid would come back later seeming bigger and tougher, making A.J. pay for his earlier triumph. Fighting was necessary, a way of life.

The violence in the streets often paralleled, but never surpassed, the level they received at home. His father, Clyde Daniels, beat them constantly. A.J. was the target of his father's wrath more often than his siblings. As a very young child, he didn't know why. He learned the truth from some of his twelve-year old playmates. Street lore had it that his mother,

Connie, had gone out to a bar after a grueling session with Clyde's fist. She met a man that night. Nine months later, A.J. was born.

When Connie insisted upon calling the boy Andrew Jackson, Clyde made the connection between his wife, the son who didn't bear the slightest resemblance to him, and a man named Jack Andrews.

All hell broke loose. Clyde battered Connie so badly that she lay in the hospital for weeks close to death. Child Services removed the boys from the home. It went back and forth this way for years until Connie collected her sons late one night and took a Greyhound bus to Dayton to live with her sister Peony.

Aunt P was a big, dark skinned woman who carried a pistol. When Clyde showed up, loud, drunk, and cussing up a storm, Aunt P asked him to leave.

"I ain't goin' nowhere 'til I Git Mah Waff!" he slurred. "Now you carry 'yo fat ass in there and git her."

Aunt P went inside the house as she was told. When she returned, she had her pistol. She shot Clyde in the face. The wound, though not serious, was enough to scare him. A.J. never saw his 'daddy' again.

The legacy that Clyde Daniels left was a nasty one. His brothers followed in his footsteps, leading lives filled with alcohol and violence. His mother died at thirty-seven from cirrhosis of the liver and other complications from years of drinking and abuse.

Determined to put as many literal and figurative miles between himself and his family as possible, A.J. attended Wilberforce University on an academic scholarship. He maintained excellent marks and was ecstatic when he received a full scholarship to Yale School of Law. He worked at odd jobs to defray the costs of living expenses and graduated summa cum laude.

He did unimaginable things in pursuit of a legal career, creating a successful practice. When the opportunity was presented him to work as an assistant district attorney in Hawthorn, Ohio, he jumped at it, leaving his thriving practice to an associate.

During his stint at Yale, he'd met Amanda Boyd and proposed to her six months later. She was proud of her aspiring legal eagle, and gave up her studies to make them a comfortable home.

They took the seven-hour ride by car so that he could meet her parents. He'd never forget the look of dismay on their faces when they met. Their daughter hadn't the nerve, or the sense to cushion the long overdue meeting by revealing to her parents that this "wonderful young lawyer" that she planned to marry was a black man.

Their shock and disappointment was more apparent as he sat through the longest meal of his life, smiling, making pleasantries, ignoring the slight green cast on the face of her mother, and the stone coldness of her father. He left their home with a renewed determination to succeed. The fire that burned in him to erase the shame of his past was fueled further by her parents' shame of him.

The low point of the meeting was a conversation that he overheard while on his way to the restroom. Amanda and her mother talked in the kitchen as they rinsed the plates to go into the dishwasher.

"I can't believe that you're going through with this Mandy."

"I love Andy, Mom. He's a wonderful man." A hard hot lump formed in A.J.'s chest as he listened to Amanda plead with her mother. "At least try to get to know him."

"I don't want to get to know him."

"Why Mother? You have no reason to act this way. Can't you be happy for me?"

"Be happy for you? Happy that you're ruining your life?"

A.J. jumped when the faucet abruptly screeched off.

"Listen to me Mandy. You're a beautiful young girl. There are plenty of decent, eligible men from good families who would be proud to have you as their wife. Honey, don't get stuck on the first man who makes you feel good in bed."

"Mother!"

"I'm sorry, Mandy, but I'm telling you this for your own good. You go away to Yale and the best you could do is come back with that grinning baboon? When I think of all the overtime your father worked so that you could have a better life, it makes me sick. Have you thought about what this is doing to him? This is killing him you know."

"Shut up, Mother! Just shut up! I won't let you talk about Andy that way. I don't want to end up like you Mother, sitting here day after day, waiting on Daddy hand and foot. He doesn't love you, mother. You're just a thing that cooks and cleans, living vicariously through soap operas."

A.J. hears a slap, then crying.

"How dare you speak to me like that? How could you do this to your father?"

A.J. swallowed the painful lump the memory produced. Not long after they wed, the relationship became one of attainment. They had to have the biggest house, the newest and fastest cars. As their lives spiraled into things acquired and accumulated debt, pieces of their love for each other were cast out from the eye of their stormy marriage as their lives spun out of control.

He watched Amanda change from a sweet, sensitive girl, to a stranger who cared only about money and position. As his wealth and position grew, so did his in-laws' tolerance of him. With frozen smiles they paraded him in front of their friends like a prized thoroughbred. Their contempt for him slid down their throats with the caviar and champagne they wolfed down at functions they begged him to let them attend.

He smiled as he pulled into the garage. The irony of the whole thing amused him now. People spend so much time hating color when the only hue that truly matters is green. He showered and slipped into white lounging pajamas just as the police arrived.

There were two of them. The one called Hurley should have been named burly. He was muscular, a hulk of a man with dark curly hair and deep blue eyes. When the detectives introduced themselves, Amanda held his hand and looked into his eyes a little too long for A.J.'s liking.

The other man, Hollingsworth, was tall and wiry. He had smooth brown skin and was attractive enough to be a model. A.J.'s jaw tightened as he watched his wife eye one and then the other.

"What's this about?" A.J. wanted to get Mr. Universe and his friend out of his house as soon as possible.

"I'm afraid we have some terrible news Mr. and Mrs. Daniels." When Rob Hollingsworth began to tell them about Jackie, Amanda Daniels grew wobbly. Jake Hurley caught her and helped her to a nearby sofa. A.J.'s eyes narrowed.

"If the two of you don't mind finding your own way out, I'll see to Mrs. Daniels."

He could barely hear the click as the lock connected. He fell into duty consoling his sobbing wife.

Chapter Four

Audrey sat out a dish of IAMS and fresh water for the cat and headed for her office. Her meeting with Ed Dixon was at six. She had plenty of time to make her appointment and decided to take the scenic side streets to her downtown office.

She approached the Academy and noticed a van and several cars parked near the main entrance. Strange there would be people still at the school after five o'clock the day before a holiday weekend. Most folks couldn't wait to get an early start, extending the break to the nth. Maybe the school was being rented out for the evening.

Thoughts of the school whisked by as did the structure itself as Audrey sped into the glorious sunset.

She arrived at the office in time to boot the system and print the spreadsheets she had created for Ed's review. She toyed with the thought of opening the new accounting software she had purchased while she waited on her client. She already had everything she needed for the meeting printed. She could afford to be without the PC during her meeting with Ed.

"What the hell." She said, cutting the cellophane wrapping and popping the CD-ROM into the disk drive. It took thirty minutes to complete the installation. When Ed still hadn't arrived, she opened the manual and started reading. She'd give him a little more time while she practiced with the tutorial doing the exercises from her software starters package.

Ed Dixon was not the kind of man to make appointments casually. He seemed very serious about getting his businesses off the ground. She hoped nothing had happened to him on his way there. She was certain he would have called to reschedule if he couldn't make it. She checked her service for any messages. He hadn't called.

She retrieved the manual from it's opened, face down position on her desk. Soon she was immersed in the 'how to', and thoughts of Ed Dixon and the meeting they'd planned were forgotten.

*   *   *

It was dark out and Ed was awakened by the far off sound of a dog barking. For a moment, he couldn't remember why he was here, in his car, underneath the old bridge. Then it all came flooding back, like the time the toilet broke and he couldn't stop the flow of waste and water from making a mess of his tidy little bathroom. Somebody had killed Jackie Daniels and his boss thought he did it.

He had driven way outside town, stopped by an automatic teller and withdrawn everything that he could. He then drove to the cemetery at Cedar Glen and hid the car under an old abandoned bridge. Things did not look good. He knew that they would catch him. When they did, it wouldn't take long for them to uncover his past. If that happened, he would be doomed for sure. He needed a good lawyer. It would likely cost his entire pension, but he was facing a murder charge.

It was quiet under the bridge. He wished that he could be transported back to his room and find himself waking from another bad dream. He could never be so lucky. He had to figure out a way to get out of this situation. One thing was certain. It wasn't going to happen with him sitting under this bridge.

Ed put the key in the ignition and the old car sputtered to life. He slowly steered it onto the main road. In the distance, the lights of a strip mall beckoned. The clothes he wore were rancid and stained. The matter had hardened from the haphazard clean up of his accident at the school, causing his underwear to rub his crotch painfully.

Turning off the desolate road into a Kmart parking lot, he parked the car among the smattering of vehicles that remained in the lot and headed inside. A static laden voice from the intercom system, announced there were thirty minutes before the store closed.

Rushing for the men's department, he selected packages of tee shirts, briefs and socks. He ran his tongue over the grit on his teeth and longed to for his tiny bathroom and freshly brushed and flossed his teeth. There was no reason that he had to look and smell like an animal. He grabbed a toothbrush and a travel size bottle of mouthwash and headed for the front of the store.

A cooler displaying water and a variety of juices near the front of the store caught his eye. He grabbed three containers of water, unscrewed the cap from one, and swallowed in huge gulps until it was empty before heading for the checkout lane.

The line moved slowly as a scraggly, fidgety woman who looked like she needed a cigarette, rang the shoppers through. Beads of sweat dotted his forehead and rolled down his face as he waited his turn. Practically throwing the merchandise on the counter when he reached the front of the line, Ed apologized to the wild-eyed, nervous cashier.

"Chill out!" he warned himself. The last thing he needed was to draw attention to himself. He peeled three damp twenties from the roll in his pocket and handed them to the clerk. Stuffing the change in his pockets, he grabbed the bags and headed for the door.

The door opened as he approached the exit. Remembering something, he stepped back into the store and went to Customer Service and requested a roll of quarters. He put the cylinder in his pocket with the ball of sweaty money and left the store.

There was a gas station at the corner, he remembered, unscrewing another bottle of water and gulping it empty as he guided the worn out jalopy into the lot. A bell clanged as he moved past the pumps and parked in one of the spaces near the restrooms.

To his relief, the door was not locked. He didn't want to risk being seen by the station attendant. Once inside, he took off his shirt, wet it, and pushed soap onto the damp material from the dispenser on the wall. He washed his face, scrubbed his armpits, and then pulled on one of the shirts that he bought.

After pulling off his pants, he rinsed the makeshift towel, re-applied soap and bathed himself until he no longer felt the sweat and stickiness. He put on a new pair of briefs and pulled his pants on over them. Gathering his old clothing from the floor, he packed them into a large metal trashcan.

There was a pounding on the door and then the sound of keys jingling. The door opened abruptly and a withered, gray haired man with pronounced veins in his arms and neck eyed him suspiciously. Stuffing the rest of his department store buys into a bag, Ed released the breath he'd been holding and he hurried past the man towards the line of parked cars.

Being spotted by the station attendant filled him with dread. Trying to run was ridiculous. There were a million ways to trace people these days. Not that he had anywhere to go. They'd track him down like a slave before he could say swing low sweet chariot. The best bet was the safe bet. He'd better turn himself in. The sooner, the better.

He drove until he came upon another gas station. It was closed. He pulled to the bank of telephones and turned off the engine. Flipped the yellow pages, he found the listing for attorneys. God, there were pages of them. It was nearly too overwhelming to imagine finding help this way. But what else could he do? There was nothing he could do but start at the beginning and work his way through.

He started calling the numbers that were listed. His efforts were met by the soothing computerized voices of about a dozen voice mail systems before his frustration led him to slam down the receiver. It was nine-thirty at night; no one would be working this late.

With no friends, and even fewer connections, what was he going to do? Outside of the people on his job, there was only one person that he had spoken to at any length lately. The quarter fell into the box, the dial tone sounded. Ed Dixon dialed the number that he knew by heart.

"Wilson Associates."

Overwhelmed by relief, Ed sobbed into the phone, "You gotta help me!"

—

Ed Dixon blurted out the events of the day while Audrey listened calmly. Now she understood why he didn't make their appointment. He told her that he was the prime suspect in a murder. She didn't know why he had called her or what he expected her to do. One thing was certain; he was a wreck and sounded crazier as the story unfolded.

"Listen to me Ed. I can't help you. You need an attorney."

"I know that. I thought maybe you might know one. I want someone who's good, who I can trust. I thought if they knew that I knew you, they'd do right by me."

Her heart went out to him. In all of their dealings, he had seemed like such a decent guy. She couldn't imagine him being guilty of murder. They had talked at length about his plans. Not only was he smart, but he was determined to change his life for the better. Bumping off a co-worker didn't fit the scenario.

"I do know an attorney Ed, and he's good. Now I'm not promising you anything. I'll have to talk to him first. Give me a number so I can call you back."

Audrey let out a huge sigh and shook her head. She really wanted to help her client out. But it was difficult for her to do what she had to do next. Emory Kimborough was the last person on earth that she wanted to talk to. But he was one of the best attorneys in town. Not only did he get justice for the innocent, he made those of questionable character come out of their trials looking like angels.

Emory answered on the first ring. Hearing his voice made her shudder. The pain of their break-up was still fresh, an open wound sensitive to the touch. Speaking his name made her flesh bubble like hot Karo syrup. Hearing his voice made her bubbling flesh crawl into a grotesque knot.

"I was just thinking about you, too." The words rolled off his tongue in the rich Barry White baritone that used to keep her wanting him. She really regretted making this call. His egotism made her weary. She figured he would think this was a booty call. She was right.

"This ain't that kind of call. This is business."

"You always were good at business. Why don't you come over here and take a little dictation?"

By now, Audrey was seething. She started to hang up the phone but instead she ignored him. The divorce hadn't changed him. He was still the same pompous, egotistical jackass that she had been married to for seven years.

"One of my clients needs an attorney. It's a murder case."

"Who is he?"

"His name is Ed Dixon. He's a janitor at the Academy..."

"Well I wish him luck finding representation. I'm completely swamped right now. I just don't see how I could fit him in."

"So why'd you ask who he was? If he were one of your high society, snobby friends, would you have room in your schedule then?"

"Oh come on Audrey, like anyone that I associate with would be a client of yours. You coming over here or what?"

He had never taken her or her desire to run her own business seriously. It was the reason that she finally put an end to their relationship. He was really pissing her off, but she had sworn to everything in the universe that she was not going to let him push her around.

"I'll let the crack about my business slide. You weren't always 'Emory Kimbrough Esquire', so let's not even go there, okay? Now I know this may not be some high profile politician, superstar football player, or Hollywood celebrity, but couldn't you at least think about it, Em?"

"What, are you fucking this guy or something?"

This time she did hang up. Her chest burned from the force of trying to remain calm. She opened her bottom drawer and removed a pack of cigarettes and a lighter and headed out the door to the elevator.

She waited. She could hear the old car wheezing its way to her floor. It seemed an eternity as she stood listening to the aged car ascend the shaft. She was about to give up and take the stairs when the door creaked open. A tall, slender man with his arms full of cartons stepped off. He seemed startled to see her and the box on top of the pile tumbled to the floor, sending papers everywhere. As he stooped to pick them up, he hit his head on the closing elevator door.

"Ow!"

"Are you all right?"

"Yeah." A shy smile teased the corners of his mouth. "A little embarrassed maybe."

"You sure you're okay?" She touched his forehead softly. "Your head is awfully red and it's swelling up. I've got some ice in my office. Come on."

She picked up one of the boxes before he could object and headed for her office. She was glad for the diversion. She needed to figure out how to help Ed Dixon. Smoking a cigarette wouldn't help either of them.

It had been so hard for her to give up smoking. She had finally given it up when she gave up her husband. Two filthy habits that she didn't want to go back to.

Once inside the office, Audrey offered the man a seat on the brown leather sofa while she filled a towel with cubes from the icemaker inside her small refrigerator. She came over to him, kneeling down with the bulging cloth. He winced as she pressed the towel to the large red lump on his head. He stared at her as she applied the cold compress.

His easy, gentle eyes were large aqua pools, deep enough to swim in. His hair was longish, slightly curly and dark blonde. He was on the thin side, clothes clean though slightly rumpled. She liked his looks.

"By the way, my name's Audrey Wilson. I'm a financial planner."

"Jules Dreyfus, attorney at law."

"You're a lawyer?"

"I'm afraid so. I moved into the first office just six weeks ago."

"Are you any good?"

Chapter Five

Jules Dreyfus returned to the office that evening because he didn't know where else to go. He didn't feel like being bothered with Cindy. This was their third year living together and their relationship was completely factious. She was constantly bugging him about getting married. He'd grown weary of her demands and sick of her in general. At thirty-two, there was so much he planned to do. The way he saw it, marriage wasn't in the program for him any time soon. He tried to talk to her about his real feelings on the issue but they always ended up fighting. His primary focus was building his practice.

He opened his own office six months ago and was barely making enough money to keep things going. It was hard. So far, he'd resisted offers to go into partnership with some of his colleagues. The most successful member of his class was Ralph Zimmerman. Ralph started chasing ambulances with an abundance of determination and zeal the same time Jules began practicing law eight years ago. Now Ralph headed the largest practice of its kind in the Midwest.

Ralph had been after Jules for years to become a partner. But Jules had no desire to go into personal injury. He'd made the mistake of telling Cindy about the offer. She jumped all over him for refusing, criticizing him for not taking advantage of such a lucrative situation.

"If you aren't going to be aggressive, how do you expect to succeed in law? Maybe you should have been a veterinarian or a rabbi."

What a nag. Her apparent lifelong goal was to marry a big time attorney. She followed the directives of her mother and her silly friends, determined that she would make Jules into the man of her dreams. She had parties and invited the Zimmermans and other lawyers who dominated their area of expertise. She hoped that she could get him to see that it didn't make any sense for a lawyer to be poor.

What she ended up accomplishing was making Jules more adamant in his belief that happiness and peace of mind are far greater treasures than anything money can buy. What he saw when he looked around the room at the so called "haves", was a bunch of up-tight, pretentious people who tried to mask their emptiness by boasting of their business and financial acquisitions and sexual conquests. They bragged of trips abroad, their famous friends, and luxury cars. But Jules heard rumors that many of these trips were to drug rehabilitation clinics. The celebs they claimed as practically kin wouldn't know them from a piece of wood siding. The luxury cars, boats, and mortgages were a month away from repo.

He loved Cindy, but he wasn't going to be goaded into making such a serious commitment. Though he knew that she cared for him, it was clear her motivation was a bit self-serving. He didn't care about the money. That's wasn't the reason he chose his profession. He wanted to be a lawyer because he thought helping people would be a rewarding way of life. He didn't understand Cindy and why she was hell bent on changing him. It couldn't be that she was worried about cash. Not only had she come from an upper middle class family but she had worked as a model since she was fifteen. Her parents were professional people who helped her make wise investment decisions.

She had grown to hate modeling and the lifestyle that came with it. She wanted to quit but she was afraid to try something different. Maybe she didn't want to do anything at all.

If he decided to marry her, it would be on his terms and they're style of living would be reflective of their earnings, not some keep up with the Jones's, look the part to become the part type of bullshit. He just wasn't going for it.

Though he hadn't reached his earning potential, he had plenty to keep him busy. He had retrieved the boxes of information from his friend Leonard Meyer, promising him to help wade through the mounds of testimony on an appeal he was working on. A sixteen-year-old inner-city boy had been convicted of murder on substantial evidence. He had been given a quarter to life. Len was working to poke enough holes in the case to get his client off.

Jules was taking the mountain of paper up to his office when the elevator door opened to reveal the most striking woman he'd ever seen. He was so taken by her smooth brown skin and warm eyes that he stumbled. The boxes he had taken such pains to balance shifted and fell. The lid came off the one on top, scattering papers all over the elevator floor.

He watched her stoop to help him collect the contents and return them to the box.

Her full, lips moved over perfect, white teeth when she spoke. She inadvertently touched his hand when they both reached for the same piece of paper. A wave of electricity traveled from his fingers throughout his system, lightening quick.

They set the boxes by his door and she motioned for him to follow her down the hall.

Jules was glad that she walked ahead of him on the way to her office. It gave him an unobstructed view of her backside and long, shapely legs, and the license to be overly obvious in his appraisal, without getting caught.

She spoke casually as she knelt beside him, pressing the cold cloth to his head. Her breath was warm on his face. She excited him. Amazingly, the heat she stirred in him didn't cause the ice to melt when she put the compress to his head.

Her light, barely there fragrance, intoxicated him as she drew near. Her full, made for caressing curves took him to a place far away and tropical. She was talking to him. He heard himself responding but it couldn't have been him. He was on some faraway island rubbing oil into her rich brown skin.

"Are you any good?" She asked.

"I'm real good." Oh my God. She is gorgeous.

"I need your help, I mean like tonight. Can you do it?"

"Sure." He heard a stranger responding to her. A wind up toy, an android, something, had taken Jules away and left a grinning idiot in his place. The android agreed to talk to someone named Dixon.

"Great! I'll call him right now."

"Okay." The android replied.

"*What the fuck are you doing?*" A voice inside of him said.

"*Shut up!*" The space man quieted the voice of reason.

"*Keep your mouth shut and do what she says.*"

"While you're getting rid of your boxes, I'll call Ed."

She was up and walking towards the door. Though he wasn't ready to leave, he followed her to the door and stood in the hallway for a few minutes before realizing she had closed it. Her perfume lingered in the air and on his hand, teasing him as he sat in his office waiting for Ed Dixon's arrival.

Chapter Six

Ed couldn't believe this guy was agreeing to meet with him tonight. He hoped he wasn't one of these washed up, boozing has beens who had just barely passed the bar. He'd make it a point to check the guy's credentials. It was a desperate situation but not one which called for stupidity. He wasn't about to give his retirement money to some shyster. Audrey said she just met this guy. It was the best she could do on such short notice. He'd asked her to check him out when she had time and make sure he was legitimate. She was a good lady. She wouldn't let him down.

He steered the rusted out gold Chevy down Granite Street to Saxon Boulevard and parked across the street from the 410 Hartley Building. This was an older part of the city, but very well maintained. Still a respectable area in which to operate a business. He could see a light on in a seventh floor office, that must belong to Dreyfus.

Entering the building, he followed the narrow corridor with its deep tan colored walls and floral carpeting to the elevator. The structure was sturdy, as were many of these hundred year old buildings. The renovator had been careful in blending the modern with replicas of the original art deco appointments. The one thing that had not been replaced was the rickety elevator. When the door opened, Ed got in and punched seven. The ride to the seventh floor was roller coaster scary. He practically ran from the enclosure when the door opened.

Dreyfus had that yuppie, liberal white boy look that usually irritated Ed. He was tall, thin and slightly disheveled. There was a huge red bump on his forehead. What was up with that? In spite of his sloppy appearance, there was sincerity in his dark eyes that put Ed at ease. He extended his hand. The grip was strong and true.

"Mr. Dixon? Hi. I see you made it past the Little Shaft of Horrors." Jules motioned with his head. "Come on in and make yourself at home."

"Shee! Ain't that thing a trip? I've been in this building several times, but never at night." Ed feigned an exaggerated shudder. "It *is* scary."

"That's why I'm here so late. If I can't get out of here before sunset, I just say screw it, and wait until daylight. I'm scared to ride that thing at night. Come on in and get comfortable."

Ed liked the lawyer right away. He knew that the man was trying to put him at ease. It's the sign of a pro. He'd had dealings with lawyers before. They were overworked public defenders whose inexperience and ungodly caseloads, left little room for personality. Jules Dreyfus knew that the more relaxed a person is the better their chances of a productive meeting with a positive outcome.

He listened intently as Ed described the events leading up to this meeting. When Ed was finished, Jules told him what he already suspected he needed to do.

"Ed, you gotta turn yourself in to the police. I believe you're innocent and I'll take your case. I know how it must feel to be accused of something you didn't do but you gotta go in and talk to them." He dropped the pencil on the pad filled with notes from their meeting, and looked Ed squarely in the eyes.

"If you don't you're just making it harder on yourself and they're going to catch you sooner or later anyway." He ran his fingers through his hair before picking up the pencil and turning to a new page on the legal pad.

"Give me the names of anyone we can use as a character witness, friends, co-workers, neighbors, and family, anyone who can vouch for your credibility. I'll put together a plan of defense and we'll beat this thing, okay?"

Ed nodded his head in agreement and approval. This was just the right man with the right attitude, but he sure had his work cut out for him. Ed could provide little in the way of positive references.

He didn't have any friends and he kept to himself at work. Fraternizing was not allowed in anyway with the students at the school, not that he cared to. An unwritten rule or some invisible line had been constructed preventing the school faculty from acknowledging him in anyway unless they needed something cleaned or fixed.

He had dated Darcy, the school cook, but they were on the outs ever since the Dicks On incident. She had heard the kids talking about it and she was jealous and embarrassed. She hadn't spoken to him in months.

He couldn't bring himself to tell him about his family in Hapeburg and why he had to leave.

"Miss Wilson, Audrey. Maybe my landlady, Miss Brownlow." He shrugged, then stammered. "I got no family here. The faculty doesn't fraternize with the help and the students are off limits of course. There's a woman who works as a cook down at the school. We used to have a thing but that was a while ago. She might vouch for me."

Ed hesitated. He didn't know if he should talk about the incident in the cafeteria. But he knew that Franklin would certainly mention it to the police. He might as well come on out with it. Better to put his spin on it before the young lawyer's mind was clouded with everyone else's account of what had transpired.

"I need to tell you about something that happened a few months ago, Jules. It was really nothing that turned into something, all because I was daydreaming and not paying attention to my work."

He recounted the Dicks On story, looking at Jules shamefully as he concluded. He even told him about the dreams he'd had for months that ended with him killing the teacher.

"I'm glad you told me about this Ed. Don't worry. Everything's going to be fine."

Jules stood up, straightening his rumpled trousers before speaking again. "Would you like for me to go to the police station with you tonight?"

"Yes, I would. Thanks. Before we go would you mind turning on the television so I can see what they're reporting about this?"

Jules picked up the remote and aimed it at the small color set in the corner of the room. The news was just coming on. They sat and watched the first ten minutes, not speaking. There was no mention of a murder at Rosemont Academy. Everyone in the township knew that this was an upscale school that only children of privilege attended. Some of the most powerful citizens of Rosemont and neighboring Hope Springs sent their children there. The teachers were of that same circle, multi-degreed and cultured.

"The police department has apparently been instructed not to talk about the murder. Who was this woman, Ed? The one who was killed."

"Didn't I tell you? It was Jackie Daniels, the daughter of District Attorney A.J. Daniels."

Jules Dreyfus exhaled, pressing his fingers into his temple trying to push away the ensuing headache.

"Holy Shit!"

* * *

Too exhausted to drive, Jules hailed a taxi and gave the driver the address to the apartment that he shared with Cindy. It was three thirty a.m. Just as he'd surmised, the story hadn't made it to the news because everyone with any knowledge of the case was forbidden from discussing it. Now that they had a suspect in custody, they would release a statement to the press.

The driver had to wake him when the cab reached his house. He put the key in the lock and turned. Cindy was asleep. The covers were thrown off the bed and onto the floor. Her gown had ridden up to her waist showing off the smooth legs and buttocks that she worked hard so they would maintain the appearance of a twenty year olds'. Cindy was thirty-three but with her fair skin, tiny build and teeny blonde ringlets covering her head, she looked ten years younger.

Jules pulled off his clothes; dropping them where he stood then crawled into bed. He had a fitful night filled with disturbing dreams. In one of them he opened a closet door and there was Cindy, petite and pretty. Wispy curls framed her smiling face. Her head was slightly askew on its broken neck.

Chapter Seven

James Franklin sat in his study pretending to be engrossed in work from the office. His wife Althea was used to his ritual of solitude after a day's work and thought nothing of his need for privacy. After eighteen years of marriage, their evenings together consisted of small talk, dinner, then each retreating to opposite sides of the house, he to "work", she to read or watch TV.

It had been a horrendous day. After the grueling session fielding questions from the police, it felt good to be home. But being home didn't seem to provide the level of comfort that he needed. This particular night, James Franklin was worried. If he ever needed the safety of his sanctuary, he needed it now. Why did something like this have to happen to him? He thought about the rocky road which led him here, his final destination. He'd come so far and now he would surely lose everything he had worked so hard to attain.

Franklin reflected all of the positive things that had happened recently. His winning educator of the year. The radio and television endorsements. Several corporations had courted him, as had numerous institutions of higher learning. Finally, he was in a position to write his own ticket.

To be close to his aging parents, he decided on the position as head of the Academy at Rosemont. The school was the wealthiest in the nation. Founded by an abolitionist in the late eighteen hundreds, the Academy was a model of excellence from its beginning. A listing of the school's graduates read like a who's who of black achievers in the most prestigious fields; medicine, law, science and business.

It was tradition to graduate the academy, strive for excellence in one's field, and support the Academy with the same level of commitment that one would tithe to his church. Ten percent or more would be submitted to the school without hesitation. Thus the school's position as the nation's wealthiest remained in tact generation after generation.

When Franklin accepted the position in Rosemont, he and Althea settled in affluent Rosemont Hills in the home of his parents. It shocked James how quickly Althea had made the house hers, planning a lavish party soon after her in-laws passed.

"It's best to get on with life, Jimmy. Your parents were so proud of you. They would want you to share your success with the people who love you."

With that said, she proceeded to invite everyone they knew. His wife had never been so excited as she brought in a stream of decorators, each gave suggestions on how to modernize the wonderful old home that James's parents had lived in since early in their marriage.

Althea couldn't decide which of the suggestions she liked best, so she ended up incorporating a little from almost every designer that she consulted with. She'd even used ideas she had gotten from pouring through a dozen magazines. The end result was at best eclectic, at worst, garrulously bizarre. Althea seemed pleased with the results. James hated it.

He kept his feelings to himself. It wasn't his job to burst her bubble of enthusiasm. Who knew what lurked in that boil? Such a rupture could disperse more of her creative ooze, adding to the decorating nightmare. The important thing was that they had their dream home in their dream community, Rosemont Hills. It seemed good fortune was smiling on them at last.

Rumors of James Franklin throwing his hat into the political arena started surfacing. Giving politics serious consideration, he had his people put out a few feelers. It seemed he'd be a shoe-in for Rosemont city government. Now this had to happen. There was no telling what kind of negative attention a murder would bring. It couldn't happen at a worse time. A pall was now cast upon the school and most assuredly upon him.

He would be seen as someone who displayed poor judgement, a manager who couldn't manage to hire competent and ethical employees. What kind of example is he setting to those in his charge when he'd hired a molester and murderer?

Franklin buried his head in his hands. Maybe they would capture that scum Dixon and put this thing quickly to rest. He may not make re-appointment, or be elected to local government, but things could be a lot worse.

Chapter Eight

After the whole ordeal with Ed Dixon, Audrey needed a drink. The clock on the dashboard read a little before eleven. Shaking off the feeling of exhaustion that crept upon her, she made a right on Lincoln Avenue and headed for the Spice Rack.

Audrey ordered two double gin and tonics. She sat at a table in the rear of the club watching her sister play to the crowd. It was Thursday night and the club was full to capacity with revelers happy to be off work the next day.

Through the smoke and candle light, Audrey saw her sister. The long, auburn tinted locks on her head, and dusty orange sarong that caressed her compact curves, attracted everyone's attention to the woman in the center of the stage. But it was her voice that held them.

Renita was a true artist. She knew how to grab her audience, tease, tickle, or touch them as she shaped a phrase, making each song her own. It always brought a tear to Audrey's eye when she watched her.

She thought back on how when they were kids they used to join talent shows with their friends Norma Jean Strange, Nicole Robinson and sometimes Judy Davis. They would be the Supremes, or the Vandellas. They'd even been Tina and the Ikettes to Renita's boyfriend Drummond's Ike Turner. The crowd would go wild as they shimmied around the stage. They ended the show by Drum feigning a punch, which sent Renita onto the ground. He'd cast the Ikettes a threatening glare and they'd pick up the pace, dancing themselves to a frazzle as the crowd roared.

She wasn't as good a performer as Renita. Audrey had been the "producer" of the shows. She scouted talent venues, made costumes, choreographed and arranged numbers. Determined how much they would charge at the door. It was hard work, but they had so much fun.

Renita finished her number and headed over to Audrey's table. Her locks bounced as she made her way through the crowd. She was stopped by several patrons, extending her hand and holding theirs, accepting the praise, or sharing a memory of an engagement in a remote city or abroad. Ten years ago, Renita was riding the wave of a successful recording career. She'd taken a break from all the traveling and stress that came with fame. Her fans still adored her. The feeling was reciprocated. She wore her celebrity with ease.

"I'm glad you came down." Audrey rose when Renita reached the table. The sisters embraced before they sat down as the waitress brought their drinks.

"Me, too. Good crowd." Audrey looked around as people pressed their way from one side to the other.

"Yeah. Judy's in here somewhere."

"You're kidding." Audrey craned her neck in an attempt to spot their old friend.

"You know if she sees you in here she's going to want us to get up and sing '*I Hear A Symphony.*'"

"I was just thinking about our talent shows." The two of them laughed. "We used to have so much fun."

"We did." Renita drew close. "Remember '*Proud Mary*'?"

They laughed again. It had been Renita's boyfriend Drummond who'd come up with the idea after reading an article in *JET* about the battling Turners. Their parents made them stop the act saying there was nothing funny about domestic violence. Parents can be a real drag.

"So what's going on? How's the world of high finance?"

"Well, I can't answer that one," Audrey frowned into her glass. "But I can tell you how the world of just getting by is. I'm so broke I can't pay attention."

"I thought you were doing better. You seem to have plenty of clients."

"I do Ren, but they just want somebody to file their taxes. Ain't no money in that. I had a client come to me yesterday who needed a lawyer. Seems he's the prime suspect and wanted for questioning in the murder of a teacher at the Academy. She was, the DA's daughter."

"Wow, you're shittin' me." Renita leaned in, her wide eyes locked on Audrey's heavy lidded ones. "What did you do?"

"I wanted to help him so I called Emory."

"Don't tell me…he thought it was a booty call, right?"

"You sure know his ass, don't you? But anyway, when he found out Ed was a janitor, and I wasn't giving up no booty, he wouldn't do it. He made some kind of crack about my clients like they're low class or something. I hung up on him. I was so pissed at myself for even calling his ass that I went outside to smoke a cigarette."

"Oh no! You worked so hard to quit. You shouldn't let that bastard turn you around."

"I didn't. On my way out of the building I met this guy who has an office down the hall from me. Goofy little white boy who just happens to be a lawyer. He talked to my client and hopefully there was a love connection."

"Wow, Audrey that's some deep shit about that guy being involved in a murder. Who says accounting's not exciting?"

"Oh yeah, it's a regular laugh riot. I got a murdering janitor for a client. He'll have me bringing the 1040s to his cell to get him to sign off."

"Money and murder go hand in hand. Don't forget what Marvin said, there's only three things for sure, taxes, death and trouble. You're doing taxes. Your client has been accused of murder. Don't *you* get into any trouble."

"Please, don't even start on the tax thing. It's a real sore spot for me right now. You're right about one thing though, money makes people do strange things. It seems people are in a tight cause they don't have enough or they got too much and it's driven them crazy. If I don't get some money soon, *I'm* going to kill somebody."

"Why, Audrey? When you get out, you're bills will still be there."

"I guess you're right. The world don't stop turning cause a bitch got sent up."

"Oh listen at you, trying to cuss. You really must be on the edge." She touched her sister's hand and smiled sweetly. "Don't worry Sis, with all the book deals and art auctions using talent from the inside, you might get you some paying clients while you're in the slammer."

"No lie. I'll have to change my business cards. AUDREY WILSON Financial Planning for the Infamous."

"It's got a ring. You could write a book, 101 Things To Do With Embezzled Funds. Well, the boys are back."

Audrey laughed as Renita stood and adjusted her sarong.

"You gon' stick around a while?" She called over her shoulder.

"Yeah, I'll be here a minute. You know the more I drink these watered down drinks the more sober I get."

Renita turned back and leaned close to Audrey.

"You ought to sneak your shit in like everybody else."

"That is *so* tacky." They laughed as Renita headed for the stage.

Chapter Nine

On Saturday morning Ed Dixon was shaken awake by a short, beefy marine-type and told he had five minutes to get ready to walk.

"What's going on?" Dixon asked when the guard returned. In response, the man glared at Dixon and curled his lip into a snarl. Another guard, slightly taller than the other one but just as thick, appeared with chains and cuffs. The door to the cell swung open and the two men began to shackle and cuff the prisoner. They led Dixon down several corridors and a long flight of stairs to the lab.

One of the guards banged twice on the metal door. A few moments later a slender man dressed in white opened it. Two men and a woman, sporting lab coats, busied themselves opening containers and preparing slides inside the bright antiseptic room.

Though they may have had some sort of medical training, perhaps even been doctors, to Ed they looked like cops uniformed in white. The woman approached him and took samples of skin, hair and blood.

"Drop your drawers." She said with all of the enthusiasm such a pissy job would incite.

"Excuse me?"

"You heard me. Drop 'em. We need urine and semen."

When he didn't respond, she said. "What are you deaf or shy? Drop 'em big boy and be quick about it. Come on, come on. You ain't got nothing I ain't seen before."

Ed looked at her as he pulled down his boxers. He didn't doubt she'd seen male anatomy before. She'd probably grown one of her own in this weird sci-fi lab.

The urine wasn't a problem. The semen would be a fete. How was he supposed to get it up with this dyke in the room? Twenty minutes later he sat in the chilly room putting on his clothes. He learned that day that a cop could get anything from you that he wants, even cum.

* * *

When Audrey returned to the office on Monday, her answering machine was loaded with calls from creditors. She thumbed through the burgeoning pile of bills. What was she going to do? Her client base was dwindling. She hadn't talked to Ed Dixon since the night she had hooked him up with the attorney down the hall. She'd thought about dropping by his office to see how things turned out, but then she saw the story on the news. According to the reports, James Franklin caught him in a 'compromising position with the deceased.' Audrey wasn't sure what that meant. But it didn't sound good. Could her client be a murderer? She supposed anything was possible. But to her it seemed unlikely that he would put himself in a position to lose everything that he was trying to build. Perhaps he was being framed.

James Franklin was the only other person in the school at that time. Could this be an attempt to draw attention away from himself? Surely there must be evidence other than the eye witness testimony tying Dixon to the crime. Maybe she could check with Rob Hollingsworth at police headquarters. It had been a long time. Over eight years since she had broken up with his brother Jerry. She had seen Rob only a few times during that period. He was always pleasant. Would he give her any information on a prisoner being held at City Hall? She felt in her heart that the man was innocent. If there was something she could do to help him prove it, she would.

But what if they really had hard evidence against him? Hell, she was his financial advisor, not a cop. Maybe she should leave it up to saying a prayer for the brother and leave it at that. If the police didn't have something hard on him, wouldn't he have been released by now?

Regardless what the circumstances, it was time for her to move on. She had helped Ed Dixon all that she could. It was time for her to start helping herself. Business was still going slow. With Dixon locked up and tax season almost over, Audrey was going to have to start beating some bushes in the hopes that some paying clients would fall out or she was going to get put out of her office. Getting a job was out of the question. Once you've tasted independence going back to slavery is unthinkable.

Maybe she would talk to that attorney she had referred Ed to. He might be in the market for an advisor. He probably knew scores of people making good money who hadn't a clue how to invest it. Audrey felt hope's promise lift the heavy feeling of despair that was cutting off her air. She tossed the pile of bills aside and marched down the hall to Jules Dreyfus' office.

She knocked several times but there was no answer. Audrey trudged back to her office trying to wish away the feelings of disappointment that surrounded her. She would try to meet with him at another time.

She would step up her exercise and meditation ritual to help her maintain a positive mind set. She had a good feeling about the attorney. Somewhere in her heart she felt a connection with him would send her on her way to a more lucrative practice.

Chapter Ten

Rob Hollingsworth had worked homicide for enough years to know when a case stank. This one just didn't smell right. First you got a teacher from black society found dead at the snotty private school where she teaches. The prime suspect, the school janitor, is found at the scene by the head of the school. He had run, but maybe he was just scared, or embarrassed. Who wouldn't be ashamed to be caught with his shit hangin' out, drooling over a naked dead girl? The question was, did he kill her? The whole thing was just a little too neat for Rob's satisfaction. There was more to this than the pervert custodian losing control and killing a beautiful young woman. Rob was intent on finding out what that something else was.

As promised, James Franklin had given them a list of co-workers and students at the Academy. Rob and his partner went down the list, spending time with each one. Everyone that they talked to painted the decedent as either a saint or as Satan. Though they didn't have a high opinion of Dixon, most of them were surprised that he would commit murder.

The first person on the list was Greta Semple, a spry woman in her sixties who worked part-time in the front office. Tiny and bespectacled, Miss Semple had the face of a yellow snapping turtle. She clutched an embroidered handkerchief and throughout the interview she dabbed at moisture that pooled in her eyes.

"Oh that poor sweet girl." The old woman pushed the wire-rimmed glasses higher on her bony nose. She clucked her beak-like mouth as she continued.

"What a tragedy. She was so young. Not only was she pretty, but she had a sharp wit and was great with her students. She worked hard to keep them challenged and motivated. It's not often that you meet young women who look like her who are that bright. I guess it must be easy for a woman with that sort of beauty to skate through life on their looks. Some of us have to work harder for the smallest things."

"Yes ma'am." Rob didn't know what else to say. The homely little woman seemed to have gone somewhere inside, maybe thinking about some long ago wrong she had experienced.

"Is it true that Mr. Dixon did that to her?"

"He's being held for questioning. We're still investigating the case."

"I find it hard to believe that he would have done that to her. I've talked to him on occasion, nothing too involved. Just talk. He didn't strike me as the sort of fellow who would commit murder."

"Well, you just never know in these cases, ma'am. Can you tell us what kind of person Ms. Daniels was, Mrs. Semple?" Jake looked even bigger standing next to the tiny old woman.

"Uh, that's Miss. Miss Semple. I never married. I was engaged to a wonderful man. Martin. It was during the war. I was only seventeen. He was going to make a career of the military. He had graduated from Tuskeegee in 1942. My Martin was smart. He graduated with honors and wanted to marry me when he got his diploma. But my parents were strict. They thought Martin was too old for me. He was twenty-one. They thought we should wait until I was at least twenty-one to see if we still felt the same way about each other. We loved each other so much. We were together the night before he was to get shipped to Okinawa.

"Though he was degreed and should have been an officer, they put him to work in the kitchen of one of those massive ships. He wrote me two letters before the Japanese bombed the boat he was assigned to. I never saw Martin again."

"I still have his letters." She brightened at the thought. She dabbed away the water that streamed down her face as the officers stood by awkwardly waiting for her to compose herself. They both eyed each other in relief when she picked up the conversation about Jackie Daniels as though she had never digressed.

"That girl was so sweet. The day she started work here we had tea in the teacher's lounge. We talked about local politics mostly. I'd known her father for years. He's the District Attorney you know."

Both men nodded. They listened as Miss Semple continued on about what a wonderful person, teacher, citizen, Jackie Daniels was. She concluded by dabbing at tears that were no longer there with the crumpled hanky.

"She had such a bright future. I can't believe that this has happened. It's such a tragedy."

Next they talked to Herman Reynolds, the science teacher. He was a pale, withered man. His blue seersucker suit hung on him like it belonged to his big brother. Heavy pomade held the bad comb-over on top of his pate in a futile attempt to hide his baldness.

"Well, if you ask me something like this was bound to happen."

"Why do you say that, Mr. Reynolds?" Rob stifled a yawn.

"Why? The woman was a shameless tease that's why. The way she dressed and twisted around here like a worm on a hot nail. You would have thought she was some Vine Street hussy," He mopped sweat from his head with a grease stained cloth as he spoke. "She made the decent men and women here uncomfortable. I'll never forget that first day she was here, that display in the teachers lounge and the way she sashayed into the cafeteria and put on a show, a show mind you. I was shocked?"

"A show?" Rob echoed.

"What would you call it when a woman opens her legs and lets the world see everything God gave her?" He patted his head with the rag.

"It was disgusting. She sat there in the teacher's lounge sipping coffee. She had on this teeny tiny skirt that rode up when she sat down and showed everything. When it was time for the noon meal, in she walks with that wiggle of hers. She drops her bag and stuff went everywhere. Mr. Jemmings and I went over to help her collect her things. The buttons of her blouse were partially undone. I swear you could see clear to China! Jemmings and I were both embarrassed but we tried to help her anyway. She didn't even thank us. She just grabbed her stuff and left."

"How did that make you feel, Mr. Reynolds?"

"It didn't make me feel anything, Detective Hollingsworth. Young folks these days are ill mannered. I no longer let that kind of thing bother me. I made it my business from that day forward to have as little to do with Miss Daniels as possible."

"Thank you Mr. Reynolds."

Next on the list was Peter Graystone, one of two teaching assistants that Jackie had.

Peter was a freckle-faced boy of about sixteen. The prospect of assisting the detectives in a murder case thrilled him to no end. He was very excited to talk to the them.

"You're here to talk about Ms. Daniels, right? I was the first person that she picked as a TA. She was really cool, not like most teachers. It's a bummer what happened to her. I knew old Dicks On was weird. But he was the stalking, porno mag kinda weird, not murdering weird."

"What makes you say that?"

"What? About the mags and the stalking?" Peter flushed slightly, and grinned mischievously. "Me and the guys found his magazine stash. Talk about kinky. He was always checking out the babes here at school too. He tried to do it on the sly, but everybody knew what he was up to. We just laughed at him."

"What can you tell us about Ms. Daniels? Do you remember the day she started working here?" Hurley asked him.

"You bet I do. We were all in class doing our usual stuff, shooting paper footballs, playing our CD's, you know, just regular stuff. Suddenly the door slams. We turn around and there is this babe, I mean she was fine. But she wasn't like these dimwit chicks at school. She was fly, but she had a lot of class and carried herself in a way that let you know she didn't take any crap.

"She put her things down on her desk and just stared at us. Everybody got quiet as she stood in front of the class and introduced herself. She gave us some hooey about what an honor to be assigned to our class and how we were the brightest group in the entire school."

"She asked each one of us our names and held our hands while she asked questions about our families, interests and our dreams. We kinda thought she was soupin' us, but she was so smooth with it that we didn't care. We were just glad for the attention. Especially us guys."

"Did she fraternize with the male students?"

"If you're asking if she screwed around with any of us, shucks naw. She was way too classy for that. She was totally different from the other teachers here. They didn't care if they connected with us or not."

"What about her appearance? How did she dress?"

"Oh she was tight. I mean, she wore suits and stuff like the other teachers, but she didn't look all stuffy in hers. She was like a hip, big sister. Miss D. was cool and we all liked her."

Tammy Coulter was pretty and petite with wide-eyed girl next door looks. Her golden hair was long and thick and she smoothed it as she spoke with them as though it were a prized pet.

She was one of the few white kids who attended the school. Tammy used a lot of street dialect, perhaps thinking that if she mastered the vernacular, it would increase her chances of being accepted. She used the interview as an opportunity to spout her resume of achievements, which she obviously found quite impressive and assumed others needed to know about it.

"My dream is to become a child psychologist. I really like kids and I know that I have a lot to offer young children. They need to know as early as possible that they can make a valuable contribution to the world." Tammy snapped the gum she was chewing to emphasize her point. "Miss Daniels selected me as one of her TA's because we had talked about my career goals and she knew this experience would be something that I could use later on. She was good at tapping into what we needed. She could just draw it out of you. Then she'd come up with a way for you to explore that side of yourself."

"So you were very fond of Miss Daniels?"

"Look, I know that I should be loyal to her cause she helped me and now she's dead and all, but I knew something like this was going to happen to her."

"What makes you say that?" Rob asked.

"Cause she was always twisting around like some hoochie. She had these big breasts and always wore her clothes tight or low cut. Usually both tight and low-cut. Her skirts would be so tight I don't know how she got them on. She wore vests most of the time. I don't think she wore any underwear. She would get 'hot' during the day and take a couple of buttons down, fanning those big ole tits." The girl stopped talking, suddenly embarrassed with the direction the conversation was going.

"It was disgusting. She would crouch down beside the boys in class when they asked a question. They could see all down her top. When she lectured, she would sit on the corner of the desk with her legs crossed or wide open. The boys said she didn't wear panties and they claimed they saw her…"

"So she was popular with the male students?"

"Let's just say class participation among the male student body was at a record high."

Tammy cracked the gum again, then blew a huge purple bubble.

"I don't know why Mr. Franklin put up with her." She continued. "I went to him to tell him the kinds of things she was doing. He didn't do anything."

"What can you tell us about the day that she started?"

"I don't know if I remember the exact day that she started, but I remember the first time I saw her. She walked into the cafeteria like she owned the place. She got a cup of coffee and sat at a table in the far end of the room with her legs crossed. Every man who came into the room thought the crack of her ass was the special of the day. Look, I'm sorry she's dead and all, but she was begging for something like this to happen."

That's pretty much the way the interviews went. There were no lukewarm feelings for Jacqueline Daniels. She was either loved or despised. The interview with her parents went pretty much as expected. Their 'baby' was a good girl who gave them the utmost respect. She still lived at home and she never stayed out late without letting them know in advance. She didn't bring men to the house. She didn't drink or do drugs. She had been an excellent student in school and was a wonderful teacher who loved her job.

From everything that he and his partner had been able to determine, this girl didn't have any close friends, only casual associates. Rob was jarred from his concentration on his interview notes by a knock on the door.

"Here's the work-up on the Daniels dame." Willie, the lab "boy" was a fifty-eight year old black man who was stuck in 1962. Willie was a brother who was striving to remain Y1K compliant. He wore his hair processed and showed all of his teeth whenever anyone white approached. He yassah'd and no ma'am'd them to death. The amount of repulsion he generated transcended racial barriers. Blacks wanted to slap him; whites wanted to head in the opposite direction when they saw him coming.

Rob thanked him and before the door clicked shut, loosened the clasp on the accordion folder. He poured over the first few typed pages and photos that lay before him.

The records contained nothing too surprising. The woman had been strangled. She had been dead less than an hour before the police arrived at the school. There was skin underneath her nails. A hair found on the body was that of an African-American and did not belong to the decedent. There were traces of saliva on her breasts. They were able to lift one good print from the shoulder. The rest were smeared to such a degree that they couldn't be used. The results from the skin, hair, and blood samples from Dixon would be forwarded as soon as the lab did its testing. Rob continued to read the report. He turned the page and stared at the information for a minute before letting out a long slow whistle.

Chapter Eleven

"Did you know that the Daniels chick was pregnant?"

The late afternoon sun beat down on Rob and Jake. They sat on a rickety green bench in the park eating loaded hot dogs and drinking sodas, discussing the case.

"Oh yeah?" Jake licked at the ketchup running down his forearm from the sloppy hot dog. "I guess our girl wasn't as lily white as some would have us believe. We got to talk to her parents again. They've got to have some idea who she was dating."

"Plus, it will give you another chance to feel up Amanda Daniels."

Rob ducked to avoid the ice that Jake threw at him.

"Man, that ole broad was fine." Jake smirked at his partner. "Don't try to pretend you didn't notice, John Shaft."

"Fuck you, Jake." Rob retrieved a ball thrown out of bounds by a group of youngsters, and tossed it back to them. "I told you about calling me that shit. I know you're not going to listen to a damn thing I say, but you better not even think about trying to tap that. A dude like Daniels has probably had people rubbed out for less than fucking his wife."

Rob was impatient with Jake trying to pull every piece of ass that he met. He looked at his partner and shook his head. He was so reckless at times; Rob didn't know why some jealous husband hadn't put a bullet in his ass.

Amanda Daniels had a lovely face, but to Rob, she wasn't that special. He hated brothers like Daniels who seemed to feel that they hadn't made it unless they shoveled some snow. These brothers had it all, power, money, and all the trappings of success. Marrying a white woman seemed to be the ultimate measure of success. The piece de resistance.

His brother Jerry was like that. But he denied it. He says the black-white thing is simply an issue of visual preference. He says that people like Rob put too much focus on something that's a non-issue. He's constantly telling Rob that he'll never be happy until he lets go of his racist views. Jerry made him angry with all his 'we are the world' bullshit. Fuck him. He was entitled to his opinion. He looked over at his idiot partner who was still talking trash.

"I bet you're right. Daniels is probably screwing everything with a hole in it, but if somebody looked at his wife sideways he'd bust a cap in his ass. But you know my brother, I might have to take that slug. Maybe I could get her to dig it out for me."

"You trippin', Jake."

"No, you're the one. You know that woman was fine." Jake wasn't ready to let it go.

"Listen. The only thing that flat booty, big titty bitch could do for me is point me to the nearest sister."

"That's cold, Rob. But I still think you're full of shit. If you thought she was game, you'd make a play for her."

"Ah muthafucka pleeze! Get your big ass up and let's go."

The rickety bench shook as they rose in unison. Finishing their dogs, they tossed the cups of melting ice into an overflowing can on the way to the car.

When the detectives arrived at the Daniels mansion, they were taken aback by the drastic change in Amanda Daniels appearance. It had been less than a week since they'd last seen her. The eyes that were bright and lively on their first meeting were dull, black encircled orbs. Her face was drawn and her hair, tangled and matted, looked like it hadn't been combed in days. When the two men stepped past her into the foyer, they detected the smell of cigarettes and alcohol, which clung to her silk kimono like a fine fragrance.

"My husband won't be joining us. He told me about the baby. We deal with our problems in different ways." She stumbled over to the bar. "Can I offer you gentlemen a drink?" She didn't wait for them to answer but busied herself instead with the clinking of ice on glass, the splash of spirits and sprits of seltzer. Rob and Jake exchanged knowing looks, then followed her with their eyes as she plopped onto the sofa.

"The memorial and funeral will be held tomorrow." She slurred. "This has been extremely difficult for both of us. My husband's doing his best to…"

Suddenly tears rushed down her pretty face. Jake offered her a handkerchief, which she took and dabbed at her face. She looked into the cloth as though she'd find the answer to some unspoken question. The sun burst in through the bay window, its glow made her tanned skin appear more golden. It did little to brighten the sadness that dulled her eyes.

"Have you ever seen the grounds?" she asked as she walked towards the window. The words were meant more for her than for them. It was as though she was talking to comfort herself.

"It's a lovely place. We have a pool, a tennis court, and a lovely garden. Unfortunately, Jackie and I were never very good at gardening, but we both love flowers. Though I'm not much of a player, we spent our girl time on the tennis court. She was quite good. She started playing when she was about six. She inherited her father's competitive spirit. Do you play?"

"No, Ma'am."

"I play a little." Rob replied.

"Well perhaps when this whole ugly matter is over and…it will never be over. Our baby is gone. I can't believe she's gone." Amanda Daniels sobs were torturous cries, a mother's pain. Jake rushed to her side pulling her to him. Rob waited until he caught his partner's attention and mouthed, "Oh, brother!"

Jake ignored him. He helped Amanda to the couch then sat himself, letting her lean into him for consolation. Once she had composed herself, Rob started asking her questions about her daughter's friends and associations. She didn't have much information to give them so they rose to leave. Jake stopped at the door and took her hand.

"Please call us if you think of anything else, Mrs. Daniels."

"I will, Detective." Her eyes brightened. A tiny smile surfaced, softening the lines on her face. "And please, call me Amanda."

Chapter Twelve

For the second time in as many days Audrey had gone to Jules Dreyfus' office to find him out for the day. Her mouth turned down in disappointment. She had to finally admit to herself that she wanted to see him for more than professional reasons. Sure she'd like to get some good contacts from him, but this was also a ruse to get to know him.

Her love life was as stalled as her business was stagnant and she thought it would be nice to have someone take her mind off the current state of things. It would also be nice to be able to say honestly that she was seeing someone when a ghost from the past resurfaced.

Her latest apparition, he ex-fiancee Jerry Hollingsworth was calling her again. He'd heard about the divorce. Expressed regret and the proper amount of sympathy with the assurance that he would do anything to help her during this difficult time. She needed Jerry's help like she needed a hole in the head.

Emory was convinced she had called the other night because she desperately needed to see him and most likely wanted to reconcile. Audrey nearly gagged at the thought. She should have given Ed his number and let the two of them deal with things. Her heart was no longer weak for him but she became angry when she thought of all the time she had devoted to someone who cared so little for her.

Instead of welcoming romantic thoughts of Jules, she threw herself into the few projects that came her way. Most of her nights were spent eating take-out food and talking to her cat, who looked at her like she was nuts.

She shut down the PC and prepared for the ride home. She dreaded going home alone with nothing to occupy her. Once there, she was in store for another boring night. Lack of activity would no doubt keep sleep at bay. The videos she'd rented a couple of days ago were still on her table unwatched. She'd slump into the couch wearing her tattered sweats, crunching greasy popcorn and watch the movies, putting herself in the role of the female lead, until sleep mercifully put her out of the day's misery.

She passed cars occupied by couples in love and on their way places. They sped past her, courteously not kicking dirt in her face as they drove off to wonderful evenings filled with unbridled passion. Or so she imagined.

"This really sucks!" she said out loud as she zoomed into the twilight.

Freedom was already on the stoop when she pulled in front of her house. His loud meow and piercing agate gaze alerted her to his cranky disposition.

"I'm not in the mood for your nastiness today, Mister." He looked up at her questioningly as she turned the key in the lock. "If anyone should be cross, it should be me."

The cat brushed past her, dismissing her like yesterday's kitty litter. Audrey sighed and pushed the door closed behind her. Ignoring the pile of bills in the foyer, she kicked off her pumps, deposited her work materials and jacket on the dining room settee, then headed for the kitchen.

Freedom circled her legs, leaving a hairy trail on the legs of her navy pantsuit while she spooned chicken gizzards into his dish. She'd have to remember to give the slacks a good brushing before hanging them up that night.

She pulled her beat up sweats from the closet, then put them back, deciding instead to shower and put on pink satin lounging pajamas. No need to look like a slug and feel like one too, she thought.

Her mind drifted once again to Jules as she dabbed perfume behind each ear and admired herself in the mirror. I look too damn good to be alone, she thought. She pulled the phone over to her and punched in his office number. What could she possibly lose by going the direct route? It always gets you right where you want to go.

"Jules, this is Audrey. Give me a call at home when you get this message. If it's not too late, I thought we might get together." She left her number and clicked the call to an end. Taking action caused the congestion in her chest to subside. She grabbed a bag of organic popcorn and poured a glass of wine.

She decided to take a pass on the movie rentals. Scanning her video library, she opted instead for *Imitation of Life,* the 1930's version with Louise Beavers, not that mammy-fied 50's nonsense with Lana Turner that runs on TV with sickening regularity.

Audrey loved the original movie and the thought of 1934 Hollywood recognizing that a black woman was capable of running a thriving business and being a partner to a white woman instead of a mammy to her bratty daughter. To Audrey, the issue of blacks passing for white was secondary to that of an African American entrepreneur. America showed its true colors in 1959, not thinking it plausible that a black woman could have a head for business. There had been a regression in the minds of the majority race in the twenty plus years since the original version. Annie was now a mammy, grateful that a white woman rescued her from herself. Poor Sarah Jane had fewer options than to pass for white.

The more she thought about the race thing, she began to regret having left the message on Jules' voice mail. He may take her for just another teasin' tan ready to throw her sex at any man who tosses her a cavalier smile. She crunched the popcorn angrily, thinking of the times she had traipsed down to his office hoping he'd give her the time of day.

"Who does he think he is anyway?" She turned the glass up, draining it for the second time before taking the phone off the hook and turning up the sound on the television.

Chapter Thirteen

Jules slammed the door of his 68' VW beetle and headed for the courthouse steps. Since the story broke, a vigilant throng of reporters huddled at the front of the building like pigeons. They pecked around desperately for any crust of information thrown from either side regarding the case.

Jules knew the DA was determined to see the whole thing brought to trial as quickly as possible. The media nearly had Ed Dixon strapped and waiting for the needle holding the lethal injection. Jules needed some good news and he needed it fast. As things stood, the case against his client did not look good. It wasn't a lost cause, but it certainly could use major shoring up.

He had literally been caught with his pants down and by a leading member of Rosemont society. To make matters worse, instead of facing his accuser, he had run. James Franklin had already been on TV talking about the case. That means the prosecution must feel confident that the evidence they have is strong enough for a conviction.

Dixon swore he had no involvement with the girl. Jules hoped he had been truthful. The last thing he needed was a surprise. The forensic tests would further link Dixon to the crime because he had touched the girl and left the stained towel as evidence of his lack of control. These things proved he was at the scene but not that he committed the crime.

He turned the corner and headed toward the city detention facility in the rear of the building. The sound of feet shuffling in his direction alerted him that the mob had detected his arrival. The feeding frenzy began.

"Can you give us a comment, Mr. Dreyfus?"

"Mr. Dreyfus, is it true that your client was found having sex with Jackie Daniels after he killed her?"

"Mr. Dreyfus, what can you tell us about your client's prior history?"

"Did you know when you took the case that Ed Dixon has a history as a sex offender."

"What about his prior convictions? Can you comment on that?"

Jules kept pushing towards the door. He hoped to make it safely inside the building without losing his temper. How did they find out he was defending Dixon? What did they mean 'history as a sex offender'? Dixon had some explaining to do and Jules had a decision to make. Did he want to defend a man who wasn't going to be honest with him? He would look like a fool in court if anything damaging came out that he wasn't prepared to defend.

He was issued clearance and led to a small meeting room. A few minutes later, Ed Dixon was brought in. A guard helped him to a chair and removed the handcuffs. The door had barely clicked shut behind the guard before Jules slammed his briefcase on the table. He scraped the wooden chair away from the table aggressively before sitting down hard and glaring at Ed. He wasn't able to contain his anger and let Ed feel the fire of his temper and embarrassment.

"You need to decide right now whether you want me to help you get out of this mess or if you're just going through the motions hoping for the best. I don't take cases to lose them. That's where I stand. I need to know where you stand before I decide if I want to go forward with this."

"Whoa! Wait a minute, man." Ed's forehead creased in concern. "What the hell are you talking about?"

"I was just informed by a group of news hounds that you have something in your past that's related to what happened last week. Now if you're some kind of serial pervert or murderer," Jules pounded the table. "you need to tell me."

"Jules, listen. I'm sorry, man. I just wanted to leave the past in the past. I didn't think it was relevant."

"Any kind of involvement that you've had with the court system is relevant Ed." Though Jules felt himself cooling a bit, anger propelled the words across the room like hot pellets.

"I want you to go back to any episodes that you've had with the law. I'm not talking about parking tickets. If you were brought in and booked, regardless of the charge, I need to know everything you can tell me about it. Start at the beginning."

Ed put his head in his hands as though he were trying to push away a bad headache. He looked down at the table for a long time before he began to speak.

"I grew up in Hapeburg, Mississippi. I went to school there, worked there until I was about thirty. I had a family and we were renting a dumpy little shack so far on the wrong side of the tracks the birds didn't even fly there. We were saving our money to buy a nice house. So I got a job working at a pulp mill nights trying to make some extra money. Me and my girl had a son together. I wanted to marry Ellise but not until we had a home. You know what I mean?" Jules nodded his head in understanding.

"I didn't want her to have to work cleaning somebody's toilets or in some rundown bar or restaurant. Plus her whole paycheck would have gone to a sitter. It just didn't make sense for us both to work. We decided that I would work the two jobs while she stayed at home and raised our son, Jooney. I made a pretty good wage on the warehouse job. If we were careful, I could take the entire check from the second job and bank it. We would be in a position to buy a home and we could get married and raise our son right.

"Ellise enrolled in one of those home study courses. She was going to be a paralegal. She was all excited about it. It would have taken her only two years to complete the course. Our goal was to get married, move to a large city and try to bust it wide open with our big dreams.

"I was good lookin' then." A sly chuckle escaped when he smiled. He was lost in another time and place. "I got a lot of attention from the ladies but I didn't pay them no mind. I only had eyes for Ellise. She was beautiful and had a heart of gold. Other women will try you though even though they know you don't want they ass."

"So you were quite the ladies man." Jules interjected.

"I didn't say all that." They both laughed. "There was this one particular female who just wouldn't quit. She was pretty. You know the kind, makes you just want to fuck her every time you see her. She worked at the pulp mill on the night shift. All the guys wanted her. They all lied about what they had done with her and to her. I would talk shit with the guys about her, but everybody knew it was Ellise and me. Period.

"I suppose the fact that I didn't give this girl attention when all the other guys did musta got off with her kind of bad. She pestered me to no end. At first it was verbal. She'd come over and say something dirty to me. I would laugh and just shrug it off. Then she started rubbing up against me, touching me. At first I would make her stop, but I cain't lie, I kinda liked it. After a while, I let her do her thing.

"She would kiss my neck, nibble my ear while she touched my shoulders, back and ass. It wasn't long before she was touching my dick. I should have made her stop but a part of me justified it by feeling that as long as I didn't touch her back, I wasn't doing anything wrong. It was like cheating but not really. You know what I mean?"

"I could see how someone could get caught up in that kind of thing." Jules asserted

"I'm not saying I wasn't wrong. I know I was wrong, but I started to look forward to what she did. But the whole thing came to a head when I found out the girl had a man who worked days' right there at the plant. Not only that, she was married, too. I completely avoided her after that. I didn't need that kind of hassle. Especially when I wasn't getting no sex from her. I didn't want things to get any more involved than they were. When she came around I would be real nasty to her. She and I even got into a couple of yelling matches. She slapped me in the face once for saying something about her being sleazy.

"A week later she was found half naked and dead behind the break area at work. She was badly beaten and had been strangled and left on the ground like garbage. It was terrible how they did that to her. It happened on my off day, but several people at the job fingered me as the killer. The cops arrested me.

"People that I worked with told the police that I was always making advances toward her and got mad because she wouldn't give me none. They told them that we'd fought at work and she'd hit me because I was pressuring her for sex and she'd refused me. They claimed I raped and then killed her. The court system in Hapeburg was all ready to throw away the key on me when the company that held the life insurance policy on the girl started an investigation.

"Turns out the husband had a two hundred fifty thousand dollar insurance policy on his wife and was paying people to lie to the police. Word had gotten back to her husband that she was chasing after me on the night shift. While she was working in the evenings, her husband and her boyfriend somehow got acquainted. Apparently they became good friends and hatched up a plot to kill this woman. They were both ex-cons and started a sexual relationship with each other. These two freaks decided that if she were out of the way they could have two fifty, and each other. What could be better than that?"

Jules and Ed looked at each other for a few moments and then cracked up laughing.

"I'm not kidding you man. Believe me, I could never make up a story that crazy." Jules looked at his client and shook his head.

"Eventually the charges were dropped and I was released."

"What happened to Ellise and the boy?"

"That's really the sad part about the whole thing. When Ellise found out that I was carrying on with this woman, things changed between us. Whenever I tried to get close to her, she'd look at me real funny and would go cold. I felt like shit." He hung his head like it was suddenly heavy with the weight of the memory. "Each day it got harder for me to face her and to face that look.

"I could understand her feeling angry and bitter. I tried to explain that I hadn't really done anything with that woman a hundred times, but Ellise didn't want to hear it. She just continued to look at me in that funny way. I had let her down. She was the best thing that ever happened to me. She put all her faith and trust in me and I blew it." He shook his head with regret, looking at Jules through eyes full of pain at the hurt he'd caused.

"I had to accept her feelings and hope that she would forgive me. But it got worse." He looked away from Jules, using the heel of his hand to buttress the tears. "When the look on her face changed from funny to out right disgust, I couldn't deal with it anymore. Every time I saw that look, I felt like a goddamn dog. We lived like that for more than a year until I just couldn't take it anymore. I left Hapeburg and haven't been back since."

"After I moved here and got settled, I wrote to Ellise regularly. She never wrote me back. I send them money once a month and cards on Jooney's birthday and Christmas. I don't know if she lets him read them. He's about thirteen now."

Ed didn't hold back the tears. He never talked to anyone about his family and the bottled up emotion sliced through him, leaving gaping wounds in its wake. He looked at Jules with his face wet, unashamed of the tears that flowed.

"I'll do anything to get out of this mess so that I can make things right with them. I still love them both. I just hope it's not too late to be a husband and father to them."

—

Still shaken by his meeting with Ed, Jules stepped out into the bright August sunshine. His initial impression of Ed Dixon as a decent man who'd just had a few bad breaks remained solid. It would take but a little for this strong man to reach his full potential. To realize his dreams. But first Jules had to get him out of jail.

The reporters met him again, pushing their microphones and questions into his face. They followed him to the parking lot where he turned and faced them.

"My client is innocent. I will stop at nothing to prove it." He climbed into the tiny car and pulled the door shut. The painted blue metal deflected the barrage of questions that were further drowned out as the engine turned over and the small car sputtered down the street.

—

When he opened the door to the apartment he wanted to pull it shut and go somewhere else. Cindy sat on the side of the bed polishing her toenails. As usual, the apartment was a mess. The sink was full of dishes showing what they'd eaten the entire week. In the entire history of their relationship, the bed had never been made. It was piled high with nearly all of the clothes that they owned. Cindy sat atop the mound of turned over covers, their dirty pajamas, and the laundry Jules dumped out this morning, looking for a clean shirt to wear.

At the foot of the bed was a plate of crusted, caked-on spaghetti and a rock hard piece of Italian bread. She had spilled the polish remover onto the rug, bleaching the blue fibers white.

"Cindy you're not working right now, why can't you clean up this shit hole? I just left the fuckin' jailhouse and it was cleaner than this."

"Do I look like a maid to you? You need to hire somebody to come in and clean this place up. This is *your* apartment, Jules. You don't really expect me to clean it, do you?"

"We live here, Cindy. You and me." He pointed at her, then himself. "Don't give me any of that 'your name is on the lease not mine' shit. I don't want to hear it."

"Well, I don't want to hear *any* of your shit. I can't clean this place up by myself and you shouldn't expect me to." Her glare cut into him. "You act like I'm the only one that leaves junk around. It's not just me who's a slob, Jules. You should stop being so cheap and hire somebody. Then everybody would be happy." She stroked the polish onto her big toe and blew on it.

"Do you know how much they would charge to clean up all this shit? I'll never make enough to have someone clean up after you. They haven't called you for any assignments in months. The least you could do is clean up a little."

Cindy lifted her eyes from her artwork and glared at Jules. He wished that he could twitch his nose, blink or have Scottie to beam him up out of the apartment and away from Cindy and her nastiness.

"You'll never make enough money to do anything, Jules. You're the sorriest excuse for a lawyer that I've ever seen. And for your information, they called me to go on the London shoot this morning. I'm leaving tonight."

"Oh, just like that. You're going to London?"

"Duh! I'm a model, Jules. I have assignments all over the world. Staying holed up in this smelly apartment in this dinky town might be okay for you but it's not for me. You never have time for me and whenever we are together we're fighting. Pierre will be picking me up at ten. We're catching the red-eye."

Cindy finished doing her nails and closed the cap on the bottle of polish. She switched on a tiny fan and pointed it at her toes. She was finished talking to Jules. He hated being dismissed like that but he was relieved that the conversation was over.

He had nothing else to say to her and he damned sure didn't want to be around when that flaming friend of hers arrived. He was beginning to feel like a stranger in his own home. He knew he had to put a stop to this soon. But he was in no mood for further confrontation.

"I forgot some files that I need to look at. I'm going to the office. I'll be back in a couple of hours."

Cindy didn't even look up as he headed out the door. There's got to be more to love than this he thought to himself as he walked down the corridor and into the street.

Chapter Fourteen

Rob was at his desk catching up on some paperwork when Jake Hurley came in. Jake looked slightly disoriented as he narrowly missed knocking over the donut wagon, then bumped into one of the desks occupied by the lower ranking detectives, on his way to the area that he and Rob shared.

"Where the hell you been man?" Rob chided. "You just drag your dead ass in here whenever you feel like it. What's going on?"

"Guess who called me last night?" Jake swaggered over to his desk and sat his rump on the corner of it facing Rob. "Amanda Daniels. She told me that their daughter had a private line." He slapped a rolled piece of paper he held in one hand, on the palm of the other. "I've been over at Western Bell. I've got the lug showing all of the incoming and outgoing calls on her number over the last six months. Most of the calls are either to her salon, several retail establishments, or to a private line in the name of one James Franklin."

"I'm impressed. Who put a stick of dynamite up your ass and lit it?" His partner looked at him and grinned.

"You didn't. Tell me you didn't fuck Amanda Daniels." Jake looked away.

"Muthafucka are you crazy or what?" Rob sprang from his seat, snatched the rolled sheets of paper and bopped Jake on the head with them.

"It wasn't like you think Rob. It was all business. She gave me the information about the telephone number. Then she just wanted to talk. She was really a wreck. Her husband won't come home and she just wanted me to sit there until she fell asleep."

"So you just sat there watching her doze off?"

"Well at first she wanted me to have sex with her. But I wouldn't do it."

"A woman is throwing herself at you and you say no to the panties? I can't wait to hear the rest of this lie." He grabbed the Rosemont Township mug from his desk. "Hold tight while I get some water. I need something to help me swallow this horse shit you're about to dish up."

"See that's why I didn't want to tell you. She's not like these other broads. This lady has class."

"All right man, I'll be cool." Rob held both hands up in surrender. "Go on and tell me what happened."

"About ten-thirty last night my phone rings. She tells me about the phone line that her daughter had. I thank her and get ready to hang up but she begs me to come over. She says her husband never comes home any more and she's afraid of what she might do in that big house by herself. So I agree to come over.

"All the way over there I kept thinking about what you said about the DA killing somebody for looking at his wife wrong. I promised myself that no matter what she said or did, I was not going to have sex with her. I get to the door, right? She opens it wearing one of those silky filmy things women like to wear that you can't really see through but at the same time you can see everything they got." Jake's eyes searched Rob's for a description, help of any kind. When he got nothing, he continued.

"Rob, I went straight to the bathroom. I couldn't take it. When we were over there earlier that day, her house looked like one of those nicely furnished homes you'd see in the magazines. When I went there that night, man she had transformed that place into a candle lit sex lair."

"So you shot a load of your heirs all over her expensive wallpaper, tipped your hat and went home." Rob said sarcastically. "Is that what you want me to believe?"

"I don't care what you believe, Rob. And it's none of your damned business what I did in the bathroom." Jake's face grew red. "Anyway, I finally left the bathroom and there she was in that thing she was wearing. Man I could see tits, thighs, the works, through this outfit."

"What was it, some kind of teddy or something?" Rob leaned forward. He was all into the story now. He was making fun of Jake but he was kind of envious. At least he was getting some.

"I don't know what the fuck that thing was man, but all women should wear that and nothing else. Anyway, she made no secret about what she wanted. She stood right in front of me holding a drink. It could have been a glass of her husband's piss for all I know. I drank it down no questions asked.

"She grabbed my hand and led me into the den. It was filled with a bunch of candles and looked like some kinda shrine. Man, when she took that thing she was wearing off I almost cried. Her body is perfect. She's gotta be in her late forties, early fifties. Everything on her looked tight, Rob."

"So you fucked her until her eyes popped out. End of story."

"No man. I told you I didn't do it. I swear. She stood in front of me butt naked. She gave me this bottle of oil and ask me to rub it on her. You shoulda seen her, Rob. She was spread out on this fur rug waiting for me to put that oil on her."

"Well?"

"Well what?"

"Did you do it?"

"Hell no, I didn't do it." His eyes were wide and he shook his head vigorously. "If I had touched that woman I'd be locked in that cell next to Ed Dixon cause I would have fucked her to death." They both laughed.

"I picked up that wrap or robe or whatever that thing was and covered her up and walked towards the door. She called me back and apologized to me. She told me that she really wanted me to stay. I told her I would if she'd go put on some clothes and behave herself. So that's what happened. We talked. I stayed until she fell asleep on the couch and I left."

Rob looked at his partner long and hard. He suddenly broke into laughter.

"What? What the fuck are you laughing at?'

"You never talked to a woman in your life. You're either making this shit up or she's playin' you're ass good." Rob was still looking at his partner. Jake wasn't laughing.

"Get the fuck outta here! Somebody finally got you're ass! Jake is in love! Wait till I tell the guys."

"Shut up, Rob. Stop fuckin' with me, man. I bring some serious information in here about the case and you so busy gossiping you don't even want to deal with it. Well somebody has to be on the job and I guess that somebody will have to be me."

"That'll be the day." Rob roared louder. Through tears he saw the humiliation on his friend's face.

"Okay, man, okay." Still snickering, Rob added condescendingly. "Let me see your little report."

He read the report, his attention completely focused on his work. Why would Jackie Daniels be talking to her boss almost every night when she saw him during the day? Rob rose, grabbed a folder from his desk and tapped Jake's arm with his knuckles.

"We need to go talk to Franklin and see what he and Miss Daniels had to talk about every night."

Chapter Fifteen

Audrey put the finishing touches on what she thought was a bang-up proposal and was about to hit the save button when the screen went blank. She sat there for a second in disbelief. Then she started cussing a blue streak.

"I can't believe this raggedy ass computer got me again." She waited for the system to re-boot and hoped she had saved her work far enough into the process so she wouldn't have too much re-work to get back to where she was. She opened the file and found that quite a bit had been lost.

"Damn!" She punched the screen but she didn't feel any better. Still needing to vent, she called her sister Renita.

"Hey, woman what's up?"

"Work. I've been sitting here all evening putting this proposal together and my computer crashed before I got a chance to save what I was doing."

"Well, let that be a lesson to you."

"What?" She raised her coffee cup to her lips, grimaced at the lukewarm liquid, at sat the cup back on the coaster.

"You should never work after six o'clock in anybody's office, even your own. Why don't you get out of there and do something with yourself?"

"Look Miss Toast of the Town, some of us have to work for a living."

"Oh, and *I* don't? I work hard, I'll have you know, not only to keep my voice sharp but to look good, too. I don't care how good you sound, don't nobody want to watch no fat ugly woman doing nothing.

Put alcohol in the mix and you liable to get cussed out and drug off the stage."

"You really believe that don't you?"

"I've seen it happen."

"Girl, you lie entirely *too* much."

A knock at the door startled Audrey. She looked at her watch. It was almost nine o'clock.

Who the hell could that be?

"Hold on, Ren. Somebody's at the door."

"Come in." She kept a small metal club near her feet. She worked a lot of late hours. A girl just never knew when she'd have to clock a fool. The door opened. It was her neighbor from down the hall.

"Hello, Audrey. It seems you got your days and nights mixed up. Business hours are supposed to be nine a.m. to five p.m. not nine p.m. to five a.m."

"Come on in." Audrey laughed. "Do you know anything about restoring lost computer files?"

"No. I'm afraid I'm completely computer illiterate. I have a part-timer help me with all that jazz. If she knew how truly lost I'd be without her she'd ask for a whole lot more money."

"Maybe I need to get her the other part of the time." They laughed.

"I got your message from the other night. I'm sorry for not getting back with you sooner. Things have been pretty crazy."

"Not a problem." Audrey hoped the words sounded nonchalant and not the cover for her embarrassment that they truly were. She remembered her state of mental imbalance when the call was placed, a state worsened by loneliness and the use of alcohol. "Listen, I think my brain is about fried for tonight. Would you like to join me at Nick's for a sandwich and a drink?"

"That sounds great." He seemed delighted by the invitation. "I'll go lock up my office and be back in a shake."

Audrey started shutting down her office as well. Until she saw the phone off the hook she'd forgotten that her sister was still holding on. She snatched the receiver from where she had lain it on the desk.

"That was pretty smooth," Renita giggled. "Who was that?"

"That lawyer from down the hall."

"Oh…a lawyer. You need to get him drunk and get some diggedy."

"Shut up, Ren. Why does everything involving a man have to be about sex?"

"That's just the way nature planned it."

"You're through. Anyway he's a white dude."

"And?"

"You know I don't go that way."

"What way? Look girl, you go on and limit yourself if you want to, you'll be making love to that raggedy ass computer for the rest of your days."

"Thank you, Dr. Ruth. Listen," Audrey whispered. "He's outside the door. I'll talk to you later."

—

Nick's was a bar on the lower level of the 410 Hartley Building. There were no other patrons that evening and the owner waited on them himself. Jules and Audrey sat in a booth towards the back. Nick brought them their drinks. The liquor warmed their work weary minds. They relaxed and listened to the full bodied tones of Diana Krall telling her lover to peel her a grape.

Jules couldn't believe that he was there with her. She was really beautiful. Her skin seemed to glow in the candlelight. He loved her laugh and the way her full lips moved over her pearly teeth when she spoke.

"How's the case going?"

"It's going okay. We've got a lot of work to do but I feel pretty confident we'll come out on top."

"I've been meaning to ask you if you were in the market for a financial planner or if you know of anyone who is. My practice is relatively new and I'm still trying to establish a client base."

"I can relate. My situation is changing rapidly with the attention this case is bringing. It's been good exposure."

"I saw you on TV. You handled those reporters very well."

"Thanks. Between you and me, I was scared shitless. I've never tried a high profile case before. It's a bit overwhelming at times. But overall, I feel good about it. In answer to your question, I do have associates who might be in need of your services. I'll make some calls."

"That would be great. Thank you."

He smiled and ordered another drink. He found it refreshing that she enjoyed talking and she did so incessantly. Mostly about herself. Within a short time he learned that she was the oldest of three, born and raised in Rosemont. She had attended the Academy, and received academic scholarships to several universities, but settled on Ohio State. She worked to supplement the cost of her college education at a few retail jobs until she got her business degree. She garnered an internship from Wyman-Franklin, one of the most prominent financial services firms in the country in her senior year. She was excited when they offered her a permanent position. She had to relocate to Albany. She worked as a staff analyst there for several years before being promoted to a financial planner position. WF relocated her to Columbus where she stayed for a number of years before leaving to start her own company.

"I was scared to death when I started at WF." She told him. "I tried hard to be grown up and not let my insecurities, of which I had many, show." She stirred the straw around in her highball glass. "It was a man's world and I was made to run the gauntlet on more than one occasion."

"That must have been tough, especially being a black woman."

"You got that right. I don't know which was harder for the establishment to deal with, my being a woman, or my being black. Though corporate America has a long way to go, things are better now in some areas. People don't seem as shocked to see diversity around the table when they enter a meeting room."

"Before I hung my shingle out, I never even thought of the term diversity, or how many minorities or women were in responsible positions at my firm." Jules confessed. "It's terrible but most of us tend to gravitate to those who look like us. When you picture the new hire, you attach many of your own attributes to this unknown person. Without realizing it, you're closing your eyes to those who are different without even thinking about it. You're not thinking that this act alone is excluding other segments of society."

"Exactly. And that's the kind of awareness that needs to happen on a broad scale before we can even think of getting rid of Affirmative Action and other programs that make companies comply. Although I'm sure some do, it's hard for me to believe that those in power sit around the table and deliberately make it a policy not to hire and promote minorities and women."

"There are a lot of idiots out there. The media would have us believe they're all uneducated, backwoods hicks." He drawled the last statement with a fake Southern twang. "You'd be surprised how many of my colleagues use starched white collars to hide rednecks."

"Doesn't surprise me a bit." She took a sip of her drink. "My field isn't exactly teeming with diversity."

"You know Audrey, I think this is the first time I've ever had an honest conversation with a black person regarding race. It feels..."

"Scary but freeing?"

"Yeah. It feels good."

The conversation slowed while they finished their meal. Kenny Garrett's sassy alto sax set their heads bobbing as they sipped fresh drinks. They talked about some of their favorite artists and performances they'd seen, picking and panning like paid critics.

They had eaten their food and the bottle of wine was empty. Audrey had let her gin and tonic go watery as Jules finished his third scotch. Audrey checked her watch. She motioned to Nick to bring the check. They quibbled for a second over who would pay before Audrey acquiesced.

"Okay Jules, but next time it's on me." She cut her eyes, surprising herself with the implication of the statement.

"So are you saying you want to see me again?" His smile teased her. Her secret was out. Audrey looked at him and smiled.

"I'm saying I want to see you again."

Jules felt as though he had just scored thirty points on Michael Jordan. They walked out of the bar together. He was the star of the game. He wondered if she could hear the roar of the crowd as his teammates lifted him over their heads, carrying him to the locker room.

"Where's your car?" he asked when they were outside.

"I'm in the lot across the street."

Emboldened by the liquor, he took her hand and they walked in the darkness to the smattering of cars parked in the lot. She pointed to a late model Saab and they headed in that direction. She put the key in the lock and when she turned suddenly he was kissing her before he had time to think. Before she had a chance to object.

Her lips were soft, quivering as he touched them with his gently at first and then more urgently. Her skin was hot, and she trembled. He held her firmly until he felt her relax. He continued his embrace until he felt her nervousness subside. When they began to drift apart, he pulled her into his arms and kissed her again.

"Nick serves some pretty strong drinks." He said when he let her go.

"So you're blaming this on the alcohol?"

"I'll take the fifth." They both laughed at the pun. He held the car door open and Audrey slid behind the wheel.

"See you later, Mr. Dreyfus."

"I hope not too much later, Miss Wilson."

Jules closed the car door, breathing in her fragrance as she pulled out onto the main road. He could still feel her smooth brown skin against his face. Her laughter rang in his ears like bird song.

Jules walked over to the old Bug and started it up. It wasn't until he exited the parking lot that he thought about Cindy.

Chapter Sixteen

Audrey couldn't believe that she had let this guy kiss her like that. She didn't even know him. Her attraction to him embarrassed her and she wasn't sure why. He had awakened an overwhelming need within her, feelings that she hadn't felt in a long time. It must have seemed to him that she was some desperate female, begging for attention.

"How could I let that happen?" she said to herself.

What started out as a quick meal, a few drinks, and a little conversation, had ended with her back pressed against her car with his tongue down her throat? She had to admit the boy had some skills. She was a sucker for a good kisser and he was one of the best she had ever experienced.

As she pulled onto her street and parked the car, Freedom appeared from out of the darkness. He whined impatiently while she fumbled for the house keys.

"Okay, fella. I know I'm late." She laughed as the cat stretched, extending his body to its full length, swatting the jingling keys with his paw. He rubbed his arched back against her leg as she opened the door, then ran inside the house and straight to the kitchen. Audrey picked up the mail that lay in a pile beneath the slot in the door and headed for the kitchen. She gave her pet some chicken scraps and refilled his water dish.

Ignoring the pile of accumulating bills on the table and the light on the answering machine, she grabbed the Grace Edwards mystery she'd started reading, and placed it near the tub. Audrey turned the faucet and poured fragrant salts into the cascade, breathing in the hot sweet steam and watching the billow of suds rise before returning to her bedroom.

As she slid out of her clothes, she could still feel the remnants of his embrace. The thought of his kiss caused a flutter of desire she didn't try to deny. Returning to the bathroom, she slid into the hot sudsy water.

The bath was sexual torture. The bubbles licked at her nipples, the hot water teased the folds between her legs. She forgot about the novel as she leaned back on a headrest and imagined Jules and his wicked kiss filling every empty part of her. She let her hands go everywhere she imagined his tongue traveling. The feeling was too much and she had to make herself stop.

She finished her bath and pulled on a soft robe. She had put off the inevitable long enough and went through the pile of bills separating them into need to pay and this can wait stacks. She hoped Jules came through for her with some new clients. It was getting more difficult to remain upbeat with her financial situation hovering like death.

With considerable dread she began listening to the messages on the machine. Several calls were from bill collectors. Two or three more were from people who obviously didn't know her situation and wanted to sell her things. There was a call from Emory, still certain that she wanted his body and the call she'd placed to him, a mere ruse.

She just shook her head. He would never change. It was funny now but she remembered a time when she laughed to mask the tears. Even with the uncertainty that the future held, she still felt empowered and better off on her own.

Before she got in bed that night, she said a prayer of thanks to God that she was allowed all of the blessings in her life. She thanked him for the blessings that were coming to her in the future and that He would help her to learn from her struggles. Audrey slept a deep and restful sleep filled with dreams of love and untold success.

Chapter Seventeen

A.J. Daniels sat on the balcony, casting an embittered stare into his glass of scotch.

Every time he thought of the newscast and the statements that skinny Jew bastard made to the press, he became angry all over again. His name was Jules Dreyfus, a young hick lawyer who had the nerve to think he was going to get Ed Dixon off. He must not know who he was fucking with. A.J. would see to it that Dixon would be sent to prison at record speed for killing Jackie. Even if it meant getting rid of Dreyfus.

A.J. would get his man at city hall to do a background check and see what they could find out. In the meantime, he had other areas of his personal life, which were taking more of his attention than he had to spare. He had to resolve his relationships with his wife and his mistress. It was almost as though there was a reversal of his feelings for the two women. It was becoming increasingly difficult to deal with Madison. His feelings for Amanda began to deepen since the death of their daughter. He felt terrible being away from her now, but Madison was really giving him the blues.

She was in the bathtub now. He considered leaving while she dozed in the bed of sweet smelling bubbles. But he would wait. There was no need to disturb her just yet. She may as well enjoy her remaining time in their apartment. She would really pitch a bitch when he told her he hadn't renewed the lease. He'd have to tell her soon because they had thirty days to vacate the premises. He'd help her find a place to live, but he was cutting off his financial assistance. After five years, he couldn't just leave her out in the cold. But he could no longer stomach her.

When she'd attended the funeral of his daughter and made a scene because he sat with Amanda, that was the final straw. Soon after Jackie's death she began insisting that he marry her. Daniels felt her demands were the height of insensitivity. His sense of loss was overwhelming and she didn't seem to care. Since Madison hadn't known Jackie, she couldn't relate to his pain, let alone do anything to ease it. His only child was gone. He did not want to lose his marriage too. If he hurried, maybe he could salvage the remaining shreds of their love and nurture it into a vibrant relationship once more.

* * *

There was an eerie silence in the house when A.J. arrived there. He went from one room to another looking for her. She wasn't there. He began to remove his clothes. It had been almost a week since he'd showered at home and it felt good. The apartment always gave him the feeling of being in a hotel. A business trip. No matter how he tried to make his relationship with Madison into something more, it always felt temporary.

He worked up a hardy lather for the third time as if the suds would wash away past indiscretions. Once satisfied the hot water had absolved all sin, he grabbed the larger of the towels he'd set out and wrapped it around him. He tousled his wet hair with the smaller one as he padded through the master bath.

He stopped to look at himself in the mirror. It seemed he'd aged ten years in the past week. The sagging skin under his eyes was dark and he noticed a bit more gray in his thick wavy hair. Moving closer, he examined the crows feet that sprang from the corners of his eyes like tributaries. He was moving in for a closer look when he spied the sheet of pink stationery on the pillow. He hadn't noticed it when he came in. He walked toward the bed. When he read the words she had written it nearly drove him over the edge.

Chapter Eighteen

Last night had been rough. Ed Dixon found it difficult to sleep as he lay in the cell listening to the sounds of the bars sliding open and clanging shut. Throughout the night he heard the pitiful cries of grown men begging for everything from their lawyers to their mothers. The smell of the jail, a combination of disinfectant, piss and vomit, thickened the air like a tomb.

He lay there motionless waiting for sleep. His thoughts drifted back to another time when he was in jail. That had been in Hapeburg. He was jailed with about thirty other men. All of them were black. The reason for their detainment ranged from petty theft to murder. To his misfortune, Ed Dixon was a part of the latter group.

He had been sitting on the porch of the small house that he shared with Ellise and Joonie. Two cops, thick, mean looking and white approached from a cruiser that stopped abruptly in front of the house.

"Yew Ed Dixon?" Meaty Mayfield asked.

"You know who I am, Meaty. What's up?"

They didn't answer him. Meaty's face spread into a nasty grin as Beau Farrow grabbed him by the neck and flung him to the ground. Dirt stung his eyes and scratched his face.

Beau Farrow's biggest claim to fame was being the quarterback at Hapeburg's predominately white Riverview High. Ed had attended the so-called black school, Douglas, and had captained its team. Beau's team had never beaten Douglas and though the boys had graduated ten years earlier, this was apparently still a point of contention for him. He and Mark "Meaty" Mayfield had been inseparable as boys. Their careers in athletics stalled after school so they resigned themselves to another arena where they got a license to kick ass, the police academy.

The two were known throughout the small community for subjecting suspected criminals to severe beatings. Now they finally had the upper hand with Eddie Dixon.

Meaty put his knee into Ed's back, grabbed both arms behind his back and forced the circles of steel shut around his wrists. They yanked him from the dirt and drug him to the sedan, throwing him in headfirst. He could hear them laughing and talking in the front seat as if he were not there.

"Blacks don't know from nothin' but killin' an fuckin'." Meaty worked his words around a chaw of tobacco. "Now take our friend Eddie back air. He was fuckin' round with Betty Jo Blanchard even though he got that cute little Ellie or Elsie or whatever her name is, at home with their little nappy headed kid."

"I guess she wouldn't do the things that Betty Jo would do." Beau replied.

"Yeah Betty Jo sure knew how to satisfy a man. But for whatever reason, she just wouldn't put out for ole' Eddie back air. That's why he killed her."

"What?" Ed piped from the back seat.

They continued talking as if they hadn't heard a word.

"Pert near every cock in the county been inside ole black Betty. I beat her ass and fucked her myself one night for mouthin' off at me. I showed her what a woman's got a mouth for."

The two men laughed. Ed could hear what sounded like a bottle being opened. They passed it back and forth between them.

"Yeah, Hapeburg sure will miss her. She played hard to get with Eddie and he went and fucked her to death. A whole lotta men are gonna be pissed at you, buddy boy."

"Did you say Betty Jo was dead?" Ed had managed to twist himself into an upright position.

"I been at home with my family. If something's happened to her, ya'll can't put it on me."

The car suddenly veered sharply down an unpaved road. Dirt and debris kicked up by the tires, peppered Ed's face. He closed his eyes trying to shield them from the detritus. His head slammed forward and then hard into the back seat as the cruiser stopped in a clearing in the midst of a thicket of oak and pine trees.

A frightened and bewildered Dixon was snatched from the car and thrown onto the ground. The two men kicked him repeatedly. The steel toe boots they sported intensified the force of the beating. He tried to roll away but there was no escaping the assault. He pulled his limbs around himself, attempting to protect his head and face. They beat him until they were both breathing heavily and dripping with sweat.

"I'm hot." Breathed Beau. He leaned against the car. "We got any more beer?"

"I'm pretty sure we do. I'll check the cooler."

Ed wouldn't look up. He heard them pop the caps and swallow liquid in loud gulps. They took turns seeing who could belch the loudest, laughing and playing like a couple of kids cutting class. Until Ed heard his name, he'd wondered if they had forgotten him.

"How 'bout a drink Eddie?"

"He looks awfully dry, Meaty, all rolled up in the dirt like a possum."

They hooted and howled like animals. Ed could hear them open more beer. They swallowed it down and took turns crunching the cans underneath their heels.

"Let's clean this ole boy up and give him something to drink. We cain't take him in looking like that. What'll folks think?"

Ed could hear the sound of zippers and feel the hot sprinkle wash over him as the men relieved themselves on him. He struggled to keep the urine from going into his eyes and mouth. The sting of the putrid liquid burned into the cuts on his face. The memory, forever etched in his mind, was as permanent as their ignorance. He could still smell the stench of their hatred. The surface wounds eventually healed, but the pain would remain embedded in his heart forever.

Now so many years later, he found himself jailed again for something he did not do. Remembering the tears that he cried then, the anger and helplessness that he felt was nothing compared to the rage that he felt now. To have this happen to him twice was almost too much to imagine.

He made a promise to himself as he lay there listening to some poor bastard who didn't have the strength or the will to fight off his cell mate.

"I'm going to change my life." He said to himself.

"I'm never going to be in a mess like this again." He vowed.

At day break he got paper and pen from one of the guards. This would be his final and most impassioned plea to date. He only hoped that it worked. He felt that if he didn't bring closure to everything in his life, then he wouldn't find fulfillment on any level. He began to write.

Dear Ellise,

I know it's been a while since you've heard from me. I've sent you letters in the past and I don't know if you read them. I sent those letters because I was in pain and I was still dealing with my own feelings. You've always been smarter than me so I'm sure you saw right through the words written to the truth between the lines. I hope that you didn't give up on me after reading all that nonsense. I wouldn't blame you if you did.

How's Joonie? I know that he's smart and a good kid because he has such a positive role model in you. Please tell him that I love him Ellise. I want to see him. I want to see you, too.

I caused you a lot of pain. You trusted me and I let you down. I was so stupid. When I cheated on you, I cheated us all. It wasn't until I was out on my own that I really began to see just what I had. I'm so ashamed for what I did and all of the hurt I caused you. I'm really sorry.

Please find it in your heart to forgive me and I swear I'll never let you down again. My current situation is not a good one. I have faith that it will work out though. When I'm stronger, I will continue to build a strong foundation so that we can be a unit the way we planned all those years ago.

I would like to come there to see the two of you but I will not disrespect you by doing this unless I hear from you first. I know that you are a strong person and I'm sure you've built a solid life for yourself and our son. I would never disrupt that.

If you don't respond to this letter or have decided that it's best we stay apart, I'll understand. But if you want to get together and talk it over, please write to me care of

Attorney Jules Dreyfus at the address on the envelope.

With my deepest love and affection,

Ed

Ed Dixon bowed his head and prayed as he held the letter in trembling hands. He prayed that he would be released soon and that he could build a life with his family. He prayed that for once, just once, he could know what it felt like to live in this country as a man.

He sealed the letter and tucked it into his shirt pocket. He would talk to Jules and Audrey about his plans when they met later that day. Ed Dixon had done something during this period of incarceration that he had never done in his forty years of life. Ed Dixon had formulated a plan for his life.

Chapter Nineteen

The blinking red light on the answering machine ushered Rob into the small, sparsely furnished room. As he moved to check it, several scenarios played themselves out in his mind.

"Hello Mr. Hollingsworth. I'm calling about your past due account. AGAIN! Are you going to pay this bill or do I have to come over there and kick your ass?"

"Hey Robby Boy! How you doing man? (his brother, Jerry) *Hey listen, I thought if you're not doing anything later, we could go and have a drink just like old times. You know, shoot the shit, do that male bonding thang!"* (read: I'm broke. Can you spot me until Tuesday for a hamburger today?)

"Hi Rob. It's Amy (or Rita, or Brenda or Lisa). *I waited for you to come* over *yesterday and you never did. Is everything okay?* (Everything is great. That's why I don't want you over here stinking up the place.) *You said you would call me back the other day and you never did. You're just like all the rest of these assholes. You lying bastard."*

"Bitches." Rob said out loud referring to them all, including Jerry. Taking off his shirt, he tossed it onto the corner where a small mound of things were accumulating that needed to go into the wash. He put his nose near his arm pit and decided that a shower was in order.

Pulling off the rest of his clothes, he rolled them into a ball and slam dunked them into the pile of dirty clothes on the way to the bathroom. The bathroom was his favorite, and most spacious room in the house. It was the reason he'd bought the place. He didn't need much room in the rest of the house, but to Rob, the room with the throne should be a place of majesty.

He never grew tired of this room. He enjoyed cleaning it. The sill of the bay window above the sunken, whirlpool tub was lined with English Ivy which crept nearly to the ceiling. The ivy theme continued throughout the large room on the border and in the accents and accessories. The woodwork was painted white and adorned with green ivy shaped Formica knobs. The curtains were secured with forest green ties, and there were miniature filigree frogs peeping from tiny matching toadstools scattered amongst the greenery.

On either side of the commode was a white wicker wastebasket and a white wicker stand which housed a library of magazines and books. He may be a little lax with his housekeeping in other areas of the house, but this room was always spotless.

Rob opened the glass doors of the large shower stall and turned on the water. He brushed his teeth. Swishing mouthwash around in his mouth, he gargled before spitting it into the sink. With his left hand he lifted his penis and scratched an imaginary itch as he admired his teeth in the mirror. He let out a yawn as he waited for the water in the shower to get hot.

Stepping into the thicket of hot, wet needles, he relaxed as they massaged away the tension of the long work day. He soaped his hair and rinsed a couple of times before turning the water off. He grabbed a thick forest green towel and began to dry his hair.

He liked the feel of the air evaporating the droplets of water on his skin as he padded around the bathroom. He applied deodorant, and body lotion, then dragged a brush through his damp hair.

After scrubbing down the shower stall and sink, Rob collected the wet towel and added it to the stinky clothes mountain he had created next to the washing machine. Turning the dial, he listened as water filled the tub.

He lifted the empty box of detergent and mumbled a curse word. Running to the garage he retrieved the bags from an earlier shopping excursion. Leaving the other bags near the door, he took the detergent with him to the washer and dumped a heaping cupful into the drum and watched as the water turned sudsy. He chipped away at the stinky clothes mountain until the tub was full. The tub was happily agitating as he closed the lid.

Returning to his bed, he lay there on his back and let his thoughts turn to the Daniels case. His initial thought was that Dixon was not guilty of the crime. His certainty of the man's innocence became even more apparent as the evidence unfolded.

He believed Dixon's account of how he found the girl and got excited at seeing her breasts exposed and shot his wad. The semen on the towel was a match with his, his print was recovered from the girl's shoulder where he had moved her hair back to get a better look. The principal found Dixon standing over the body, and that was the extent of the evidence against him.

The skin found underneath the girls nails, a single hair, and more unidentified prints could not be tied to Dixon. The skin and hair belonged to an African American. The hair was natural with no chemical dyes or processing. That would narrow the focus considerably. Most of the students and faculty used every process imaginable to ensure they fit society's standard of beauty. Rob surmised the usage of relaxers, dyes, green and blue contact lenses, and maybe even skin lightener among these people was higher than anywhere in the tri-state area.

Several loud knocks interrupted his thoughts. Rob looked out of the bedroom window and saw Jerry at the front door impatiently shifting from one foot to the other. Rob walked toward the door shaking his head as he grabbed the knob and turned.

"Hey man, I been calling you all day. You could call a brother back sometimes."

"Sorry Jerry, I just got in and I wanted to shower before I checked my messages."

"Anything new going on with the Daniels case?"

"You know I can't discuss that with you Jerry." Rob stood between the doorway and Jerry, blocking his entry. He really didn't feel like being bothered. Jerry peeped over his shoulder and around his arm.

"You got company?"

"No."

"Are you 'gon let me in or make me stand in the door like a beggar?" Jerry pushed past his brother who stood there pondering the question that had been put to him.

"I came to see if you wanted to hang out with me tonight. We could watch the game, shoot the shit, throw down a few drinks…"

"Jerry I'm tired. It's been a long day and I'm not in the mood for that."

"You 'gon play me like that huh? I'm your brother, man. I come all the way over here cause I miss my baby brother. You know we only have each other and one day, well, who knows what might happen."

"Man, just shut up. You know where I keep the Jack. Help yourself." Rob made his way to the kitchen. He could hear Jerry rummaging around the liquor cabinet before he caught up to him and pulled out a chair at the table.

"I was getting ready to throw some shit into a pan for dinner." Rob turned to his brother, waving a stainless steel pot as he spoke. "You want some?"

"Uh, sounds appetizing bro, but I've had all the shit I can take for one day. I'll pass on that offer."

Rob shrugged and began slicing chicken, peppers and vegetables. He scooped up the chicken and dumped it into the heated wok. He filled a pot with water for the pasta and selected a crisp white wine from the cabinet. He was a good cook and planned to go to culinary school in the fall. When he received his pension in a few years, he'd open up a restaurant.

Jerry was on his second shot of Jack Daniels before he made his pitch. "Listen Rob, I got an opportunity to get in on the ground floor of this sweet deal. You're the first person that I'm telling about this. You can make a ton of money but we have to do it now. All I need is…"

Chapter Twenty

James Franklin sat in front of the television in the den drinking his third double bourbon. Relief replaced his nervousness when the story made the local news. There was no way the story would have broken before they were sure they had a solid case against Dixon.

Here it is again, he thought, his interview with Channel Six. He looked pretty good if he did say so himself. Were it not for the slight graying at his temples, he could easily pass for a man in his mid thirties. He worked out religiously, beginning each day with a six mile run. The full gym in his basement allowed him to keep his body fit and trim. He never let on how flattering it was when the youngsters at the school commented on how good he looked. He pretended not to notice the admiring looks from the female members of the faculty. He wouldn't give most of them the time of day. His wife Althea had given up trying to fulfill his needs a long time ago.

She was home now. He could hear her upstairs flitting around, a ball of energy, always in motion. She burst into the room rushing to her husband's side like a mother hen, trying to comfort him.

"I just heard what happened at the school. Are you all right?"

He ignored her, swiveling the recliner towards the wall. Althea was asking him all kinds of questions about Jackie Daniels and Ed Dixon and "what really happened?" He hated to hear the name Jackie Daniels. All this fuss over that little tramp. It made him sick. How many lives had she affected by living her life like a slut and then dying like one? He knew that this would definitely change things at the school and not for the better.

He'd had way too much to drink and wasn't in the mood for Althea's histrionics. She flew to him like a magpie, twittering her concern. The alcohol had nearly put him in a peaceful place. Like an ice bath, Althea shocked him into the present. Why didn't she leave him alone?

"Why didn't you tell me about this? No wonder you've been acting so strangely. I know that this is putting a lot of pressure on you. I'll bring you something to eat."

She flitted over and snatched the empty shot glass from the table and headed towards the stairs, talking all the while.

"I'll bet you've just been sitting down here worrying and drinking. That's not good for you. You've got to take care of yourself honey. I'll fix you a plate and a nice hot herbal tea."

"Would you just get the hell outta here?" James shouted. "And give me back that goddamn glass."

Franklin had to move quickly to avoid having the glass hit him. It splintered into a million pieces on the wall just above his head. His heart pounded as she ascended the stairs and slammed the door. He had to give Althea credit, she sure had balls.

*　　　*　　　*

The crowd was light today just as Althea liked it. That's why she preferred to go to the club in the early afternoon during the week. The weekends were unbearably crowded and she tended to stay away from here Friday through Sunday.

After putting her bags in a locker and stripping down to a fuchsia leotard and tights, she snapped the padlock shut and headed for the weight room.

"How are you today Mrs. Franklin?"

Althea smiled and nodded at Sue, one of the trainers who was usually there in the afternoons. She headed for the mirrored back wall and the assortment of free weights and spent the next two hours moving from one apparatus to the next, enjoying the sight of her muscles flexing and relaxing. She concluded her workout by returning to the weights, her favorite of all the items there. She liked the effects of resistance training, the definition in her triceps and biceps brought her many compliments.

She curled ten pound weights to her chest, then brought them down beside her muscular thighs. Beads of perspiration dotted her forehead as she worked through the final reps. When she was putting the weights back into the rack, she noticed that she'd nicked the acrylic coating on one of her nails. She'd have to get the nail repaired when she left the club, she thought. She did a series of stretches before heading for the showers.

Making a stop at the locker, she retrieved shampoo, conditioner, and her shower shoes from her bag. She looked at herself in the mirror and smiled.

"You a bad ass bitch!" she said in self-admiration. One of the other patrons eyed her curiously, quickly changed clothes and left the locker room. Althea just laughed. She used to hate working out. She'd always had a good body and didn't see any point in tampering with perfection. Her husband had always been athletic. As he began to distance himself from her, she took up swimming and running to try to get closer to him. Swimming wreaked havoc on her hair and running caused her joint pain. But she liked the way exercising made her feel so she joined a health club.

She'd tried half a dozen before she found one that she really liked. This place suited her needs perfectly. There were certified nutritionists on staff. If one chose, patrons could indulge in a light meal after partaking of the other services there. Massage therapists, skin technicians, and personal trainers were available for members as well. The closed changing and shower areas provided the privacy she craved after her workout.

She smiled at her reflection in the mirror. She was still trying to adjust to having her hair relaxed again after so many years of wearing the short afro. As long as she kept it in this short style, it wasn't too difficult to manage.

The shower was hot and washed over her muscular back, down her tight arms and legs. Her overworked body relaxed under the pulsating spray from the shower head. The scratches on her hand, made more pronounced by the intensity of the water, stung slightly. She pushed away the irritation that she felt remembering James and how rude he had been to her last night. How she had responded by throwing the glass. She examined the abrasions again. It seemed whenever she responded to him in anger, she always ended up hurting herself.

Her husband was a very vain man. He needed to look good. He also needed to have a good looking wife. And Althea did look good. She was pulled, primped, and pampered. She wore the finest clothes and exercised everyday. She took classes to expand her mind and remain on par with her husband who needed his mate to be an extension of himself. He was after all, the head of a prestigious academy. There were always benefits, fund raisers and other public affairs to promote the school.

But once the camera was off, the banquet over, the hands shaken, the checks received, James Franklin was through with his wife. Until the next time. So Althea stopped going to the salons and wearing the wigs and the flowing loungewear. The cut her hair and started wearing her hair natural. She gave up the fake nails and just kept her own buffed to a high gloss. James was shocked at her appearance, calling her everything from dog to dyke.

The two of them hadn't been intimate in years. There had been a couple of occasions during this hiatus that Althea had taken a lover. She slept with these men as much for spite as to fill a physical need her husband no longer felt obliged to provide.

But the trysts left her feeling empty and lonely. Afterwards, she desired the closeness of her husband more than ever. In spite of this, she continued to try to satisfy her love hunger in ways that did not include James. She even bought herself some sexy underwear and a vibrator and tried to 'love herself', but she felt so stupid lying there pinching her own nipples while jabbing the apparatus into her vagina, that she had to laugh at her own pitiful self. She threw the device into the trash can.

So her clandestine rendezvous were to the club to meet the rowing machine. She moaned as it pushed her to work every muscle. Her nipples hardened as she firmly gripped the dumbbells, working her pectorals. Her heart skipped a beat, its rate accelerated by thirty minutes on the treadmill. The water from the shower kissed her tenderly, soothing every tired muscle.

The lighted mirror reflected bright, even skin. Althea Franklin could have been a cover model for women over forty who had it goin' on. She smiled at the familiar face and applied blush and lipstick. She parted her short, slick hair and molded it into a cute style on her small head. She stepped into a short orange dress and matching sandals. She smiled again at her image in the glass. She had started taking care of herself because her husband had stopped wanting her. She would have done anything to keep him.

"Well, you finally got him." She said out loud as she exited the lounge, a flash of orange on golden brown skin.

Chapter Twenty-One

On Monday evening A.J. Daniels sat staring at the TV screen that had blued out after the video had ended. He pressed the rewind button, waiting for the click indicating its completion before pressing play. Though some of the scenes were out of focus and the quality of the film was poor, in no way was the appeal of the subject captured by the videographer diminished. There was something special about her even then. Thick auburn curls surrounded her cherubic face. She'd already developed a sense of timing. Of all the children performing at the recital, Jackie Daniels was a natural.

Her father watched the footage and listened as she sang her solo, the other participants and parents looking on. She was really something. When Amanda enrolled her in dance and vocal classes, she was little more than three years old. As an infant she'd shown signs of musical talent. The parents were quick to do whatever necessary to develop this faculty.

Jackie had rewarded them by attacking any opportunity put before her with great alacrity and determination. She would practice a particular step for hours until she got it just right. Any areas where she lacked natural ability, she more than made up for in intensity and hard work. She never gave up.

Throughout her life Jackie was involved in a variety of activities. It was music and drama as a youngster. As she matured, she developed an interest in politics and teaching. She loved children and devoted a lot of time to her students.

Daniels continued to watch the screen and the image of his little golden princess, his baby. Tears clouded his vision, making it difficult for him to see. When he clicked off the machine, it was as if the same switch controlled his emotions. Huge sobs wracked his body. He allowed the wave of pain to wash through him. First Jackie, now Amanda, gone. They had been married in name only, shared a distant union that had no name. Knowing she'd really left him sent daggers of pain through his heart that he hadn't expected. How could he have lost them both? A lonely feeling descended, darkening everything around him. Not since A.J. had been a small child had he felt so alone. He sat looking at the blank screen for a long time, wondering what he should do next.

Chapter Twenty-Two

Audrey and her brother Bobby had been working together to form a partnership which would utilize both their areas of expertise. It had become apparent several years ago that Bobby's best years in the pros were behind him. He'd run from Audrey and her suggestion that they partner, thinking that there was no way a union between the two of them would work. They had always clashed as kids. Bobby didn't see how things had changed that much and couldn't see how they could work together without being at each other's throats.

The business plan she'd put together was viable and she was anxious to get started. Her brother saw things differently. As they sat in her office that Monday evening, nothing had changed. No sooner had she begun laying out the newest version of the plan than Bobby started shooting down everything that she said.

"That's it?" Bobby sounded unimpressed.

"Well, if you'll let me finish…the best way for the athlete to maintain better control in contract negotiations is not going in like some money ignorant chump."

"Whoa, wait a minute. I think I know a little bit more about how an athlete thinks than you do." He huffed. "You might know how to present this kind of stuff to those stuffed shirt wannabe's that you deal with, but most of these brotha's come from very humble beginnings. They're not comfortable around all that big talk about IPO's and investment portfolios." He wagged his finger at her emphatically.

"You're going to have to break it down or you'll lose them before you even get started."

"I disagree Bobby. Why coddle them?" She shrugged. "They get enough of that from the schools and the league. I think you're selling these guys short."

"I *am* one of these guys."

"That's my point. Look at you. Since you got such a late start dealing with the business aspect of the sport, you can see where you made a lot of mistakes because nobody ever told you that the real game is played in the board room. If we're able to pitch this plan to these guys when they're being scouted or maybe the first year that they sign with the pros, then they will be so much better off when their careers come to an end. There are a lot of guys out there that don't make it to superstar status like you did. You can still go pretty far on your name. But what about all those other guys? Many of them won't be so lucky. What are they supposed to do?"

"I'm not saying you're wrong in what you want to do, I'm just saying your approach is all wrong." Bobby reasoned.

"Well then," she came around the desk and propped her butt on the edge of it. "You tell me…how do I approach them?"

"You don't approach them. I do."

"You?" She snorted. "You don't know a thing about investing and income planning."

"Well, judging by the enormous influx of clients I see streaming through your door, you may not know all that much yourself."

"Excuse me? That's a low ass thing to say Bobby." She shouted. "You know I'm just getting started. I'm doing everything that I can to build my client base."

"Including pimping me to bring big moneyed ball players into your organization." He was standing now, hovering over her like a dark, angry cloud.

"And what's wrong with expecting my brother to have sense enough to know that we can scratch each other's backs? I resent being characterized as a pimp when for years you've let managers and promoters help send your black ass to bankruptcy court." She poked his chest with her finger. "You never thought of them as pimps, but that's exactly how a lot of folks see those nasty blood suckers. You don't see any of them reaching out to players once their playing days are over."

They were both winded and took a few minutes to catch their breaths and to think up new arguments. Their meetings always turned out this way. The two siblings had carried on a heated rivalry since they were kids. Audrey, being the oldest, had taken her place as the trio's matriarch, scolding them when they misbehaved and telling them the right thing to do. Renita was the calming force. She was in the middle in sentiment as well as in birth order among the siblings. As the youngest of the bunch, Bobby was the spoiled only son, the baby of the family. This gave him certain privileges as did simply being male. He rebuffed his oldest sister at every opportunity from about the age of twelve until this very day. She could still hear his pre-pubescent voice screaming at her.

"Just because you're the oldest don't make you the boss!"

"Look, Audrey." She looked up. Her brother towered over her. His forehead wrinkled in displeasure. He was pissed off and the meeting was over.

"This is never going to work." He shook his head. She felt the warmth of the heavy sigh he released. "You know we can't get along. We never could. You never respected my ideas because you still see me as Little Bobby. I'm trying to explain my experiences to you in a profession that you know nothing about." His tone had softened some, but it still smoldered from the fire of his anger. "You should at least give me the courtesy that you would any other professional. When you're ready to talk business, give me a call. But don't bring me here again to waste my time." He slammed the door so hard behind him that Audrey thought the glass would break.

Chapter Twenty-Three

The information was on his desk when he arrive at the office Tuesday morning. Anger coursed through him like a river of lava as he looked at the vile photographs. A.J. Daniels slammed the folder down with such force that several loose papers left their resting places on the oak surface, scattering to the floor like dancing leaves on an autumn day. Was she trying to humiliate him? The pictures the investigator left with him burned into his brain. Amanda had taken the cottage he'd bought for Jackie's use and turned it into something nasty. And with a common, ten cent, flat footed cop at that. The pictures said it all. The two of them in various stages of undress, there was no mistaking what was going on. She had gone way too far this time.

Daniels looked at the pictures again. His stomach felt queasy. According to the report, in the two weeks since Amanda had moved out, the cop had practically moved in with her. He remembered this guy. He was the big cop who'd come over to tell them about Jackie. He remembered the uneasy feeling he had then as his wife looked at him, flirting shamelessly. Their daughter hadn't been dead a month and she had formed a relationship of this nature with this man. They were carrying on like common trash.

She'd be sorry, though. That boyfriend of hers would be lucky if he could get a job as a security guard in a mall parking lot when he was through with him. A.J. let the anger rise up in him. As the bitterness and hurt subsided, reasoning took its place. Perhaps the whole thing had been his fault. After all, he had been involved with Madison for more than five years and scores of other women before that. It was over between him and Madison now. He was ready to be a husband to Amanda and wasn't about to let this man stand in his way. He looked at the pictures again. He read the expression on her face in the one close-up. Her eyes told him more than he needed to hear. Unless something happened to change the current situation, Amanda would be lost to him forever.

Chapter Twenty-Four

Jules' confidence in the outcome of the case was bolstered by the lab results he'd just reviewed. This was the kind of news he had hoped for. The semen that was on the girls body and the discarded towel was a positive match with that taken from Ed Dixon. That was no surprise. The man had already admitted ejaculating near the body. The good news was that there was at least one other source of the evidence which was collected at the scene. Without an identity to attach to the samples, and the fact that his client was not connected with the evidence, was certainly enough to place reasonable doubt in the mind of a jury. If it went that far.

According to the evidence, Jackie had fought pretty hard with her assailant. Ed Dixon had no scratches, abrasions or other evidence that he'd been involved in such a violent confrontation. They were not able to match the skin taken from the nails of the decedent to the samples collected from Ed Dixon. There was one fingerprint match, but the others belonged to someone else. It would be an embarrassment for the state to bring the case to trial as it stood. Their only chance would be to get the judge to disallow the samples that did not match Dixon.

If this was not enough information to make them release Dixon on the spot, they would a least have to seriously consider someone else's involvement and redirect their efforts.

They were in the process of testing sample tissue from the fetus. If the father of the baby wasn't the killer, he would at least be questioned so that any involvement on his part could be ruled out.

For whatever reason, the DA had his mind set on Ed Dixon's guilt. He was applying pressure and the city responded by being as difficult with Jules as the law would allow. They only released information if it was requested. He got no more than what he asked for. Once he understood the game they were playing, Jules just relaxed and let them have their fun. He was wise to the game playing that seemed to be a necessary part of his profession. He remained resolute, keeping his focus on the task at hand. No matter what their tactics, his client's innocence would be proven. It was time for him to see Ed. He grabbed his files and the information he had requested earlier from the fax machine and headed out the door.

He spent the rest of the afternoon going over lab results with Ed, making sure that he understood that once the DNA results were in on the fetus, they would have to release him. They just didn't have enough concrete evidence to hold him. If he had to, he would make them get a sample from every male that Jackie Daniels knew until they found a match.

Ed didn't look too convinced. He had been locked up a long time. Too long. Depression was setting in. Jules hoped that the other information that he had for him would lift his spirits. He handed Ed the documents that had been faxed to him earlier from the two realty companies.

"Read over these Ed and let me know what you think. We'll discuss the next step in a few days. That is, if you want to proceed with the purchase."

Ed Dixon scanned the facsimiles, looking hopeful for the first time that day.

"You're familiar with the building on Hartley, right?" Jules asked. "It's the same building where my office is located. The residential rental property is old, but it's in a solid working class community. I think it's a good investment. There's a nice apartment in the building all ready for you to move into. They sent pictures and diagrams of the sites. Look 'em over and let me know if you have any questions."

"Jules, you don't know what this means to me. I really appreciate it." He shook the lawyers' hand who replied with a hearty slap to Ed's back. "This more than anything shows your confidence in me and your belief in my innocence. Thank you."

"Ed, this is business. I take you very seriously. As a matter of fact, I have a proposition for you once we're through with this case."

Ed Dixon gave his lawyer a quizzical look as the two shook hands and the younger man left the room.

* * *

A wave of hunger washed over Jules as he entered copious notes into his laptop. He'd returned to his office after the meeting with Ed Dixon. The rest of the day had been so full he'd forgotten to eat. The bagel he'd brought in that morning remained on its plate. The single bite had changed the circle to a "C". Considering it for a moment, he picked it up and tossed it into the trash can. His head pounded. He tried to remember when he'd eaten last.

He'd stayed up last night bagging Cindy's belongings. He'd left several messages at her mother's that she needed to come get her stuff. He was ready to move on. The sooner she removed the last vestiges of their relationship from his life, the better.

He missed Audrey. He hadn't seen her since their last encounter. Though the case was consuming, a small section in his cluttered head was reserved for personal thoughts. Visions of her chewed away at this space until he found himself thinking about her more and more. Her smooth brown skin, easy manner and warm smile, sent a current of heat coursing through his veins. Thinking of her soft lips on his made him dizzy.

When she opened her luscious lips to say his name, his rumbling stomach drowned out the auditory attached to the daydream. He turned off his computer, grabbed his wallet and headed out the door to an eatery down the street.

It was hot in Roselli's. The oven filled an entire wall of one side of the tiny restaurant. The smell of fresh baked bread and sizzling vegetables and meats cooking made his stomach churn. They couldn't fix his order fast enough. He grabbed the box containing the large loaded pizza like a hungry dog being offered a bone. His next stop was the nearby wine shop where he purchased two bottles of Merlot. The food and drink was a great excuse to see her. It was presumptuous of him he knew, but it was late and he gambled that she'd be working and hadn't yet eaten dinner.

It was eight o'clock when he knocked on Audrey's door. It opened so abruptly that he was practically knocked off balance. He struggled to keep the containers of food from falling on the floor.

The man was tall, perhaps six feet seven, maybe taller. His build was powerful and athletic, crowned by a lean face with full, handsome features, and deep brown skin. He scowled at Jules, who flinched. The man smirked, shook his head and boarded the rickety elevator which had waited for him as though even it were intimidated.

Jules pushed open the door to Audrey's office. He could feel the heat of her anger before he saw her face. She looked up and either didn't see him or chose to ignore him. He entered and closed the door. He wanted to run to her, protect her. But the thought of her visitor returning sent fear through him. Although he wanted to protect her, somehow he felt he'd be useless against the man who'd dwarfed his six foot, two inch one hundred eighty pound frame. He touched her shoulder.

"Are you okay?"

She ignored his query.

"I just thought you might be hungry. I got a pizza and salad."

Still nothing.

"I'll just leave this stuff here and when you feel better, give me a call." He put the packages on the table and turned to leave. He opened the door, walked through it, then turned back.

"Shit, I'm the one who's hungry. Give me my food back!" He started collecting the packages and headed for the door.

"Wait! I'm sorry Jules. I'm just so pissed off right now I can hardly think straight."

"I don't think anything's wrong with your thinking. I noticed as soon as I said I was taking my food, you snapped right out of your funk."

Audrey laughed. That intoxicating tinkle of bells that he loved. Jules wasn't going anywhere.

"So are you saying that I was just being rude?" The aroma of hot bread and rich sauce seemed to relax her.

"What do you call it? I've been standing here for the longest being completely ignored." He feigned irritation. Being there with her made his heart pound. He inhaled, trying to separate her fragrance from the smell of the food.

"I was not ignoring you." She replied. "I was just trying to get my head together."

"There's never a good reason for bad behavior. But if that's how it is, two can play that game." He moved the box to her coffee table, opened it and dramatically pulled a gooey slice towards her, then away. "I'm starving. I haven't eaten in two days and I'm going to stay here and eat my dinner. And you know what? I'm not giving you one bite!" He rolled the slice into a cylinder and took a healthy bite.

"How mean could one person be to another?" She moved toward the box, but he blocked her.

Jules ignored her, giving all of his attention to the greasy pie. He popped open the box again. Hot, spicy aroma filled the room. He took a huge bite of the second slice. A long, rubbery string of cheese quivered between his mouth and the juicy slice of pie. He wrapped the cheese string around the slice, which he'd rolled like the last one to keep the heavy toppings from falling onto the floor.

"All right. I apologize for being rude." Audrey put her hand near the box again. He slapped it and closed the box shut.

"I said I was sorry," she pouted. "You're not leaving this office without giving me a slice of that pizza!"

Jules opened the box. She didn't know it, but he would have given her anything at that moment. She had given him more than she knew just by being near him.

They ate pizza and salad, and drank wine until their stomachs were heavy and their moods were light. They sat on the floor. The empty food containers lay on a coffee table that Audrey had protected with a lace cloth. The first bottle of wine was gone and Jules was pouring the remnants of the last bottle into their glasses. He was enjoying her company, but he was slightly distracted. She hadn't mentioned the guy who was here earlier and he didn't want it to seem like the incident was still on his mind after almost two hours. But it was. Who was that guy and why had he upset her so?

"Well, that's the end of the wine." Jules said, turning the bottle up and letting the remaining drops trickle into her glass. "Do you want me to get some more?"

Audrey looked up at him with intoxicated eyes and put a finger to his mouth.

"No. I think you've had enough for tonight." She said. Before he realized what he was doing, he was kissing her fingers. Then he was kissing her hand. She withdrew it. Her eyes were now clear. She began to pick up the containers from the table. She took the glasses over to the tiny sink and began to wash them. He watched her determined movements as she wiped up the excess water with a cloth. The towel was soaked. She turned around with the glasses in her hands, tiny rivulets of water fell from the glasses to her smooth dark fingers and onto the floor.

Jules grabbed a roll of paper towels. Pulling off what seemed like half the roll, he brought them to her to use on the glasses. But she didn't. She couldn't. Jules' arms were encircling her, his mouth was on hers. She responded passionately. To him it felt as new as their first kiss and as passionate as if it would be their last. It was the kind of kiss that made up for a lifetime of searching. They remained in their embrace even after the glasses slipped from her hands and crashed to the floor.

Chapter Twenty-Five

"Mr. Daniels is expecting you. Please come this way."

The detectives followed the willowy woman with wispy bleached hair into the inner sanctum which was the office of A.J. Daniels.

The DA extended a curt nod to Rob and Jake. He didn't offer them a seat so the detectives remained standing. Rob didn't like the feel of this. The man's demeanor was beyond cold. Most of his hostility was directed toward Jake. He must have found out about Jake and Amanda. Jake told Rob that Amanda had moved into another place and that he was over there every night. She told him that her marriage was one in name only and that her husband didn't care if she had lovers. Rob tried to tell him he was stupid to deal with this woman, but Jake wouldn't listen.

"We're in love with each other, Rob. She's going to get a divorce and we're getting married."

No amount of reasoning with his partner would make him reconsider what Rob saw as professional suicide at best. Worse case scenario, Jake could be the victim of a mysterious accident, or just disappear. Rob had met men like Daniels before. A.J. Daniels was dangerous.

"I've seen the lab results gentlemen and I'm not pleased. I want a conviction! If that black savage bastard gets off after what he did to my baby, you'll both be picking up aluminum cans for a living."

Rob glared at the DA. It didn't seem to matter to him if they had the right man. He wanted a conviction. Rob realized this situation was way beyond a man losing his daughter. To Daniels it was a personal affront as well as an embarrassment to the department. It sent the message that someone could kill the daughter of the District Attorney and get away with it.

"I want a progress report on this case as it develops." He looked at the duo expectantly. "Well?"

"Sir, the case against Dixon just isn't that strong." Rob said. "He's being released tomorrow."

There was an uncomfortable silence. The DA's icy stare made the room feel one hundred degrees hotter that the artificial setting of seventy.

"We're interviewing the names from your daughter's private telephone line. We're hoping we can match someone from that list to the DNA evidence from the crime scene and with that of Jackie's unborn child." Jake stammered in response. His usual confidence had left him. The powerful man *was* intimidating. The fact that Jake was screwing his wife didn't help things either.

"I already know all that you dumb bastard! I read those fucking reports before you do." Unable to hold the man's icy glare, Jake Hurley looked away. He searched his partners eyes for help but Rob quickly averted his gaze. 'You're on your own my man.' Rob thought as Jake sweated through the ordeal. His bright blue eyes clouded as Daniels took several steps forward, facing Jake. The DA's ominous tone surrounded him like an approaching storm.

"How long have you been a detective?" It was almost a whisper. To Rob the man seemed much more threatening now than when he yelled at them. Rob couldn't remember the last time someone had sent a chill up his spine. He could only imagine how Jake was feeling. This muthafucka was scary as hell.

"Seven years sir." Jake responded. "I've been with the department sixteen years total."

"Do you like your job?" Daniels smiled in a strange, sadistic way, taking great pleasure in Jake's discomfort.

"Most definitely sir."

Daniels stood in front of Jake, dead silent. Droplets of sweat from Jake's forehead trickled downward, connecting with the pool that dampened his collar. They stood there mere seconds but it seemed that everything had slowed down. A frightening hush filled the room. The detectives were afraid to move or speak.

"Go." He gave the dismissive wave, shooing them like two pesky flies. They almost tripped over each other running to the door.

Chapter Twenty-Six

The small gray office smelled of cigarette smoke and was furnished with cheap gray furniture that was probably older than the men who filled its space. Papers cluttered the dingy metal desk. An overflowing ashtray and a plaque which read 'THE BUC STOPS HERE', were the finishing touches to the cop chic décor. Police Chief Ned "Buc" Buchannon dropped the lit cigarette he was smoking into the cup of cold coffee. Jake Hurley, one of his best detectives, had given notice. It was Wednesday, several days since Daniels last meeting with Hollingsworth and Hurley. The resignation would be effective immediately. Considering the circumstances, he wasn't surprised that Jake would leave, but he hated to see any good cop go.

He'd called Rob Hollingsworth in to get his take on the situation with Jake. How much did he know? They were both good men, but Hollingsworth was the sharper of the two. Hurley had gotten himself into quite a predicament. Though he skirted around his true reason for wanting out, Buchannon knew the score. So did practically everyone else in the department.

"Has Hurley told you of his decision to leave the department?"

"We discussed it sir."

"What's the deal with him anyway?" He searched through the clutter on his desk until he found a battered package of cigarettes. "I completely extended myself to him. I told him that every resource available to the department is his for the asking. He could have taken a leave, started getting counseling, gone on light duty, any number of things." He fished a bent cigarette from the crumpled pack, pushed it into his mouth and lit it. He took a long drag before he continued. "Why would he give up everything that he's worked for when he's so close to retirement?"

"I'm as shocked about this as you are, Chief. But there's nothing I can do. Jake's made up his mind."

They talked a few minutes more before Hollingsworth returned to his office. Buc looked after him, making sure that he was involved in the work on his desk before picking up the phone.

"The information that you got on Hurley. Bring it with you tonight. Yeah, the usual place. Five o'clock."

* * *

Rob left Buchannon's office feeling tired and a little sad. He understood why he was leaving his job and he felt bad for his buddy. If he had the DA on his ass, he'd leave too. Things had started to go bad for him there. Some of the detectives were beginning to give him the cold shoulder. His relationship with Amanda Daniels had somehow become public knowledge and no one wanted to be associated with a detective who had the DA as an enemy.

Rob tried to humor him, get his mind off his worries. But there was no dealing with Jake on anything of substance and he wasn't in the mood for jokes. The look of dread on his partner's face led Rob to believe that Jake was dealing with some issues that he couldn't or wouldn't discuss.

The two of them sat in the car looking straight ahead letting sounds of the street replace conversation. Rob drove with no destination in mind. He thought if he got away from their district, Jake would be more apt to open up to him. Lush green lawns and clean streets were inevitably replaced by gray, sterile ground and concrete as they left

Rosemont Hills for some of the less fertile surrounding communities. Wealthy to middle class, to poor.

He soon crossed over into Gatewood. A low income, high crime area in east Rosemont. This had been Jake and Rob's original patrol area when they became partners years before.

They had overcome a lot, getting used to each other as policemen and then as men. After clashing about everything from race to religion, people to politics, they finally became friends. The two men were a dichotomy in every sense of the word. But when Rob saved Jake's life right on the street they were traveling now, their relationship changed. They were almost inseparable since then.

"Are you all right?" He asked Jake.

"I'm cool man."

"You still haven't told me why you're quitting the force. I know you're under the gun and you care a lot for Amanda, but this is your career." He struggled to keep the mounting irritation from spilling out with the words. "You worked hard to get where you are. If you leave now, they'll give you next to nothing. You're pissing away your retirement."

"I may not have a choice." The words came out as little more than a hopeless whisper.

"What do you mean?" Curiosity wrinkled Rob's brow.

"I've been getting a lot of strange calls at work and somebody's been tailing me. It's either a high-end PI or a group from some other arm of the government. The stuff I've been seeing isn't from the local level."

"I don't know what you're talking about."

"Good. The less involved you are, the better." Jake looked out of the window at litter strewn streets and graffiti laden walls. "I'm doing what I have to do, Rob. Trust me. I'm kinda regretting I had any conversations with Buchannon. I should have just left without a word."

"You think Buchannon's involved in what's been happening to you?"

He shrugged in frustration. "Who knows? All I do know is that this heat is major league. I know when to fold and that's what I'm doing."

"Where are the two of you going?" Jake told him that he and Amanda would be leaving the area. It was the only way he could see they would be safe from A.J. Daniels.

"We're not sure yet. When I know I'll let you know. I love her man. That's one of the few things I'm certain of anymore."

"I know, man. Look, I made a bunch of dumb ass remarks about you and Amanda and I'm sorry for that. I know now that the two of you really love each other. That's important. It's hard to find someone who really cares. I hope you guys find a place where you can be happy."

"Thanks, Rob." Jake's smile was fragile but sincere. "You've been a great partner to me and an even better friend. I'll miss you a lot."

"Ah, don't go soggy on me, man. See, you wasn't like this before you fell into love."

"What do you mean 'fell into love' like it's a booby trap or something." Jake's laugh possessed the spirit of his old self.

"Shit, it is. Remember those old Tarzan movies when the trappers would step into that rope booby trap that would leave its victims suspended upside down from a big ass jungle tree? That's what love is."

"You're sick, man." Jake smiled at his friend then turned and looked out of the window. He didn't want to think about working without his friend.

"Amanda has filed for divorce. As soon as the ink dries I'm going to ask her to marry me. I want you to be my best man."

"Thanks, man. You know I'm right there with you." Rob found this whole thing so hard to believe. Who would have thought that Jake Hurley would fall for anyone? Let alone Amanda Daniels. Go figure.

They didn't speak for a while. It had started to rain and they watched rivulets stream down the windshield. Dark clouds thickened as the precipitation intensified. The rumble of thunder played in the distance. Rob turned the wipers up a notch to increase visibility.

"Stop here a minute Rob. I want to run into the convenience store and get a bottle of wine for dinner. Hey, why don't you come over? I want you and Amanda to get to know each other better."

"Shit man, if she get to know me she'll leave your weak ass. Why you gotta stop on this side of town? Can't it wait until we get back to The Hills?"

"I'll just be a minute." He was already opening the car door when Rob pulled into a parking space. Jake darted into the store. The grimy, iron barred door clanged shut behind him, swallowing him in the establishment's gloomy abyss.

The rain was coming down in sheets now. Rob sneaked a donut from Jake's box on the dash and grabbed the newspaper from the back seat, pulling out the sports section. He was halfway through the paper when he heard the door to the store slam shut. He hurriedly wiped crumbs from his face, hoping Jake wouldn't notice the donut box was a couple of pastries light.

The sudden horrific sound of flesh meeting steel sent a wave of nausea through him. He threw the paper aside and in a flash was out of the car into the cold wet street. Sound seemed muffled and motion had slowed to a crawl.

He never saw the vehicle that hit his partner. Scarcely remembering how he got outside the car, he found himself kneeling before the lifeless, bloody, distorted body of his friend. Blood gushed from a gash in Jake's head. Rob lifted it, cradling Jake's lifeless torso close. He rocked him in his arms, futilely consoling his partner and himself. The rain washed his friend's blood into the speeding street river, carrying it with leaves and trash into the gutter.

He held the battered body of his friend and cried. It saddened Rob to think that Jake's true form and spirit were no longer there. His body, crushed bone inside flesh, as shattered as the bottle inside of the bag he still gripped in his hand.

Chapter Twenty-Seven

The glare from the screen illuminated Jules' face as he pecked the keyboard. It was almost six o'clock. He should have been finished working a long time ago, but his mind wandered. It had been several days since he'd seen Audrey. Memories of their last encounter dominated his thoughts. The woman was a puzzlement, a distraction he scarcely needed. He told himself after their last meeting that he would just forget about her. He had long ago given up trying to understand women.

One minute they were standing in her office in a passionate embrace, the next, she was asking him to leave. From their first encounter, she had been a paradox, friendly one minute, aloof the next.

He heard the muffled sounds of footsteps in the hall during the day and wondered if it was her. She hadn't dropped by to speak to him. It was like their encounter had not occurred. Perhaps the thing to do was just forget about it. If she was interested, she'd let him know. He told himself to just let it go. But thoughts of her still whispered gently in his ear, lightly tickling his thoughts. She must have strong feelings for him. The signs were all there. The flirting back and forth, the eye contact. What about that kiss?

He considered going to her office, not leaving until he'd convinced her to own up to her obvious attraction to him. Upon reconsideration, he decided it best to wait her out. Besides, he had the Daniels case and several others that he needed to focus on.

His last few meetings with Ed had been very positive. There would be a hearing tomorrow and in all likelihood, Dixon would be released. There was nothing definitive proving his guilt in anything but having weird sex fantasies with a corpse. He wasn't the father of the unborn child. The semen on the towel and the eye witness testimony had been damaging, but there were too many other things that did not match. There was no connection between his client and the hair, skin and fiber evidence. The prosecutor knew that his case was weak. They had no choice but to let him go.

Saving the document that he was working on, Jules clicked off the computer. He picked up the remote control and aimed it at the television. As he straightened his desk, he half listened to the intro to the six o'clock news.

"Our top story tonight is a reported fatal hit and run collision which took the life of Rosemont Detective Jake Hurley. Hurley was one of the lead detectives in the Jackie Daniels murder case. The detective was leaving a store when he was struck while crossing the street. The driver of the light colored or white truck never stopped and the detective was killed instantly."

"Detective Hurley joined the police force more the sixteen years ago and was promoted to detective in 1993 after transferring from the Hope Springs precinct. He is survived by his parents, a sister and three brothers, all of Hope Springs.

A press conference this afternoon answered questions that cropped up amid rumors of moral misconduct on the Detective's part, which led to his leaving the department recently.

"At six we'll be talking to Police Chief Buc Buchannon about the death of the detective and how this new development affects the Daniels case."

Chapter Twenty-Eight

The day was filled with questions and reports. Internal Affairs sent two of its most loathsome bloodhounds, Skofield and Meyers, to conduct the interrogation. The men took turns hurling questions at Rob, hardly giving him time to think. They grilled Rob like he had so often badgered the thugs he and Jake brought in off the streets. His head pounded and he wanted to lash out at someone. To them it was gossip, something to kick around with the guys over a beer. Or it was part of the job. They had to file detailed reports, so the questions were asked again and again. Rob hated them all right now. It seemed none of them cared that Jake was gone.

"What were the two of you doing in that area?"

"Why did you stop at that particular store?"

"What were you doing while Hurley was in the store?"

"Why didn't you get an ID on the truck?"

"Is that the best description you can give us?"

"Nobody else saw the vehicle. Is that right?"

"Did Hurley say anything before he left the car?"

"Did he say anything before he died?"

"Were there any witnesses?"

"Okay, one more time from the top." Skofield gnawed on a toothpick eyeing the clock overhead like he'd rather be somewhere else. "What were the two of you doing in that neighborhood?"

It had been raining like hell. No one was outside. Rob had been inside the car reading the newspaper and barely caught a glimpse of the truck as it sped around the corner. He didn't even know what color it was. Was it light blue, tan, white? No matter how hard he tried, he just didn't know. The only thing he was sure of was that Jake, his partner and friend, was dead. He had been right there and hadn't seen anything that would help them catch the person who did it. He put his head in his large hands and tried to push back the pain and anger that consumed him. When he closed his eyes he could see Jake's smiling face, hear his profanity peppered conversation about most anything. Then the soft expressions of love for Amanda.

It was nearly four o'clock when they let him go. He filed the report and reviewed the latest information Jake had regarding the Daniels case. They were planning to conduct interviews based on their findings from the phone company. For Rob the only way to get past his pain was to work through it.

"You sure you don't want to take some time off, Hollingsworth?" Ned Buchannon crushed out a cigarette in a stained white ashtray, full to the brim with butts and ashes.

"I gotta finish this Chief, for Jake."

"That's a noble gesture Rob, but you look like you could use a break." Buc looked at his subordinate who stood there stone faced.

"All right, go on. Take Smiley and McPherson with you."

—

Rob pushed the bell three times before Althea Franklin opened the door. She opened the door a crack like she was afraid to let anything in or out. She eyed them suspiciously without speaking.

"Good evening ma'am. I'm Detective Hollingsworth. This is Officer Smiley and Officer McPherson. Is Mr. Franklin in?"

"What's this about? My husband is lying down and doesn't want to be disturbed."

"I'm afraid I'll have to insist ma'am."

The principal's wife let out an abhorrent sigh. She stepped aside and let them into the foyer.

"Come in and have a seat." She said, making a sweeping motion with her hand in the direction of a room to the right of the vestibule. The beautiful room they entered had been completely bastardized by its décor. The pattern on the green and gold flecked wall paper displayed embossed cannons, muskets, and swords. There was a hideous gold bust resting on an ornate gilded stand in the center of the room. The furniture was from several different periods. With nothing to pull the eclectic pieces together, the overall effect was early flea market. The room was further vitiated by ornately framed paintings of pink cheeked ladies with lacy parasols and stiff collared gents seated in horse drawn carriages. The few tasteful reproductions of the masters were wasted among the collection of obscure artists' weak renditions of Toulouse-Lautrec, Renoir and Delacroix. Althea's attempt to show culture and refinement fell miserably short. The trio of law enforcement was still standing, held captive by the collection when Mrs. Franklin returned.

"Mr. Franklin is getting dressed. He'll be with you shortly."

"I'm a bit of a collector and history buff." The woman asserted, assuming their looks were of appreciation rather than wonder at the portraiture, pastoral scenes, American Revolution and the Civil War. The mingling of antacid pink, sea foam green with gold accents, swirled throughout the room, daring them to keep down their lunches. Mrs. Franklin was still prattling on about the history of her acquisitions when her husband entered the room.

"Detective Hurley?" Franklin approached Rob with his hand extended.

"Hollingsworth." A sharp pain stabbed his heart at the mention of Jake's name.

"We need you to come downtown with us sir and answer a few questions regarding the Jackie Daniels case."

"What?" Franklin stood there, his hand, which Rob never took, was still extended. The unanswered shake fell limply to his side.

"Do you mind coming with us, sir?" Rob said.

"Do I mind? Do I have a choice?" Franklin raised his voice in indignation. "Are you arresting me?"

"We would like for you to come downtown with us for questioning. You are not under arrest, sir." Rob motioned to the officers who moved over to Franklin, flanking him. Daring him to make one false move.

"Why can't you talk to me here?"

"Mr. Franklin if you want, we can get a court order, or we could arrest you on suspicion of murder. Take your pick. Now would you come with us?"

The detective eyed 'Martha Stewart' who seemed totally oblivious to the situation at hand. But as Rob looked deeper, he realized that it was not a lack of awareness on her part, but a lack of concern.

"You're more than welcome to call your attorney when we get to the station." Smiley said. They all walked from the mausoleum, towards the door. Althea Franklin was quickly closing it behind them.

"Call Horace Owen and tell him to meet me downtown." The door closed on the rest of his plea to his wife.

Chapter Twenty-Nine

James Franklin sat at a small table in a cramped room without windows. His eyes darted around the space nervously. The smell of cigarettes and urine clung to the stale air. It was more than an hour before Horace Owen entered. Franklin rushed the man like an expectant puppy approaching its master.

"Let's sit down, Jim."

Horace Owen had been his lawyer for years. He considered him a friend as well. Today the man was noticeably detached. He eyed his client in a way James Franklin had never experienced in their past dealings. Owen placed his briefcase on the table before sitting in the chair across from Franklin.

"Tell me what happened."

"This is some kind of crazy mistake, Hoss. Daniels is going after me for political reasons. He's got nothing on me."

"Jim now is not the time for holding back, especially from your lawyer. Jackie Daniels' telephone records have already incriminated you. In addition Tammy Coulter has made a statement which supports the circumstantial evidence that you had a sexual relationship with her and the teacher. Miss Coulter's parents are filing a criminal suit for wrongdoing and also filing charges for statutory rape among other things. The prosecutor is going to want to do a paternity and DNA testing against the evidence collected from the scene. There's nothing I can do to prevent them from proceeding with this."

"What? What do you mean there's nothing you can do? What the fuck...Tammy Coulter? She's a student at the school. What is she saying? I never..." Franklin looked at his lawyer who looked away as his client's shoulders quivered. Tears streamed down his face. He collapsed into a mass of sobs.

"Look Jim, I'm not a criminal attorney. There's nothing that I can do to help you, and quite frankly, if you slept with a minor and killed that girl..."

"Wait a minute! I didn't kill anybody." The heat of his passion dried the tears that fell.

"I didn't kill Jackie." He desperately searched the eyes across from his for acceptance. Owens gaze was judgmental, unbelieving. "I swear it, Hoss."

"Okay, I admit having sex with Tammy. She may be sixteen but she's no kid. She came to *me* man. She'd come to my office every day and..." He stopped in mid sentence, looking over his shoulder as though he was ashamed for anyone to hear what he was about to say.

"It started last year." Franklin mumbled.

"When she was fifteen, Jim?" Owen hissed. "For God's sakes man, what the fuck were you thinking?"

"Hoss, I know how it sounds. I don't know what I was thinking. It was like it was happening to somebody else. I thought it was my imagination. She would pass me in the hall and brush against me. She'd give me these seductive looks. I wasn't used to that kind of behavior in students and I didn't know how to deal with it." He looked away from his lawyer, unable to withstand the pressure of Owens contemptuous gaze.

"There's a program in place for exceptionally bright and ambitious students where I help them with their career goals. She started scheduling appointments to meet with me. We'd talk about the usual stuff you know, grades, universities. During one of these sessions, right in the middle of a discussion, she got up from her chair and stood right in front of me. She pulled off her top. I told her to put her shirt back on and leave. But then she unhooked her bra. She was right in my face. I was telling her to leave and she pushed her breast into my mouth. Before I know it, I'm touching her and she's touching me. She unzipped my pants and made me ruin my slacks. I was absolutely frantic. She laughed at me while I tried to clean up the mess." Franklin brushed his hand over his wavy hair, then swallowed trying to moisten his tension parched throat.

"She put on her clothes. I was ashamed of myself but I hadn't been so turned on in years. I canceled the next appointments that she made but I thought about her a lot. When I'd see her in the hall at school she'd look at me and I could feel myself losing control. Thoughts of her and our encounter began to consume me. I was determined that I was going to regain control of this situation. When she made her next appointment, I didn't cancel it. I lied to myself that we would talk business, but when she arrived she closed the door and rushed me. I let her…she, that's when it really started."

Both men sat in silence for a moment. Franklin wiped sweat from his face with a clammy hand.

"Though I felt like a dog afterwards I always looked forward to her visits. Sometimes she'd be hiding underneath my desk when I returned from a meeting or lunch. She'd wait until I got on the phone and unzip my pants and give me the time of my life. She was fifteen, sixteen and doing things to me that my wife had never done. She had a kind of power over me. I just got caught up."

"She's a fuckin' baby, Jim. What kind of…"

"I'm a bastard, Hoss. I know it." He hung his head shamefully.

Horace Owen felt no remorse for the man before him. "What about Jackie? When did the two of you become involved?"

"When Jackie Daniels started teaching at the school we spent a lot of time together because I knew her parents. She saw me as a mentor. It was completely professional at first. She was enthusiastic about teaching and she worked hard to be good at her job. And she was. Her students admired her and there was an improvement in their test scores. She was really making her mark with them. I helped her in any way that I could.

"The more time we spent together, the more jealous Tammy became. She thought there was something between us and started to make trouble. Jackie thought that if she took the girl under her wing and helped her reach her professional goals, Tammy would feel better about herself and concentrate on her future." Owen checked his watch. He was sick of Jim Franklin and would be glad to be out of this stuffy room listening to this unbelievable story.

"It seemed to work for a time. By this time Jackie's and my professional relationship began to turn personal. Tammy went ballistic. She threatened to tell my wife, go to Channel Six, all kinds of other stuff. There was no reasoning with her. She was totally out of control. When I thought things couldn't get worse, Jackie became pregnant.

"I was angry at first. I felt she was trying to trap me. It wasn't her style to do that but I was worried. We stopped seeing each other for a while. I was married and the head of a prestigious institution. How would it look?"

"So your sense of morality finally awakened?" He looked at his client like he was a vile form of lower life.

"Hoss, I know I used bad judgment, but things were happening so fast. I have nothing to say in defense of my behavior with Tammy. But I really loved Jackie. When we broke up I missed her terribly. I finally called her and told her to keep the baby. I would leave my wife and we'd be together."

"Did you tell Althea?"

"I wanted to wait until the time was right. Jackie and I discussed how we were going to handle the whole thing but we never agreed on how to broach the situation. In the meantime, we were still having problems with Tammy. She came to my office and tried to seduce me. I hadn't told Jackie about us, she thought the girl had a crush on me. Tammy told me she was going to talk to her. She threatened that if I didn't meet with her, she'd go to Jackie and tell her everything. We arranged a meeting. She came to my office and tried to get me to have sex with her. It was a set-up. Tammy had contacted Jackie and she walked in on us. It was a mess. But when Jackie didn't let the situation rile her, Tammy couldn't take it. She began her threats with renewed vigor, started calling both of our houses, saying all kinds of nasty stuff. My relationship with Jackie started to deteriorate as Tammy's childish behavior continued."

"Well considering the fact that she was a child, how would you expect her to behave?" Owen shook his head in disbelief. "Jim I've gotta tell you, this just doesn't sit right with me. Your conduct was lewd, immoral, and unethical."

"Don't give me that fuckin' shit about ethics, Hoss. You're the guy who set his own wife up with another man so that you could take the children from her. You knew that losing the kids would crush her. Hell, you didn't even want them. You shipped those kids out of state to school before the ink was dry on the agreement."

"This isn't about me Jim." Horace Owen looked at his client as though he were something slithering on the floor. He closed his briefcase, snapped the brass locks shut and told James he would refer his case to several colleagues who were experienced in criminal law.

"I know this isn't your kind of case, but you've been around. What do you think my chances are? Can I lose my position with the Academy?"

Owen was tall, about six four. He leaned his expansive body towards the seated man. His eyes held no emotion.

"You still don't get it, do you? People are not going to just let this go. I have a sixteen year old daughter myself, Jim. She could be a student at your school."

"But you're my friend, Hoss. I wouldn't do that to a friend."

"What about A.J. Daniels? Is he your friend?" He shut the door quietly on the way out.

For a considerable retainer, Matthew Feuer agreed to take Franklin's case. He met with the educator the following day and listened poker faced as James recounted the story he had told Owen.

Though his client could not read his face, the loathing that Matt Feuer felt for Franklin was immeasurable. The nerve of this spade taking advantage of that poor girl who was entrusted to him. Feuer didn't give a damn about the DA's daughter. Just another case of these black animals fucking and killing each other. They have no morals, the blacks. A.J. Daniels was an asshole anyway. It was surprising that someone hadn't punched his ticket a long time ago. Somehow he always managed to extricate himself from the swirl of corruption that he was most assuredly at the eye of.

He sat across the table from Franklin, picturing the filthy black ape with his hands on that innocent white child. Race mixing. The very thought made him sick. What if it had been little Tammy who carried the seed of this monster?

They had no strong evidence, really no evidence that said Franklin committed the murder. Had the situation been different, Feuer could have worked a deal so his client wouldn't have been locked up one day. But Franklin repulsed him. He had used his position to take advantage of a child. He was going to pay.

He sat at the table crying like a bitch, begging for compassion. To Franklin's misfortune, he agreed to let Feuer represent him. Feuer, a brilliant lawyer, had a command of the study of jurisprudence that many in his field didn't possess. He was extremely savvy in the courtroom, using his words like an artist uses his brush to paint a halo on the head of Satan, resulting in an acquittal. He could also clip the wings of an angel, smear him with soot, and stand by as it crashed and descended into the bowels of hell. He didn't like James Franklin and would see to it that this scum never had another chance to sully the pure and innocent again. Several days later, they stood before the judge. The principal was released on a two hundred fifty thousand dollar bond. He went home to await his trial date.

*　　　　　　*　　　　　　*

"Where do you get off asking me some shit like that?" James Franklin looked at his wife as though she'd lost her mind.

"Well, somebody killed that woman. I used to hear you on the phone with her." Althea hissed. "You got her pregnant and got mad when she wouldn't get rid of it."

"That's a lie!"

"Which part of it, the fact that you were fucking her or the fact that you wanted her to have an abortion?"

"Just shut up, Althea. It's none of your goddamn business."

"It's none of my business? Our marriage is nothing but a big lie and you tell me it's not my business?" Althea stood before him defiantly, arms crossed tightly in front of her chest. "Forget about that Daniels' slut, what about that baby you were fucking? She's sixteen and you're damn near sixty."

"I'm not sixty. I'm fifty-four."

"Oh excuse me." She snorted. "That makes a *huge* difference. You're such an idiot. I guess it would have been too much for your monstrous ego and your minuscule penis to find an adult to screw. You disgust me."

The blow didn't hurt Althea as much as it surprised her. It sent her reeling into the wall. She sat in a crumpled mess on the floor, trying to get her bearings. She touched the sore place on her head and drew back bloody fingertips. The sight of her own blood set her in motion. She rose so quickly that James flinched.

"All right you bastard, come on with it." Althea gave him two sharp kicks to the stomach, doubling him over. She drew her knee upward, smashing his face. Moving quickly behind him, she shoved her foot into his butt, sending him headfirst into the wall.

She looked down at her husband who lay on the pink, green and gold rug. The lamp had fallen over, encircling him like a spotlight. Althea looked at him and shook her head.

"I don't know why I bother. You never were man enough for me."

Chapter Thirty

The view from his office was the best in the city. From the expanse of glass, A.J. Daniels looked out on the Midwestern skyline. The sunset was magnificent. Blue, lavender, and mauve painted the heavens, splashing color bursts throughout skyscrapers from the palette of a yellow-orange sun.

He paid little attention to the empyrean splendor. He'd gone through almost an entire bottle of bourbon but it hadn't numbed his pain. Amanda was gone. He never thought of her as someone who would take her own life. He found it harder to believe it could have anything to do with Jake Hurley's death. Though the note she'd left him made that plain, he refused to accept it. Perhaps it had been a delayed reaction to Jackie's death.

Though she was not the protective, hovering type, he knew that she loved the girl more than anything. Amanda wasn't the type to wear emotion on her sleeve. She seemed to accept Jackie's death, had continued to live her life in spite of her deep sadness by what happened to Jackie. Perhaps being with the detective gave her a sense of connection. Hurley could keep her apprised of the goings on in the case like few others could. She had little else to hold onto during that time. God knows A.J. hadn't been there to support her the way he should. But how was he to know she was so troubled? She never discussed her feelings when they spoke and, from all appearances, she was going on with her life. If signs were there, he had completely missed them.

She shot herself dead with the pearl handled revolver he'd purchased for her many years ago. The note read, in part,

'I'm grateful to have found real love if only for the briefest moment. Jake Hurley was a wonderful and loving man. With him and my daughter gone, there's no reason for me to stay here. Thank you, Andy for giving me the means to free myself from the hell you've put me through.'

How mean spirited of her to use something that he had bought for her protection as the tool for her own destruction. When had they changed from two people who loved each other into lifeless beings who cared so little for one another?

He remembered when he bought her the pistol. Jackie was about two. They had just moved into their first real house. Their home was spacious, a big responsibility for the new wife and mother. A.J.'s job required a lot of travel and Amanda was afraid of being in the big house alone with a small child.

When he showed her the revolver, she recoiled. Amanda abhorred guns and violence of any kind. The idea of having one in the house was a source of great discomfort for her. He couldn't get her to go near it. Finally, A.J. coaxed her into taking lessons. Once she'd learned how to handle the weapon she felt much more confident, perhaps even grateful to own the gun.

He remembered telling her, 'You never know when this baby might come in handy.' He never thought that she would use it in this way. He had left her to her own devices for years as he bandied from one mistress to the next. It could have been spite but it was most likely boredom which drove her to finally start taking lovers of her own. Could she have fallen for another man to such a degree that she would end her life? He just didn't understand how she could let that happen.

He remembered when she started her life without him. Amanda had become cold and distant. He suspected what might be happening and hired a private detective. It didn't take long for the man he'd hired to bring him the damning proof of his wife's frequent liaisons. He knew the source of her wanton behavior over the last few years had been in retaliation to his philandering. Humiliated and angry, she decided to embarrass and disrespect him whenever she could. Because she knew it would anger him, she brought her lovers to the house. It didn't seem to matter who. She seemed to prefer the average working man, the type of individual that A.J. considered beneath him.

There was the UPS man who made daily deliveries after his shift ended, the florist who had the house looking like a funeral parlor. She'd kept company with a pizza boy who was a year younger than Jackie. A.J. could always tell when he'd been there by the greasy red stains he left everywhere. There had been an Asian gardener who came to Rosemont from God knows where. She'd stopped seeing the muscle bound fireman when he left her for a Fabio look-alike from his job.

He was shocked when she initially took lovers with such recklessness. But he could fault no one but himself. It was he who introduced others into their marriage. Over the years their lifestyle had become ritualistic. Though suitors were collected like snowflakes uniting to form a drift, the precipitous slide to their inevitable separation was something that his ego would not accept.

He knew things were different when she met Jake Hurley. Could Amanda really have felt more than lust for someone so gritty? His whole world consisted of the violence she'd once found so repugnant.

When he first learned of the affair, he thought of it as the ultimate embarrassment for a man in his position. He was the district attorney and his wife was sleeping with a subordinate of the lowest level. When she left him and moved Hurley into the cottage, he knew that this relationship was different. Amanda needed the security of a man. He must have had quite a powerful hold over her. She never would have done anything as brazen as having such an open affair without male succor.

After Detective Hurley had that unfortunate accident, Andy was certain his wife would run home to him. Instead, she used his gift to her as the elixir to fix her broken heart.

It was he who took their marriage down this ugly road. She'd always resented him for that. Her words in the note and the use of the gun were her final dig at him.

He drained the remaining contents of the glass and turned his attention to the manila folder containing the latest report on the case. Of all the people in the world, Jim Franklin would be the last person he would imagine to be involved in something like this. He had attended many social functions where Franklin had been a guest or the host. He'd been a guest in their home on occasion. The entire time he'd known this man, he'd smiled in his face and shook his hand heartily, all the while having a sexual relationship with his daughter. The bastard had gotten out on bond yesterday but Daniels would see to it that he was soon put away once and for all.

Chapter Thirty-One

On Wednesday morning, Ed Dixon pulled out of the grocery store parking lot, cardboard boxes in tow. He needed them to collect his things from his apartment. Jules had been kind enough to let him spend the night at his place. It was one a.m. when they'd released him from the cell that had been home for more weeks than he wanted to remember. He wasn't sure what to expect from his landlady. He already knew that she planned to rent his room to someone else. If she hadn't already done so.

Had it not been for the new opportunities he'd forged in his relationship with Jules Dreyfus, he surely would have left this bad luck town. Having been locked up for over a month, his desire was to run and never stop. But he didn't. He was afraid that if he ran he'd draw attention to himself. But that was a silly thought. Fortunately for him, the eye of the media was on Franklin now. Nobody cared that he had been wrongfully accused or the harm it had caused him. Who cared what happened to a janitor?

He wound his way towards the small dark apartment building on East Colson Lane. His landlady had already moved his few belongings. She told him when he called that she put the boxes containing his things in the storage area. He hated facing her but she had to let him into the cellar.

He rang the bell marked 'MANAGER'. As soon as it was released her voice crackled over the intercom.

"Mr. Dixon?" The words were clipped and impatient.

"Yes ma'am."

"I'll buzz you in. The cellar is unlocked. Your things are on the right as you enter the storage room."

The intercom clicked off and a buzzer sounded. He pushed the door and it gave way.

"Ole' bitch" he thought. She didn't want to face him either. She made it clear to him in his telephone call to her that she no longer wanted him in her building.

Opening the heavy outer door, he lifted the empty cartons he'd brought, and trudged down the worn tiled hall to the cellar. Pushing open a lightweight wooden door, he stepped inside. For a fleeting moment he was back in the utility closet at the school looking at Jackie Daniels partially exposed body on the floor. He rubbed his eyes with the heels of his hands, pushing away the memory.

Once again focused on the boxes, he looked at them and shook his head. This couldn't be everything, he thought. It was hard to believe that everything he'd accumulated since he'd taken up residence in the small room could be summed up and packed away in two eighteen by twenty-five inch boxes.

Stooping down, he loosened the folded flaps to make sure all of his stuff was there. His main concern was his books and papers. Inspecting the first box, he was satisfied it contained all of his documents and books. He cared little about the few clothes and shoes that she'd put in the other box. He decided to leave the cartons he'd brought with him there. He heaved one packed box under each arm and left his former residence.

A sudden wave of emotion washed through him as he walked to his car. He placed the boxes in the large trunk of the rusted out old car and slammed the door. Ed Dixon smiled in anticipation of the new life he was about to start.

"Hot Damn! I'm a property owner!" he laughed out loud as he slid behind the steering wheel. He was finally free and going home.

Chapter Thirty-Two

"Come on Ren, I always have to wait on you whenever we do anything." Audrey pouted as she sat in Renita's living room clicking the remote. The screen flashed a variety of children's shows and infomercials, none of which interested her.

"I told you over the phone that I had to get ready." Her sister called from the bathroom.

"That was over an hour ago."

"Your point is?"

"Why does it always take you so long?" Audrey fidgeted in the round, burgundy chair. "You know Wednesday is One Day Sale day. If we wait too much longer we won't be able to find a parking space."

Audrey took out her aggression on the oblong contraption in her hand, mashing the buttons forcefully with each word she spoke to Renita.

"Look, we get there when we get there." Renita responded. "I'm not like the rest of you sheep, doing that boring nine to five thang. It'll take me a minute to make myself beautiful. I been laying in the bed for the past four days, just getting' up to eat and pee."

"You forgot shower." Audrey mumbled, checking out Chuck Norris' muscles as he demonstrated the Nordik Track.

"I didn't forget. I ain't had drop one hit my ass since Saturday night."

"What? That is sooo trifling."

"We live in a trifling society."

"Excuse me?"

"I'm merely a product of our society." Renita walked out into the living room to face Audrey as she spoke.

"Every time you turn on the TV you see shit to spray your shower so you don't have to clean it anymore, shit to spray in your toilet, so you don't have to clean it anymore. Don't get me started on that shit you put on your clothes so you don't have to take them to the cleaners." She patted her neck. Realizing she wasn't wearing her necklace, Renita returned to her bedroom.

"I see your point. Pretty soon they'll develop a spray that you can apply to your ass so you don't have to wipe anymore." Audrey stopped channel surfing when she found QVC displaying precious stones.

"That's disgusting." Renita responded from the bedroom. "But you're right. Americans are lazy. Who has time to go to the bathroom anymore?"

"Just hurry up and get ready before I leave you. It's almost eleven o'clock."

"I'll be out in a sec." Renita's muffled voice floated from the back of the apartment. "Hey, come back here a minute would you?"

Audrey sighed and stomped to the back room like a spoiled child. She stepped into Renita's bedroom and looked over her shoulder at the large square she held at arms length.

"Oooh, Ren! When did you get that?"

"El brought it by yesterday."

Audrey admired the painting of a tall, muscular black man and his tiny son who ran in his shadow on the beach. El Jones was a local painter Renita met during one of her stays in Europe. They developed a close friendship built mostly on mutual artist admiration. When El moved stateside, Renita made it a point to purchase at least one of her works a year and display them in her home or at the club. This piece spoke to Audrey. The subject matter was simple, yet poignant. You could almost hear the waves crashing against the craggy shoreline and the giggles of the fat brown boy.

"I love this! Do you think I can get her to make one for me?"

"She's pretty busy. It took me a year to get this from her. I'll check with her though." Renita practically pried the painting from Audrey's covetous hands. "I'm ready."

The mall was packed by the time they got there. Renita was looking for a gown for an upcoming formal event with the band. She'd seen a beautiful dress in *Vogue* and was looking for an inexpensive knock-off. Audrey was so shocked at her sister making a departure from her usual sarong and sandals that even she was excited about the shopping trip.

She sat outside the fitting rooms of nearly a dozen stores while Renita tried on gowns. A fitness buff, Renita's frame was firm and compact, just right for the exquisite dresses she chose. She finally settled on a strapless, satin burgundy number with a beaded bodice that they both agreed was perfect for the occasion. Renita paid the clerk and struggled to include the bag with her other parcels.

"I'll get it for you, Ren."

"Thanks. I knew there was a reason I asked you to come with me."

Audrey slapped at her playfully as they headed for the bistro in the lower level of the mall.

The glass and stainless steel décor was very twenty first century. The hostess seated them near a window that looked out on the parade of shoppers juggling packages or hushing cranky children.

After taking their drink orders, their waiter rattled off the day's specials and twisted off to fill their requests. He soon returned with two large salads, the club sandwich and bowl of fries they would share. They sipped ginger ale between bites, talking about everything that was happening in the small town recently.

"I heard they picked up the headmaster of the Academy for that teacher's murder."

"Can you believe that? When we went to school there back in the day, there was never that kind of drama." Audrey worked her tongue between her molars trying to dislodge a trapped piece of ham.

"Did you see the picture of A.J. Daniels' daughter? When did the Academy start hiring lap dancers for teachers?"

"What picture were you looking at? In the pictures I saw of her she looked like a young business woman."

"Yeah, the porn business. So I guess that means your client, what's his name?"

"Ed Dixon. They released him." Audrey sawed at a tomato wedge. "If it weren't for Jules pressuring the prosecution the way that he did, things might have turned out differently."

"Well now that he's out of jail, does that mean he will resume paying you? I'm getting kind of tired of buying you lunch."

"What? You need to quit, you ungrateful, stankin' cow. All the free meals you got off me when your lounge lizard ass couldn't find work. I started to claim you as a dependent."

"Excuse me Miss Wall Street, but I could find plenty of work. I was just taking time to connect with my inner self."

"Yeah? Well you need to have your 'inner self' get a credit card so the next time ya'll want to bond ya'll can leave me out of it."

"You cold Audrey." Renita bit her sandwich and chewed it before continuing. "How's things going with the business?"

"Jules referred several of his law buddies and Bobby and me are still working on some things so it's looking up."

"This is the second time you mentioned Jules. What's the deal?" Renita asked between mouthfuls of salad.

Audrey hadn't mention her last encounters with Jules, nor had she mentioned his increasing appeal to her. She knew that Renita would start asking her all kinds of questions that she wasn't ready to answer. She was attracted to him and she didn't want to admit to herself the reason why she wouldn't let the relationship progress. Here she was, over forty years old and afraid of what people would say or think if she dated a white guy.

"It's nothing, Ren. I hooked Jules and Ed up because Ed needed a lawyer. I really didn't know anything about the man, I was just trying to get Ed off my back. It just kinda worked out. With Ed out of commission, I was really starting to miss that little piece of change I was getting from him, so I asked Jules if he needed an advisor or if he could refer me to some of his associates."

"Is he good looking?"

"He looks okay." Audrey shrugged, then raised her glass to sip.

"Well if he looks okay, and he's a lawyer, you need to jump on that. He's not married or gay is he?"

"How the hell would I know Ren?"

"You should ask." Renita nudged her hand. "You guys went to Nick's that night. You should've found out then."

"I should just walk up to somebody I don't even know and ask if he's married or gay? Girl you been hanging around them damn weed heads too long. There's no way I would grill a man I just met in that way."

"*There's no way I would grill a man like that.*" Renita mimicked. "Why not? He's not a stranger. The two of you had dinner together. Why didn't you ask him about himself then?"

"I don't know, I just didn't."

"That's what's wrong with a lot of women. We're not direct when we meet guys. We get all caught up with some illusion that we've conjured up and try to make them 'Mr. Right.' Then we find out they're married, cross dressing ax murderers. By then it's too late. We all in luuv."

"You think you know everything don't you?" Audrey smirked. "Why don't you get a radio talk show? So many of us could benefit from the Wisdom That's Renita."

"Make fun if you want, but you know I'm right."

Audrey laughed nervously. Once again, Renita had hit the nail dead on the head. It was already too late to check her feelings for Jules. They gushed through her like a torrent. She hoped he wasn't some freak.

"Why don't you ask the man out? You ain't had none since the last lunar eclipse."

Audrey didn't respond. She had grown tired of her sister's constantly berating her about her love life. Why does everybody make such a big deal about sex? Why do we pressure ourselves into using sex as the indicator of the success or failure in human relationships?

"You're not exactly a spring chicken." Her sister clucked.

"One day you're gonna wake up and your shit is going to be sealed like a tomb. What are you saving it for? You scared he ain't gon' want your old gray kitty cat?"

"My kitty is not gray. And I'll have you know, we got together the other night."

Oh shit! Audrey put her hand to her mouth. Now she was going to have to spill it.

"AH HA!" Renita's eyes gleamed. The corners of her mouth turned down smugly. "I knew something was up. Every time I talk to you lately it's 'Jules this' and 'Jules that.' You fucked him, didn't you?"

"I did not!" Audrey drew back in indignation.

"All right, you didn't fuck him. He fucked you." Renita punched the air with her fist for emphasis. "Gon' white boy. Lick it and stick it!"

"What? That's disgusting! Why don't you stop using such filthy language?"

"Just tell me what happened, and don't leave anything out."

Audrey shook her head, looking at Renita in amused wonder as she told her about the pizza dinner they'd shared in her office. She couldn't hold back any longer. She told her about the kiss they shared that night and the night at Nick's.

"That's all?"

"What do you mean, 'that's all?' It wasn't none of that peck on the lips stuff. This was the kiss of all kisses. There was a little groping going on too."

"Why you little cunt!" Renita bucked her eyes in feigned disbelief. "How could you live with yourself?"

"Shut the hell up, Ren. I'm just being cautious."

"For what?

"I'm just not sure I want to get involved right now. The ink is barely dry on my divorce decree. I need some time to just chill."

"Bullshit! That's the weakest excuse you could have given." Renita bent her head, giving attention to her salad. "Tell that shit to somebody who don't know no better. If those kisses were all that, the two of you might as well have fucked. What are you waiting for, an engraved invitation signed by his pecker? Girl wake up and smell the new millennium."

"There's a big difference between kissing a man and sleeping with him. I don't care what you say, Ren. I'm not going to do anything that I'm not ready to do."

"Okay. I'm not going to ride you about it. He's probably a freak anyway."

"Shut up and pay the check so we can go."

Chapter Thirty-Three

On Wednesday night, Rob sat in the cramped theater seat watching Rita grab handfuls of buttered popcorn. At her request, he'd bought the super sized bucket. She held the large greasy tub on her lap protectively, shoveling the oily kernels into her face like there was no tomorrow.

"Monica said this was a good movie. She's my girl and everything, but she sure has got fat. You remember her don't you Rob?"

"Yeah." He didn't.

At first she was mad at him for bringing her to this theater. She'd wanted to go to the big multi-cinema to see one of those crying, my man done me wrong movies. But he wasn't having it. She'd apparently gotten over the fact that he brought her to the dollar movie when he splurged on the big bucket of corn and a drink so large he couldn't fit his hand around it.

"Well you wouldn't recognize her if you saw her now. I try to get her to go to the gym with me but she just won't do it. She would look like Angela Basset if she would lose about fifty pounds or so."

Rita stopped talking long enough to force in another mouthful.

"I keep telling her, don't no man want a hog for a woman. But she won't listen." Chomp, chomp. "She think she fine just the way she is. She'll tell you so too, in a heartbeat."

Rita took several large, loud gulps of the super size diet cola, belched, then continued.

"That girl can eat 24-7. Her fat ass don't never get tired of eating. That's my girl, though."

Rob eyed her with disgust as she plowed into the bucket. What the hell am I doing here? He thought to himself. He had spent so much time dealing with the case and with Jake's death that he began to feel like he was losing his mind. The weight of exhaustion and depression anchored him. If he didn't do something to divert his mind from the constant tension, he would have a breakdown. That's just how bad he felt.

When Rita called him that evening, asking him to take her to the movies, he reluctantly agreed. He knew if he didn't step back from his problems for a minute, he'd lose his ability and desire to be effective at work. He'd heard that *The Hurricane* was a pretty good flick. If he could immerse himself into somebody else's hard life, maybe his own wouldn't seem so bad.

He missed his friend more than he'd ever thought he would. They'd spent so much time together that the loss of Jake was like losing an appendage. As the case unfolded, he kept having to remind himself that Jake was not there. They had developed such a rapport, each filling in where the other was lacking. With whom could he discuss strategy now?

He smiled thinking of the kick Jake would have gotten out of recent developments in the Daniels case. Who would have thought the headmaster was not only the killer but had a thing for the teen-aged girls who attended the school? Jake would have really appreciated that.

He also found himself haunted by Jackie Daniels. He never knew her so he couldn't imagine why she was in his head so much. It was almost as if she were trying to lead him to some undiscovered truth.

He found himself wondering what kind of person she really was. There was such a dichotomous view of the woman from everyone who knew her. He wondered what his impression would have been. Would he have found her the quiet, solitary type, or the kind who talks nonstop through movies while cramming popcorn into her face?

He and Rita were the only people there for the screening which was nice. Too bad he wasn't here with someone who he really cared for. Rita was basically a thing he used to relieve built up tension. She was real good at that.

Strangely enough, he would have left her that evening after their love-making had it not been for Jackie Daniels. As he lay there on the kitchen floor, Rita but a breath away, he wondered. Had Jackie Daniels ever had sex on the kitchen floor with some guy just to relieve tension? He wanted to leave Rita right there in the kitchen as one would a dishrag after it's function is met. But he could hear Jackie whispering to him.

"Don't go, Rob. Spend some time with me tonight."

He wondered what kind of men she liked. What if she liked men who looked like him, he thought, taking extra care in grooming himself. He rubbed pomade into his clean, neatly trimmed hair. His smooth face was clear and refreshed after the shave and hot witch hazel towel wrap he'd gotten at his barber's that day.

He selected an olive colored silk shirt and black slacks that caressed his tight buttocks, accentuating the healthy bulge between his muscular thighs. The full pant legs touched the tops of his butter soft, calf skin loafers. He looked so good he wanted to kiss his damned self.

After another quick self approving glance in his full length mirror, he grabbed a black leather blazer and heading out the door.

Rita opened the door to her apartment on the first ring and planted a juicy, red lipped kiss on Rob's mouth. Moving her hands over his body, she pulled him inside, effectively ending his visualization of a date with Jackie Daniels.

"You ready to go?" he asked, ignoring her obvious intentions.

"Why don't we catch a later show baby? I've really missed you, Rob." Her hands traveled his muscular chest. She wrapped her arms around his neck. "You come over here lookin' good enough to eat and then don't wanna give a sister a bite."

Damn she looked good. Rita sported a tiny black leather skirt, and a red button down blouse. The shirt was tight, accentuating the implants she'd gone into debt to acquire. Rob tried to ignore the vision that pushed itself into his mind that caused the stirring between his legs. He wanted to throw her down and get the release that he needed. But that kind of self satisfying behavior only led to problems later. Women always made him feel guilty if he didn't play the sensitive role before and after sex. Showing insensitivity now would mean she'd take him through hell before she gave him some again. His feelings for her weren't that deep but the sex was great and he wasn't ready to let that go.

"Rita, I'm kind of tired. Can't we just go and see the flick and come on back?"

Looking hurt and embarrassed, Rita turned and walked slowly towards the bedroom. He watched her round rump twist in the skirt. She had no idea how weak he was for her right then. She could have taken out his gun and whipped the shit out of him with it and he would have kissed her ass all night long.

"I'll get my bag and be right back." Her high heels clicked on the parquet floor as she left the room. She brushed past him stiffly, returning a minute later with her handbag.

"Let's go." She said through clenched teeth. A pang of guilt moved through him and he pulled her to him.

"Rita, I'm sorry." He lifted her pretty face. She averted her gaze but not before he saw the redness in her bright eyes. He gently touched her face and her soft hair before kissing her lightly on the lips. She remained stiff and guarded. He held her until he felt her resistance ease.

"Maybe this wasn't such a good idea. I'm in a bad mood and I shouldn't have come over here making you feel bad." He moved away from her toward the door.

"Wait!" Rita said. It came out so loudly, so quickly, she looked away so he wouldn't see the embarrassment in her eyes.

"Please don't go, Rob." Her words reminded him of Jackie and the plea he'd imagined earlier. "We don't have to go to the movies if you don't want to." Rita was saying. "Have you eaten? I'll bet it's been a while since you've had a home cooked meal." She kept talking as though afraid that when she stopped he'd be gone.

"I made baked chicken, greens, black-eyed peas and cornbread. Come on in the kitchen and I'll fix you a plate."

Rob hoped she didn't hear his stomach rumble as she recited the menu. She was right, he hadn't had a real meal, home cooked or otherwise in a while. He sat at Rita's little kitchen table while she prepared his plate. As she piled on each course, Rob looked around the small, tidy room, inhaling the aroma of delicious Southern cooking.

Rita's kitchen was decorated in various shades of yellow and accented in white. The sunny colored walls were bright and welcoming. Sheer goldenrod curtains were pulled back with sunflower ties letting lacy white panels peek through. The tiles on the floor and the countertops were the same yellow and white checkered pattern. A clean lemon scent filled the air until it was overridden by the heated food.

The microwave dinged and she set the steaming plate before him. She removed a vase of bright yellow daisies from the small dining room table, and put a healthy slice of chocolate cake and a glass filled with ice cold milk in its place.

"Aren't you going to eat?" Rob was so busy shoveling the food into his mouth it took him a minute to notice Rita sitting there watching him.

"Already did." She pulled a chair away from the table, turned it around and straddled it.

"This is really good." He said before swallowing the last forkful of cake. He drained the glass of milk. Unable to suppress a belch, he smiled sheepishly.

"Now I'm too stuffed to move."

"Good." She said. Moving behind him, she began to massage his temples. She slowly moved to his shoulders, kneading them firmly until she felt the tightness soften.

"That feels fantastic." Rob let her work the tightness in his shoulders free.

Rita smiled, continuing to press, rub, and push all the tension away. He let his head fall back so that it rested on her breasts. She massaged his neck, then moved her hands to his face and kissed his closed lids, his nose, then his mouth.

He reached for her, pulling her around to face him. She straddled his lap, their tongues thrusting deeply, leaving room for only a moan, an impassioned cry. He moved his hands up her thighs, diving his fingers into the hot, wet pool between her legs. She threw her head back, crying out as he yanked at her panties. He quickly slipped out of his trousers. His massive erection sprang forth, eager, looking for satisfaction. Rita pulled him into her mouth. She massaged his tight, round ass, forcing him deeper into her throat.

"Oh shit! Oh, baby!" He ran his fingers through her hair, never wanting her to stop. When he felt her easing away from him, he tried to guide her back to him, but she rose and removed the rest of her clothes, every part of her, wanting him. Rob cupped her buttocks, pulling her up so that he could taste her firm breasts. She purred and clawed at him as he took her to the heights of her passion before putting his rock hardness deeply inside her. A pleasure filled laugh escaped, her legs straddled his back, moving up and down until they glistened with sweat.

They laughed as he took a few crab like steps with her still attached. He lay her on the kitchen table which creaked a rickety song as they rocked. Wanting to prolong their pleasure, he pulled out of her, burying his head between her thighs, he kissed her, his lips on hers, his tongue deep inside her, tickling, licking.

"God damn! Oh it's good."

"You like it?" he whispered.

"Yes! I love it." She breathed between moans

He kissed her before rising and ramming himself into her with such force her breath caught in her throat. She softly whispered his name. They held each other, shuddering. She cried out. He shouted as he felt himself throbbing, pulsing, warm, hot inside her.

He pulled her down to the floor where they lay, glistening. They listened to each other's breathing and the soft hum of the refrigerator until they fell asleep.

Rob dozed for a few minutes before getting up and heading for the shower. The water felt good as it pelted his face. He hadn't realized how much he needed tonight until now. He felt grateful for the meal and the physical contact. He wished he were home so that he could relax in his own bed. But now he felt obliged to take Rita to the movie. She'd given him more than she'd realized that evening. Spending a few more hours with her wouldn't be so bad.

He was feeling around for the soap when he felt cold air on his back. Rita had entered the shower and pulled him into her mouth before he could object. Her tongue worked him with such skill it made him wonder how many dicks she had to blow before she got this good at it.

Instead of being excited, Rob was annoyed that she had disrupted his time in the shower. Why did women do this kind of shit? They watched them ole' bitch movies with some fag who probably never had a woman in real life, fuckin' some chick in the tub or the swimming pool and they expected us to do that shit in real life, he thought. He knew that there was only one way to get her to stop that wouldn't hurt her feelings.

He picked her up and slammed himself inside of her until she cried out from the pleasure or the pain of the assault. He dropped her in a heap on the floor of the shower, grabbed the soap and finished his shower. When he stepped out of the stall, she was still crumpled on its floor. Her face was turned up toward him, begging, needy. He felt his stomach churn.

When she walked into the living room, he was straightening his clothes, looking for his keys.

"Hey, we're still going to the movie, right?" She asked in a tiny, desperate voice.

"Sure Rita. Get dressed. We can still catch the eleven o'clock showing."

Chapter Thirty-Four

"What a surprise. I guess you've been pretty busy in the wake of the Daniels case." Audrey's heart pounded. She hadn't realized how much she missed him until just that moment.

He stood in the doorway of her office that Thursday evening, hesitant. She didn't blame him for being cautious. She'd been uncharacteristically vacillant. It was surprising he hadn't given up on her all together. But behind his nonchalant front, a hopeful glint flickered that relaxed Audrey. He still wanted her.

"Yeah, it's been pretty crazy. How 'bout you?"

"Things could be better. With the economy doing so well, and more people letting the Internet do their number crunching for them, financial planners may become obsolete."

"Nonsense. Who do you think is doing the work for these web sites? Believe me, nobody wants to sit around crunching numbers if that's not their area of expertise. Hang in there. It'll come together for you."

Jules looked at Audrey and smiled. He's really kind of cute, she thought. They were silent for a minute. She didn't want him to leave, so she engaged him in a conversation about their mutual client.

"Have you heard from Ed Dixon?"

"Ed's doing fine. He's staying in town as you probably know. The residential property that he purchased needs some minor cosmetic work. He's doing the maintenance for this building, too."

"Oh? I didn't know that."

"Yeah. In addition to the real estate he's acquired, he's also forming a janitorial company." Jules leaned his long, slender body against the door jamb. He looked sexy as hell. Audrey could feel her face turn warm.

"Ed's not messing around. The man is on a mission. He's going to need someone to manage his finances so if I were you, I would take this as a breather." He gave her a reassuring smile. "Pretty soon you're going to have more work than you know what to do with."

Audrey felt her breath catch in her throat. His eyes gleamed devilishly. She wanted to rub her tongue over his straight white teeth until she tasted his tongue. She was looking at him, lost in a dream when she realized he'd stopped talking. Had he asked her a question? If he did, she damn sure didn't hear it.

"Wha…what do you think about uh, James Franklin being in the center of all that trouble at the Academy?" She stammered like a blooming idiot. "I never would have guessed that the headmaster of the school would be involved in this. Do you think Franklin really killed Jackie Daniels?"

"The prosecutor's office seems to think so. We'll just have to wait and see what happens at the trial. He's got excellent council in Matt Feuer. Having Matt, plus his good standing in the community, if he's innocent, he'll get off."

"But how will this whole thing affect his position at the school?" She picked up a pencil, drummed it distractedly, before putting it back down. "The fact that they would take a case on him this far has to mean they have something on him."

"You never know." He held her eyes as he spoke. "Look at what happened to Ed Dixon. He wasn't guilty and they practically had the needle with the lethal mix poised at his arm."

"Ed Dixon wasn't exactly without guilt. Standing over a naked woman with your privates out isn't exactly moral behavior." Her chest heaved up and down in rhythm to her beating heart.

"It isn't exactly murder either." His glance cut through her. She wanted to feel his lips upon hers, but she didn't want to make that move. The next time they embraced she was certain she'd be unable to hold back.

Audrey struggled to maintain an air of nonchalance in his presence, but Jules made her heart race. She found herself more attracted to him each time they met. When she didn't see him, she thought of him more and more. Her longing for him invaded even her dreams lately. She blushed remembering the fantasy, shifting in her seat to distract her fluttering heart and the tingling that crept between her legs.

She told herself it wasn't just a sex thing. He possessed an easy, confident manner that she found very appealing. She had decided that she wouldn't do anything to advance the relationship in hopes that whatever she felt for him would fizzle.

Instead, it had the opposite effect. The more she tried not to think of him, the more he interrupted her thoughts. It's like any other form of deprivation. The more a smoker tells herself she won't smoke, the more she wants a cigarette. When the dieter tells himself he won't eat any more fatty foods, everything fattening seems to taunt him.

She had been so busy trying to keep her lust at bay, she didn't realize that he was still talking. She hadn't a clue what portions of the discussion she'd missed or when he'd moved away from the doorway to stand in front of her desk.

"Well, I'll let you get back to work. Things have gotten so hectic I just needed a break."

Due to the notoriety he'd received during the Daniels case, Jules had become a bit of a celebrity. Though there had been no trial for Ed Dixon, the young attorney was attractive and media savvy. The camera loved him and media moths seemed to hover around his flame. The phone started ringing after his first television appearance and hadn't stopped yet.

As for Audrey, she'd had plenty of nibbles, but no bites. Her lease would be up in a couple of months. Things had gotten so slow that she decided to close shop and find a much cheaper space or maybe work from home. She hardly needed an office for the types of services she supplied to the few clients that she had. It just made good sense to cut any additional expenses where she could. Jules was so busy now that she hardly ever saw him. Since she had decided not to renew her lease, she thought this would be the perfect way to dissolve any feelings still lingering between them.

When she'd heard his soft knocking that evening, her heart sang. She welcomed a distraction from the mound of bills that she was working her way through. They talked shop until the electricity between them burned like a taser.

Jules turned to leave, then came back.

"Hey, I was thinking about grabbing some Chinese from the place down the street. If you haven't had dinner, I'd love for you to join me."

"I'd love to get away. But I've got a better idea. Have you ever been to the Spice Rack?" Audrey suggested.

"Yeah. I love that place."

"Why don't we eat there? If we hurry we can catch the first set."

Twenty minutes later they were in the cabaret seated at a small table near the stage. The bright décor exuded an island flavor. Rattan and bamboo shored thatch walls and ceilings. Grass skirted tables held coconut shells with lit candles inside. The flames flickered festively, dancing gaily on vibrant lemon, mango, and kiwi washed walls.

Lloyd Eckstine and crew were on the stage warming up. A wide-hipped waitress in a black spandex ensemble, took their drink orders. They sipped in silence, until the band closed the gap that remained when their small talk was expended. Once Lloyd started touching the piano keys, the ringing telephones, shrill of fax machines and whir of copiers seemed to drift away. The sound of deep mahogany and blaring brass accented the ivory as the bass and saxophone players joined the pianist. Jules and Audrey were whisked away to a tropical island, the music merging with the breeze that rippled off the blue water, kissing them as they lay upon the shore.

The musicians segued from their intro to '*Weeping Willow*' featuring Lloyd and the raspy nuances he rendered, taking the listeners to a place sad and far away. His once youthful voice, now rusted out by too much scotch and nicotine, was delightfully jazzy. The couple was halfway through their dinner when the band started to play '*Girl From Ipanema*'. Over the strains of the Brazilian tune, Lloyd announced the featured vocalist. The crowd broke into wild applause as Renita Wilson approached the stage.

She was small in stature but there was nothing diminutive in her presence. With bold features set in smooth skin the color of Brazil nuts, her look whispered Kenya, Somalia and Zanzibar. Rhinestones decorated her locked, shoulder length hair. Multicolored kente cloth draped one arm, cupped her small breasts like a desperate lover, before twisting around her full hips. On the exposed arm was a single gold bangle which glinted in the subdued lighting.

Her voice, though younger and stronger, was a feminine version of Lloyd's. She picked up the melody, moving her round hips, becoming the character in the song.

'Tall and tan and young and lovely
the girl from Ipanema goes walking
and when she passes each one she passes goes ahhh'

She moved into the front row, stopping before select men, teasing them with her voice, her hips inviting, then casting them aside. The trio, a perfect compliment to her vocals, followed every inflection. Together, they harmonized like jazz birds.

"I love Renita Wilson!" Jules was so excited that Audrey couldn't help but laugh. He was completely enraptured. When the set was finished, Audrey waved to Renita. Jules sat bug-eyed as she approached their table.

"You know Renita Wilson?" He squealed excitedly, making Audrey laugh.

"Sure." She smiled. "We grew up together"

He was amazed. When he saw Renita squeezing through the thick crowd that filled the aisles or sat at small tables, as she made her way toward them, he was even more astonished. She greeted appreciative patrons along the way, stopping to talk to a few. By the time she reached their table, Jules was completely dumbfounded.

"Hey, Audrey. I'm glad you came down. Lloyd told me he'd seen you."

"So why didn't he bring his skinny ass over here and give me a kiss?"

"Who you callin' skinny?" They looked toward the sound of the raspy voice and there was Lloyd. He held a cigarette in one hand and a drink in the other. He bent down and kissed Audrey on the cheek.

"Silver Fox. How's it goin'?"

"Great guns, pretty lady. Great guns. I've never been happier."

"Aren't you going to introduce us to your friend?" Renita's eyes bore into Jules salaciously. She was a terrible flirt. Her smile could only be interpreted one way. Jules blushed like a kid. Audrey thought he would pass out.

"This is Jules Dreyfus. Jules, this is Lloyd Eckstein." Jules nodded at the reedy, silver haired man and hurriedly turned back to Renita.

"And this is my sister, Renita."

"Renita Wilson is your sister?" Jules put his hand to his chest. Audrey found the gesture quite comical.

"She didn't tell you?" Renita moved in closer to him. "What am I, the family's dirty little secret? If anyone should be shamed to claim, it should be me."

"Oh, please." Audrey sipped from her glass. "The luckiest day of your life was the day you learned that I was your sister."

"I'm so glad to meet you, Miss Wilson. I've been a fan for years. I have both of your records." Jules gushed, ignoring the sisters playful snipes at each other. He was mesmerized, amazed to be in the company of the great Renita Wilson.

"Please call me Renita. And thank you for the compliment. I've been out of circulation so long I'm always grateful when someone remembers me."

"Why did you stop making records? You were on your way to the top. You were among my favorite female vocalists. Diana Krall, Nnenna Freelon, Cassandra Wilson and Renita Wilson. I used to think you and Cassandra were related until I read that article about you in *Upbeat*."

"Yeah, I used to get that a lot, not only because of our last names but because we have similar styles and phrasing. Hell, I've been linked to everyone from Nancy Wilson to Flip Wilson. I don't care if they link me to Wilson Pickett, I'm just happy for the support and recognition."

"Well you're just as good as they are and they're winning Grammy and every other kind of award. I don't mean to sound...well, what are you..."

"Doing in a dump like this?" Renita laughed.

"Our mother was diagnosed with cancer a few years ago." Audrey answered him. "Renita put her career on hold and moved in with Mother."

"Renita put her career on hold and moved in with Mother."

"I'd worked as a registered nurse for several years before I could make a comfortable living as a singer. Shortly after the release of '*Soaring To New Heights*' and the promotional tour, Mother told us the news. She wanted me to proceed with my plans. I finished the U.S. leg of the tour but I wouldn't sign the contracts that would have taken the tour international. I've done that before. I would have been out of the country two or three years and I just didn't want to do that again. Mother wouldn't talk to me about it, but I knew that she was getting weaker. I had to be there for her.

"She'd done everything for us. She worked three jobs after our father died so that we could advance ourselves in whatever endeavor we chose. It was time for me to give something back to her. So I walked away from it."

"Wow. That's really something." Jules was bewitched. "Was it hard for you?"

"Not at all. My career or my mother? It was a non choice. I didn't even miss it. Touring is the most exhausting thing. You have to be *on* twenty-four seven. You're not just getting up there singing every night." She shook her head ruefully, sipping her gin and tonic. "You have to deal with staffing issues, management trying to jack you up. People quitting on you or deciding not to go on ten minutes before the show starts. All kinds of egos and attitudes. It takes a toll on you physically and emotionally. It's not glamorous. It's a lot of hard work."

"In her own way, my mother really helped me. If I'd kept going at the pace I was going, I would have hit a wall. Hard. Besides, I didn't give up singing. I would sing for my mother. She was always my biggest fan. Towards the end, as I bathed her, washed her hair, prepared and fed her meals to her, I sang constantly. She called them her private concerts." Renita smiled. A faraway look washed over her. "I got more joy from being with her those last few months than I could ever get from a room of cheering people."

Renita stopped to dab away a tear. Jules, Lloyd and Audrey sat misty eyed as she continued.

"It wasn't just me though, all three of us were with her in those last months. We took turns shoring each other up so that we could be strong for her. We refused to let her see us crying or worrying about what her struggle was doing to us. During all of her years of working in a bank every day, cleaning office buildings at night, and doing people's taxes on weekends, she never complained once. Now that she needed us, we tried to show her that we had learned by her example." Renita looked into her glass, swirling the liquid around before turning it up.

"It was very difficult for us to smile for her when we could see her getting weaker each day. We would do all kinds of stuff to divert our thoughts from our own pain and focus on keeping her spirits up. Right Audrey?"

Audrey shook her head. Jules gave her his handkerchief. Their drinks had turned warm and watery from the melted ice. Jules motioned to the waitress for another round.

"You said there were three of you." Jules said, breaking the silence. "Is there another strong Wilson sister out there making a mark on the world?" Audrey winced at the characterization. Strong black woman. Why can't a black woman cry in boardroom meetings and fall when running from villains in the movies like white women? Who was the first sistah to play that strong role and had everybody type cast black women forever more? Renita knew what Audrey was thinking and stopped her from going on a tangent.

"Oh no. We're the only girls." Renita's face lit up, her lashes still wet with tears, but her eyes brightened. "We have a brother, Bobby Wilson who's a center for the Cleveland Cavaliers."

"You never mentioned Bobby Wilson was your brother." He looked at Audrey like he'd just discovered she was an agent for the other side.

"Yeah, well, he's just Bobby to us. He makes me so mad sometimes I could break his neck. We've been trying to build a consulting service which centers around athletics."

"That sounds like a great idea."

"Yeah? Well tell it to Bobby. He doesn't want to hear anything that I've got to say on the subject. Since I don't know sports, he thinks I don't have an understanding of the needs of athletes and wouldn't know the right way to approach them." She glanced into the crowd, shook her head, then looked back at Jules. "Every time I try to go over my proposal with him, we end up fighting. That's why I was so upset when you saw me at the office a few weeks ago. Bobby frustrates me to no end."

Jules remembered the man who stormed from her office that night. He'd towered over Jules like a Georgia pine. He laughed to himself as the feelings of threat dissipated but were quickly replaced with other questions. If that wasn't her man, who is? There must be some reason why she was so distant with him.

He looked over at Renita who looked towards the front of the club distractedly. Lloyd had already left the table and the rest of the band was repositioning itself on the stage.

"It was really good meeting you, Jules." Renita held his hand and smiled. Jules stood as Renita rose and headed for the stage.

They stayed for the remainder of the set. Leaving the club, they walked in relative silence to Audrey's car. Conversation was infrequent during the twenty minute ride back to the office.

Audrey pulled up beside Jules' old VW bug. He turned towards her. The smoke from the club masked the fragrance of his after shave. She was a bundle of raw nerves. Her body desired him, but her mind gave off an air of aloofness which made Jules draw back.

"Well, I guess I'll see you later." He said.

"Bye."

He closed her door and walked over to his car. It seemed to take the longest time for him to get the key into the lock and turn. Audrey thought for a moment that he would run back to her, open her door and pull her into his arms. Her chest burned, remembering their kisses. Why was she so afraid of him?

The rumble bang of the tiny car's engine turning over drowned out her thoughts. She saw him watching her. He rolled his window down. She pressed the button on her left so she could hear what he had to say.

"You know I'm nuts about you don't you? Why won't you give me a chance?"

"Jules, I just got out of a marriage that just about killed me emotionally. I just can't get involved with anyone right now." Why was she lying? She'd had relationships since she'd been separated from Emory.

"I'm sorry if I've been too forward. I can't help it if I think you're the prettiest woman I've ever seen. I dig the hell outta you, Audrey. Why don't we get together and talk about it? I promise I won't touch you." He removed his hands from the wheel, holding them out so she could examine his empty palms.

"See. No tricks."

"Okay." She laughed. "We can talk about it. But not tonight. I have an early day tomorrow and I really need to get some rest."

Jules didn't try to mask his disappointment. He shifted the car into drive and sped away.

Chapter Thirty-Five

"Damn!" Althea Franklin looked down at the chipped nail, a patch of white peeked at her from the smooth pink enamel covering her fingertips. She dialed the number to the salon, making an appointment to have her hair and nails done that afternoon.

It would have been simpler if she had kept her nails bare and her hair natural. But circumstances had made her new look necessary. She'd done it all for James. She thought that if she went back to the look she had when they were in love it would turn things around for them. But he didn't care. Hell, he didn't even notice the recent changes in her appearance. Her new look was bringing her plenty of attention from outside her marriage. If James no longer found her desirable, other men certainly did. So it turned into a positive thing after all.

She sat in the study, his room, deep in thought of a more peaceful time. She watched the painted impressionist view of city life from a gaudy frame hanging over the sofa. Seated behind his large wooden desk, she reached underneath the middle drawer and could feel the listening device she'd placed there when she first suspected him of having an affair.

The tiny apparatus had helped prove her suspicions when he was away from home all those nights. This was how she found out about the late night trysts with Jackie Daniels. With all the pressure coming from the DA's office, they would be sure to convict James even if all the pieces didn't match. The fact that Jackie Daniels carried his child was motive for wanting her silenced. The scandal would have ruined his career. He had plenty of reasons to want her dead. He would be convicted and put in prison for the rest of his life. Was life imprisonment too severe a penalty for committing adultery? Perhaps, but that's the price he'd have to pay for breaking his marriage vows.

Althea walked to the powder room. Clicking on the light, she stepped inside. She loved the tiny room with its rich fabrics and Gothic trim and décor. She proudly displayed this room to guests who would nod and smile through pained expressions. The little room was truly atrocious.

In keeping with the garish theme of the rest of the house, the walls were painted pastel pink with flecks of gold sponged alternately with baby blue. The bathroom fixtures were gold plated trolls who vomited water at the turn of a claw. Tiny, hideous gargoyles commissioned as cabinet handles kept most nosy visitors from peeking inside.

She looked at herself in the ornately framed mirror and smoothed her short, straight hair into place. A quick check of her watch revealed her appointment was more than an hour away. She was about to turn on the television when the phone rang.

She accepted the collect call from her husband. An evil smile planted itself on her face as she listened to his anguished cry.

"Althea? Althea you know I didn't do this, don't you?"

"I don't know what you're capable of James. I would never have thought that you would involve yourself with a student, a minor, but that's exactly what you did."

"Please, forgive me, Thea. I know that was stupid and there's nothing I can say to defend it."

"Can you imagine what this has done to me? Couldn't you just once think of anyone but yourself? The Daniels were our friends. How do you expect me to hold my head up in this town after what you've done?"

"I know baby, I know. You didn't deserve any of this. I refused to work with you to salvage our marriage. I should have gone to the counselor like you wanted. I know you wanted a baby. I wouldn't even give you that. I'm sorry. If I'd only tried to make you happy, none of this would have happened."

"Listen baby, I was talking to my lawyer." He talked fast. Althea envisioned beads of sweat forming on his brow and running down his face to his lying lips. "He said that if you take the stand and testify on my behalf, it would help to strengthen my case. You'd be like a character witness. You'd have to tell them what a good husband and provider that I was to you."

"So in other words, you want me to perjure myself?"

"No! I mean, well, I want you to speak positively on my character."

"What damn character? Where was your character when you laid that baby down in your office and slammed your fifty year old dick in her?"

"Althea, it wasn't like that." He stammered.

"Where was your character when we attended social events where the Daniels were present? You smiled in their faces and held their hands with yours after you had just pulled it out of their daughter's ass."

"She was an adult. I…"

"Where was your precious character," she spat, "When you stood before faculty and student body, continually preaching about morals and ethics? You were going to let that man go to prison, maybe even be executed for something that you did!"

"I didn't kill that girl!"

"Where was your character all those nights you left me here alone, and then lied to me about it?" She pulled the phone away as tears sprang to her eyes. It angered her that he caused her so much pain. She slammed the receiver into its base and stared at it for a long time, afraid that if she moved her eyes it would attack her like a snake.

"Fucking bastard! You never think of anyone but yourself." She yelled at the telephone, the instrument that had been used to hurt her. It was an abettor in her husband's deceit.

She picked up the phone and flung it into the wall with all of her might. Her hands clenched into fists as she paced the room, muttering to herself about all of the abuse she had taken.

"I'm not going to let you use me James Franklin!" She glared at the telephone. The instrument used to set up his rendezvous. The tool used to lie about it later. It lay upon the floor. The screeching warning of the phone off the hook became the voice of James whispering to his lover. She covered her ears but she couldn't shut out the sound. They were laughing at her, taunting her.

"I need to see you baby."

"What if you can't get away? Won't she make trouble for you?"

"Don't worry about her. She's an idiot. She doesn't know a thing."

"But what if she finds out?"

"Who gives a shit if she does?" Laughter. *"I can't wait to see you."*

"Stop it!" Althea put her hands to her ears, trying to shut out the voices. She yanked the telephone cord from the jack. The voices chased her still. The porcelain figurines and brass miniatures teased her, making fun of her antics. She grabbed a sword from its mounting and started swinging it at the laughing faces in the frames.

She raked the bric-a-brac from the shelves, sweeping the broken curios to the floor. Grabbing hold of a tall etagere, she pulled it onto the floor sending glass everywhere. The deafening sound of the crash seemed to shock her back to the present, back to sanity.

Panning the room, a sense of horror rumbled through her. Portions of the wallpaper hung in sheds from the wall. Tattered artwork, glass and wood was strewn around the room. Althea looked at her prized possessions, welling up, she slid to the floor.

"What happened to my things? My lovely things." She sobbed.

She sat against the wall. Pressing her knees into her chest, she rocked back and forth, trying to calm herself. Someone else took over then. The one who always came at times like this. The one who consoles and comforts her. She sat for a long time, her eyes childlike. Reaching inside, she comforted her child self in an attempt to rescue the little girl from the maelstrom whirling through her mind.

Chapter Thirty-Six

It had rained for the last three days and it was raining now. Rob stepped off the curb into a huge puddle.

"Shit!"

He lifted his foot slowly as though reducing the speed of his actions would lessen the damage the water caused. He stepped down gingerly, each step a deliberate attempt to avoid puddles.

Through the expansive restaurant window he could see Jerry seated at a booth smoking a cigarette. Someone was seated next to him. He was positioned in a way that Rob could not make out his companion's gender, but knowing his brother, it was most likely a woman.

Jerry called him earlier wanting to meet at Freddy's that evening for a drink. He wouldn't tell him the reason for the meeting. With Jerry, there was always a reason when he wanted to get together.

He assumed his brother was up to one of his money making schemes. Being a stock broker fed Jerry's financial insecurities. He was always within reach of multiple millions, but the millions never seemed to make their way into his grasp. This evening's meeting was probably to ask Rob to make an investment in his newest scheme. He'd want seed money for his potential harvest, or something of that nature. He'd play along with Jerry until he got to the punch line. He'd laugh, wish him luck, finish his drink and get the hell on down the road.

He opened the door to Freddy's. Steam clouded the lenses of his glasses. He pulled them off along with his hat as he made his way into the restaurant, squinting in the direction of the booth where Jerry and the woman were seated. Her dark brown hand patted Jerry's golden brown one. They whispered intimately, their heads lightly touching. Rob was still holding the dripping hat and glasses when he approached the table.

He cleared his throat a couple of times before they looked up. Recognition replaced the question in his eyes as Jerry's companion rose. She leaned over the table to accept Rob's kiss and hug.

"Audrey Kimborough! Where have you been hiding?" Rob pressed her to him, breathing in her clean hair and floral scented skin. She was as lovely as ever. He pulled away to fully visualize his brother's ex.

"It's been a long time Rob." She smiled as she spoke.

"I wouldn't have thought it was possible for you to get any prettier. Time is definitely on your side. You look fantastic." Rob held her hands in his and admired her.

"Look who's talking, Mr. All American, college football hero. Looks like you're still following your old regimen." She gazed at him approvingly. "Jerry tells me your still single. What's wrong with these sorry ass sisters that they would let a fine brother like you go home alone at night."

"Who says I'm alone at night?" he let go of her hands, feigning insult. "I'm single, not a monk."

"Excuse me. I hate to break up this meeting of the mutual admiration society, but I do have an agenda." Jerry smiled at them.

"Don't you always." Rob chided his brother. "I left my wallet at home so don't bother trying to lift it."

"Just shut up and sit down, you're getting water all over the table."

The two men hugged before taking their seats. Rob thought back in time. How long had it been since he'd seen Audrey, two, three years? It had been even longer ago than that he thought she was going to be his sister-in-law, but it never happened.

Audrey and Jerry had been in love with each other since they were little more than kids. They'd each gone away to college and when they returned they began a relationship which culminated with an engagement to be married. Audrey was very ambitious and quickly advanced her career in finance. Had she been a man, she would have been considered for a partnership at Wyman-Franklin years before they actually made her the offer. Had she taken it, she would have been the first woman of color to hold such a position with the firm.

Jerry drifted from industry to industry in lower lever financial positions until he secured a position as broker with the regional office of an international firm. He seemed content at first, but as Audrey's career blossomed, it became apparent that Jerry was not moving through the company ranks at all. He'd had one promotion in his first two years, after that, he'd been passed over for several higher level positions. To make matters worse, his commission rate was slashed. He was always insecure about money. When he learned that Audrey was making more than twice the amount he was getting, he became withdrawn and unbearable to be around. He just couldn't deal with his woman being more successful than he.

It was apparent that Audrey would be a star in her field. She had many options and could write her own ticket. She would constantly be in the company of people just as successful as she was. Through her association with WF, her world was full of rich business leaders and powerful politicians who made deals on the golf course and over champagne brunches. Jerry's world, in contrast, consisted of people whose aspiration was to make it to noon so that they could sneak a beer for lunch. Her life was top drawer. His was a cardboard box in the back of the closet.

While Audrey took her life in stride, Jerry was constantly questioning her about who she met, what meetings she attended and whether she was sleeping with anyone outside their relationship. He repeatedly accused her of waiting until she latched on to one of her rich clients so she could dump him.

Inevitably, his insecurities led him to the beds of other women. Though all of the obvious signs were there, Audrey tried to deny what her mind was telling her. When she dropped by his apartment unannounced one evening, she could no longer deny her suspicions. Distraught, and humiliated, Audrey had showed up at Rob's and collapsed into his arms, telling him the whole story.

Rob didn't know what to do or say. There was nothing he could say in his brother's defense. He'd been a fool, plain and simple. Audrey was a wonderful woman who didn't deserve to be treated that way. When she left his place that evening, Audrey was a ghost of her usual self. Rob felt so bad for her.

Suddenly Jerry and Audrey were no longer an item. It seemed only weeks later he remembered reading about the impending nuptials in the society section of the newspaper. There was a picture of his would be sister-in-law with prominent attorney Emory Kimborough.

The break-up left his brother with a sadness that seemed to mature him. He painted Rob a sketchy drawing of what had happened and then never spoke about Audrey Wilson again. He tried to behave as if the relationship never happened.

Rob would see Audrey in passing over the years. They'd speak briefly, each instance an embarrassing reminder of the incident that ended her engagement to Jerry. Then she seemed to have fallen off the edge of the earth. Now she sat here with Jerry as though time had stood still and nothing negative had ever happened between them. He watched her bright eyes and smooth chocolate skin, looking at Jerry with stars in her eyes.

"All right, the suspense is killing me." Rob looked from one to the other curiously. "What are you two up to?"

"We ran into each other a few weeks ago and decided to give it another try. We're older now and not as insecure as we once were." Rob cut his brother a discerning glare.

"Okay, *I'm* not as insecure as *I* was then." He averted his eyes, grinning sheepishly. "It was all my fault that we broke up. We started talking to each other because we both realized that we needed to heal. I never stopped loving Audrey." He touched her hand lovingly. "I just didn't know how to show her. I called you both here today because I wanted my brother, who I love, well, like a brother, to be here when I ask you to marry me Audrey."

Rob almost spit his water across the table. The frozen smile remained on Audrey's face while the melanin seemed to drain from her skin leaving a weird gray cast behind.

"What?" The word slipped through clenched teeth.

"You said you still loved me Audrey. I've never stopped loving you. Let's not lose each other again. Please, be my wife."

Audrey sat in stunned silence. Rob tried to think of a way to bail her out.

"I hate to be the ant at the picnic, but aren't you forgetting one small detail? If I remember right, isn't there already a Mr. Audrey Wilson at home?"

"Already ahead of you Bro. Their divorce is final. She's free and clear."

'I'm sorry things didn't work out for you, Audrey." Rob looked at her and shook his head sadly.

"Well I'm not! If she hadn't broken up with old what's his name, I wouldn't be here with you guys today."

Rob looked at his brother and frowned. He loved him dearly, but he'd never have enough class for Audrey Wilson.

Chapter Thirty-Seven

Audrey opened the front door of her brownstone just in time to hear the ring of the telephone. She picked up the receiver to retrieve her messages. Emory had called again. So had Jerry. What was up with these guys? It was like they had an agreement among themselves: let's see who could be the first to break her down.

She had agreed to meet with Jerry because she felt that maybe her hesitance in opening up to Jules had to do with negative feelings she harbored due to her past relationships. The first time or two that they talked, it had been cathartic for them both. He finally admitted to his insecurities and infidelities. She released the bitterness that she felt and forgave him.

Seeing him again opened old wounds and conjured up long buried pain. It was like going back in time. That day she came to his apartment was so present she could smell the incense cones burning in his ashtrays, hear the giggles, the splashing water.

Using her key, she opened the door and brought in the packages containing the ingredients for the meal she planned to fix them that night. She heard a noise upstairs and ascended the spiral staircase leading to the master bedroom.

The covers had been thrown upon the floor. Various articles of men's and women's clothing were strewn about. She followed the trail of clothes, laughter, and intermittent splashing to the bathroom.

There was Jerry, the man she loved, the man she was to wed, sitting in his sunken tub. A wet, pinked skinned blonde bounced up and down on him in frenzied fashion while he slathered suds from her backside to her breasts.

She had no idea how much time had elapsed. Jerry and his playmate were completely involved in their aquatic activities. They didn't even notice her. It seemed to her they were moving in slow motion. She remembered the wide open smiles, their laughter as the woman threw her head back, then Jerry pulled her forward, slipping a dark pink nipple into his mouth. That's when he saw Audrey.

That was the end for her. She had put up with his self doubt, his feelings of inadequacy because she thought that in time, her love for him could overrule everything else. But this was the last straw. She walked away from him that night, never spending another minute of her time on Jerry Hollingsworth.

Of the scores of men who she met through her business dealings with the firm, none impressed her more than Emory Kimborough. Kimborough was a partner in the Midwest's most prominent African American law firm. He was everything Jerry Hollingsworth wasn't. Emory was self assured, rich, and powerful. He seemed proud of her achievements, not threatened by them. He had pursued her relentlessly until she told him of her engagement.

When she ran into him at a conference the week after she walked away from her relationship with Jerry, the two of them talked. He asked about her engagement and she let him know that the marriage would never happen. Emory saw this as his green light. He plowed ahead leaving time nor space for her to change her mind about Jerry or meet someone new. He showered her with gifts and affection. Whatever she wanted and needed, Emory Kimborough either did it or got it for her. They began being seen in public and six months after her relationship with Jerry ended, Audrey was married to Emory Kimborough.

Audrey was happy at first. After a number of relationships with men who were insecure, insipid, or just plain stupid, being with Emory was like a breath of fresh air.

He was a big man. Everything about him was imposing. When he spoke, the rich baritone possessed not only a depth in timbre but in substance as well.

He had a take charge attitude that Audrey needed after dealing in a world where she was the decision maker. Emory made her feel soft, delicate, feminine. Ever the gentleman, he opened her door, poured her wine, massaged her feet, carried her to the bedroom, drew her bath and then gently bathed her. His lovemaking was strong and passionate. He was almost perfect.

Emory Kimborough had one bad habit. He needed to be in control all the time, no matter what the situation. She witnessed him in the courtroom. His smooth style impressed everyone from the judge to the jury. He'd have the prosecution playing the cards he had masterfully dealt before they even realized they were in the game.

She soon learned that Emory was a control freak. As their relationship progressed, he began to make her over. There were little things at first. Her name was no longer Audrey but 'Honey' or 'Babes'. He always wanted to add his own touch to everything that she did.

"Honey, don't you think that dress shows a bit too much cleavage for this occasion? You're my wife now. You must remember that you're representing me and the firm now. Let's look the part."

"Is that what you're wearing? Why don't you put on that little black number that I bought for you?"

"Hey Babes, you should let your hair grow long. Don't get me wrong, you're beautiful with short hair, but long hair is so sexy."

"Babes, have you ever thought of coloring your hair? If you went just a few shades lighter, you'd be gorgeous. Not that you aren't now. Just try it. Plus it would cover that gray that's sneaking up on you."

He imposed himself on everyone and everything. He told the gardener how to garden, the plumber how to plumb, the office staff how to be more efficient in the office. Everyone and everything was at risk. He was always there with a watchful eye, an assisting hand. The benevolence of Emory Kimborough in his quest to correct all that was amiss in the world caused Audrey to run from the room at times screaming.

The first time that they went to the Spice Rack together, he was in rare form. Renita didn't know Emory very well and looked forward to the two of them coming to the club. Emory wasted little time commenting on everything from the décor to the attire of the patrons. He asked to see the chef after they'd completed their meal to give him suggestions on preparing Chicken Kiev.

"Try whipping the eggs slightly. When you beat them too long, the result is, well, what we had here tonight. Also, the trick to a good risotto is to make sure your rice is firm not gummy."

The man looked so far down his nose at Emory that his eyes crossed. The fiery glare was lost on Emory. He was so busy telling the chef how to take care of his business that he didn't notice. Emory conducted his "how to clinics" with the same flourish as his closing statements. Patrons at surrounding tables couldn't help but hear the discourse. Audrey was so embarrassed after the cooking lesson that she wanted to crawl underneath the table.

During Renita's first set, he took out a pad and started taking notes on how she could improve her technique.

"What are you doing?" Audrey was two seconds from walking out of there.

"Your sister's quite good. I mean she has the right voice for this type of music. With a little coaching, she could be an exceptional singer. It could take many years but she has promise."

"For your information, Renita is a world renowned artist. She's got several recordings and been the featured singer at major venues nationally and internationally."

"Oh,yeah? So what's she doing in this dive?"

"Renita sings here because this is what makes her happy."

"Is that what she told you? Balderdash!

"*Balderdash?*"

"No artist worth his salt would waste their time in some seedy nightclub when they could do better."

"Everybody doesn't need material trappings that others say are the signs of happiness and success."

"Listen Babes. I know what I'm talking about. With the right direction she could do a lot better. She'd better make it snappy though, she's getting to be a bit long in the tooth."

"What? Renita is my baby sister. If she's old, what does that make me?"

"Honey, I didn't mean that she was old. It's just that in her business the competition is ruthless. It takes a lot of energy to stay ahead of the pack."

"She's on her way over." Audrey cautioned. "Please don't say anything to her about this Em. All right?" Her eyes searched his for a level of humanity that didn't exist.

"Why not?" He touched her hand and smiled at her condescendingly. "Don't you want to see your sister be the best that she can be? Fortunately for you, you have me to work with you. Your sister's a lovely girl. She has some natural abilities which could use some cultivating. Don't worry Babes. She'll thank me. You'll see."

By the time Renita joined them, Audrey was steaming. She had scooted her chair so far away from her husband that she was sitting at a different table. She was debating whether to make a break for it. She knew that if he started talking that shit to her sister, he was going to end up with a shot glass up his ass.

"Renita, that was wonderful." He greeted her as she approached the table.

Renita looked at her sister quizzically. Judging from the fact that she was no longer sitting with her husband, Renita assumed they had been fighting. Audrey seemed pissed but her new brother-in-law was just as gregarious as when she'd met them at the table earlier. He seemed very eager to speak with her. He was handing her the slip of paper that he had been writing on.

"I took the liberty of making a list of suggestions that I know will help you in your struggle to become a singer."

"Excuse me?" Renita looked at him like his hair had suddenly caught fire.

"Go on, take it." He smiled as she opened the note and read it.

"You're joking right?" She smiled. When she wanted to, she could take a joke as good as anyone.

"About as much as you were when your up there, uhm, singing. But don't worry. If you follow the guidelines as I've listed them, I guarantee you'll never have a problem. I've included the names of a couple of vocal coaches that I'm acquainted with. They're good men, I'm sure they can help you." He smiled, waiting for thanks that wasn't hardly even about to come. "You show a lot of promise. If it's not too late, you may be able to make something of yourself yet."

Renita was still staring at him. She reviewed the scribbled instructions on the piece of paper again and cracked up laughing. It was loud, raucous, gut-busting laughter that caused patrons throughout the club to direct their attention to them.

"I'm not feeling well, Emory. Let's go home." Audrey was afraid that if they stayed there much longer, somebody was going to get hurt.

"No, I want to hear what Mr. Kimborough thinks of my performance."

Renita was really scaring Audrey now. She was laughing so hard tears streamed her face. Emory looked stunned, then he seemed to be insulted. He went into further detail about the problems with Renita's singing. With the exception of an occasional "Oh, really" or "You think so, huh.", Renita made no comment as he gave his views on everything from renovations to the café to opinions on how she should dress.

Audrey was proud of Renita. She was the picture of poise and composure. She listened to Emory and not once did she fly off the handle. There was no cussing, no screaming, no blood letting, nothing. Emory should have quit while he was ahead. But no. He had to go and talk about her locks.

"No matter how you sound, you're a beautiful girl." Audrey winced at his use of the chauvinistic term. He probably didn't detect the slight narrowing in Renita's eyes. He kept going.

"You're much too pretty to wear such a dreadful hairstyle. Often times we try to let our outward appearance make our statements for us. A preferable approach would be to verbalize our principles. It's far more effective. That hairstyle offends people, not just whites, many blacks are turned off by women who refuse to straighten their hair. It's not very becoming on a man or woman. In your case, wearing that ugly style really detracts from your natural beauty."

Renita glared at Emory, tossed back her bourbon and slammed the glass onto the table. The band was warming up for the next set. Renita made a movement like she was leaving the table, then she turned back.

"It detracts from my natural beauty? This *is* my natural hair, you ass. How would you know what offends black people? You've been trying to pass for so long you forget that it's the hair straighteners, skin lighteners, and tinted contacts that take away from our natural beauty. Everybody doesn't feel the need to whiten up so that they can be more acceptable to a race that excludes them. It's really scary, no sad, that many educated blacks have such ignorant views about so many things."

"Now I have a piece of advice for you." She drew near him, looked in his eyes coldly. "Stick to your law practice and leave the social, fashion, culinary, gardening, and all other commentary to the experts."

With that, she tossed her *ugly, unbecoming* dreads in his face and headed for the stage.

Audrey exhaled. That wasn't too bad, she thought as she watched her sister whisper to Lloyd who summoned the rest of the band for a brief huddle.

"Ladies and Gentlemen, I'd like to dedicate the next song to my brother-in-law, Rosemont Township's foremost attorney, Mr. Emory Kimborough. Stand up Emory and say hello."

He stood, flashed his million dollar smile, and waved to the crowd. The soft sound of the band was the backdrop to the audience's slight applause. Lloyd began to tickle the piano keys. The applause subsided as the band picked up the melody of what had become Renita's signature song *'Girl From Ipanema'*. But soon after Renita started singing, Audrey found to her surprise, and Emory's dismay, the words had been changed.

"Overweight and slightly balding the man called Emory goes walking
and when he passes each one he passes goes, AAAHHH!
When he talks it's time for slumber because his words have so little substance
and when he's talking each one he passes goes, UGHHH!
Nobody asks his opinion but you can bet he still gives it.
He thinks we're shy and we're timid.
When he ordered a glass of Remy
The bartender added some pee.

The audience roared. Some members of the audience snickered. The regulars were used to Renita's antics and raised their glasses to her. She was a genius with verse, making up lyrics on the spot for birthdays, anniversaries, or any occasion. Emory Kimborough didn't know who he was messing with. The chef came out of the kitchen and blew Renita a kiss. The bartender lifted a glass and winked at Emory. Everybody fell out laughing.

She watched him siting across from her, glaring at Renita, heat shooting from him like rays. She knew he would scold her for letting her sister take such license with him. But he'd asked for it. By this time

Renita had the audience participating on the *AHHH's*. Audrey had to bite her tongue to keep from joining in. She was having more fun than she'd had all evening.

In spite of his arrogance and conceit, Audrey stayed with Emory for seven years. She was good at putting on a confident and professional face to her clients, but in her personal life she had some insecurities of her own. Emory identified her shortcomings early in their relationship, and used the knowledge to manipulate her. She had always been the big sister, the business woman, strong, tough. She never felt that she could show her softer side without being taken advantage of. When she came home after a hard day, Emory allowed her to collapse into him. He listened intently to everything that she said. He took her side no matter what the situation was, empowering her to face the next day. He had given her this gift that no one else ever had. When situations became too difficult to bear, Emory allowed her to cry.

Emory Kimborough was strong, financially successful, good looking, and generous. He was loving and attentive. She overlooked his tendency to feel it was his obligation to "help" those less fortunate than himself. In his mind, that was everyone.

For more than six years she bit her tongue, looked away, closed her ears, shut down her mind, as he criticized, antagonized, judged and opinionated. When he mentioned starting his own firm, she left WF to assist.

Seeing him taking such a leap inspired her to go out on her own. When she talked to Emory about her dream, he not only discouraged her from going into business for herself, but belittled her professional capabilities. It was then that she decided to leave him. She could overlook his criticism of externals, but she had worked hard in her profession. In her field she knew there weren't many who rivaled her. She realized that in order for Emory to maintain his feelings of superiority, he needed to make everyone else feel lesser than he. Audrey couldn't let him dog her like that. She drew a line in the sand. To cross it would have meant betraying her own soul.

She hadn't regretted leaving him one day. And going it alone had been rough. The many clients who'd sworn their allegiance to her during her association with WF abandoned her. Things were so bad that she wondered if her former company and Emory were in cahoots to sabotage her career. In any event, she was on her own now and glad that Emory Kimborough was a closed chapter in her life.

Somehow he didn't seem to think she could possibly make it without him. He called her repeatedly during their separation and he was still calling her, but there was nothing that he could say or do to make her go back to a life with him.

Now she had a different problem. It was true that a part of her heart still belonged to Jerry Hollingsworth. But their recent meetings and telephone conversations confirmed that she was right to walk away from him when she did. She could never go back. She realized that he really hadn't changed that much. She knew that he was incapable of giving her the support that she needed.

She realized even before the three of them left the restaurant that evening that she'd have to tell him that a marriage between them would never work. Her only purpose for meeting with him was to replace the rough ending to their love relationship that his affair had meted out.

There was one other thing. All the time she'd spent with Jerry recently, Jules had been there too. Thoughts of him and their last meeting flitted around her head like a pesky moth. Her lips still tingled with the memory of their last kiss. Her heart still ached, yearning for a chance for real love.

Chapter Thirty-Eight

The door closed quietly behind the visitor. Buc Buchannon stared at it and popped several antacids. His ass sagged in the busted seat of the gray leather chair. Having suffered years of pressure, the cushion, like Buchannon, was now rock-like and inflexible.

With his elbows propped upon the metal desk, he pressed his fingers together, forming a tent. He looked into the cavity his hands created as if he'd find an answer there. The meeting had been a disturbing one. Daniels wouldn't like this new development at all. Hell, he couldn't even tell him.

He got up from the desk and gave the waste can a ferocious kick. Garbage went flying around the room making Buchannon even angrier. It was one more reminder that every time he got involved with that asshole, he was the one left cleaning up shit. But he could blame no one but himself. He had done one favor for A.J. Daniels, the wrong kind of favor, and he couldn't stop. The money was too good. The retribution that he meted out to the unfortunate enemies of A.J. Daniels provided him a sense of power that gave him an incredible rush. He'd found his calling. Buc Buchannon was in too deep. Like being bitten by a vampire, hitting the crack pipe, or taking money from a loan shark, once you're in it, you become a slave. He was a slave for life.

As a boy he'd watched the *Untouchables* on TV and knew then that he wanted to be in law enforcement. But once a member of the small unit in Rosemont Township, he quickly learned there was much more to being a cop than you see on television and in the movies. The job brought with it intense pressures. It seemed he had to answer to everyone, his superiors, other cops with more seniority, as well as the community.

Buchannon found the politics of his career challenging, but he was able to adjust to the rigors and routine of the job. What he could not get used to was the pay. As a single man it had been tough enough, but when he married Betty and the kids came along, it was hell just making it through each week.

To make matters worse, Betty was always on his back about the long hours that he worked, the fact that he wasn't there to help her with the kids, and that there was never enough money. The boys always needed something for school, or wanted something that everybody else has. Then there were the trips to the doctor, new shoes, clothes, it never stopped. The pressures continued to mount reaching a climax one day about five years into their marriage. Her words were still as fresh as the morning.

"Buc, can we start a college fund for the boys?"

"A college fund?"

"It's when you put money into the bank so that your kids can use it to go to college."

"I know what a college fund is, you idiot. What I don't know is, where do you expect the money for this college fund to come from?" He remembered his anger rising like mercury up the shaft of a thermometer.

"We could take from somewhere else maybe?" She replied timidly.

"Somewhere like where? My pockets are inside out." He pulled them out of his pants for effect. "I'm working two jobs, Betty. What do you want me to do? We can just barely afford to send them to public school, now you want them to go to college."

"You see how things are these days. A high school diploma won't guarantee they'll be able to find work. By the time they grow up, everybody will have college degrees."

"Oh, here we go again." He threw his hands up in exasperation. "Everybody else has one, why don't we?"

"That's not what I meant, Buc."

"Well just what do you mean? Betty I'm doing the best that I can."

"Well your best ain't even putting food on the table half the time." She slammed the mixing bowl she was drying so hard it shattered into the sink. "The boys deserve better than this. If we start saving for them now, they can go to college, get some kind of degree or something so they won't have to get some lousy cop job or worse when they grow up."

Buc had never hit a woman in his life. His father beat his mother nearly to death. He swore he'd never be like his dad. He felt the sting of his open hand meeting her face before he could think. She fell backwards into the wall, ending up in a crumpled heap on the floor.

Shame and disbelief drove him from the house. When he returned later that evening, he reeked of alcohol and handed her a flattened box of candy. He had accidentally crushed it with his foot when he dropped it getting out of the truck.

He swore to her that he would never hit her again. He kissed her swollen lips and promised he would find a way to get some money for the boys to attend college. But that wasn't the last time he hit her.

The beatings became a part of their routine. Promotion didn't happen, Betty was beaten. The captain chewed him out at work, he found some reason to hit her. If the lights got turned off or the kids got a bad report card, Betty was punished.

From that point, their lives together changed. The house was never clean when he got home. Betty didn't try to look nice for him anymore. Her hair was nasty, her skin was discolored from old and new bruises. The tattered house dress she wore which used to be yellow, was now so full of unwashed stains, blood, sweat, food, semen; it was no color and every color.

The kids started running wild in the streets. They asked for everything that they saw on TV. When they didn't get what they wanted, they'd steal it. That's when the violence spilled over to the children.

Their life was the stuff you read in tabloids or saw on morning talk shows. Buc dealt with it by creating a life with someone else. Betty and the boys floated through life, dealing with whatever happened to them when it happened.

When A.J. Daniels became the district attorney, he sought out staff members who were hungry, desperate and greedy enough to be a part of his special projects force. When Daniels called upon him to be a part of this elite team Buchannon thought his luck was finally changing. He eagerly took on special assignments and waded through the political mire which quickly led to his appointment as Chief of Police for Rosemont.

In the beginning the extracurricular assignments gave him some much needed breathing room. With the extra "benefits" that he got from Daniels, he was able to get out of debt and relieve a great deal of stress at home. But there were intangible costs associated with his new lifestyle.

He turned his attention once again to the visit and his relationship with Ted Masterson. They'd grown up together in Glenwood, the roughest part of town. Joining the police academy had been Buc's out, but he'd never lost touch with many of the gang from the old neighborhood. There was always someone there who could do you a favor. For a price.

Masterson was Buchannon's hired gun. Whenever one of the assignments called for special attention, the work was contracted to Masterson. They had worked like this for years without problems. But this thing with Jake Hurley had been trouble from the start.

Daniels had given Buchannon fifty thousand dollars to "take care of" Hurley. Buc had given the assignment to Masterson. He was to be paid five thousand dollars up front and another five upon completion of the job. Somehow, Masterson discovered how much Daniels had paid for the hit and wanted a bigger piece of the pie.

Buc didn't know how the hell Ted had gotten his information, and he denied there was that much money involved. This angered Masterson who not only wanted the other forty thousand, but an additional ten.

Buchannon didn't have the money. He'd used it to discharge gambling debts and to catch up past due mortgage payments on his second home in Dover Hills. He couldn't return to Daniels for more money. He wouldn't take kindly to being dragged into the details of how Buchannon's work was completed. There was no way he would be extorted. The mere thought of approaching Daniels with this turned the beads of perspiration that had gathered on Buchannon's forehead cold.

"You know me Buc. We go way back. I'm not greedy, I'm just asking you for what's fair. We're talking about a cop here. If this shit hits the fan, it's going to splatter on me. You were stupid for not getting more from Daniels. If I had known when we set the price that this guy was a cop, the job would have cost you fifty anyway. Maybe more."

"What do you think this is, Findley Street market? The price was set. You don't bargain with men like A.J. Daniels. He set the price, you agreed to it. That's that."

"He set the price low because he knew you didn't have the balls to contest it. I tell you what. Why don't you call up ole' A.J. I think I can reason with him." Masterson glared at Buc icily, handing him the phone.

"Look man. The cost of the job was fifty. It's over. You agreed to ten thousand and that's how much you were paid." He tried to maintain a bold front but he knew Masterson. He would not slink quietly away. This was bad.

"Well, I changed my mind. I want the rest of that money."

"There is no 'rest of the money.' There were other costs associated with setting up this deal."

"What fuckin' costs? You picked up the phone and you called me. I'm the one who incurred costs. I didn't charge you for the dent in Luke's truck. And what about our gas fare and cleaning costs?"

"So how much did you foot for gas and washing that raggedy ass truck? Thirty bucks? Look, you had a job to do, we agreed on terms, you were paid. End of discussion."

"Oh no, my friend. This discussion is not over. Far from it. What do you think will happen to you and your good buddy when this hits the press? If he off'd the cop for fuckin' his wife, what do you think he would do to you for fuckin' him? I got a tidy little package all ready to go to Channel Six with you pointing the finger at Daniels."

"You're full of shit." Buchannon sputtered.

"Oh you think so? When have you ever known me to bluff?" Masterson was cool and controlled. The icy cold glare he cast was unwavering. "I don't play games Buc and you know it. Now here's how I see it. You get the fifty to me by midnight tomorrow or you won't be alive to see the sun come up the following morning."

Buchannon tried to hide the fear he felt. He was more afraid of the killer in the DA's office than the one he faced now.

"Listen, Ted. I don't have fifty thousand dollars. Let's try to work things out…"

"Ain't a damn thing *we* got to work out. It's simple. You get that money or you got big problems."

There was no way Daniels would give him anything else. The mere mention of this situation would be risking his life. A.J. Daniels was the most dangerous man he knew. He had to find an alternative way of getting himself out of this mess.

He had only one very long shot. He had provided for her all of these years, giving her nothing but his best. Perhaps the investment would now pay off in ways he never could have dreamed of.

* * *

Dava Storm blew cigarette smoke from red painted lips set in a sun wrinkled face. The bright, lemon yellow kitchen with its lacy curtains and squeaky clean windows darkened when Buc Buchannon entered, plopping his girth at the kitchen table. Dava sat a cup of hot tea before him laced with his favorite brandy.

"Buc, I've been with you a lot of years. I gave up a lot. I never married. I don't have any kids. I've listened to you talk about your wife and kids and it hurt. I always put you first, comforting you in spite of my own emptiness and pain."

"You never told me Dava."

"I'm not blaming you. I made my own decisions. Now I'm old. All I got is the clothes on my back and a little money that I managed to squirrel away. This house, that car out there, those are your things. I own nothing." Her empty eyes fixed on his.

"I'll give you the money, but before you leave here to day, I want you to sign over the house and the Cadillac to me. We'll make everything legal before the week ends. That's my offer, take it or leave it."

* * *

The couple took the Interstate going east out of town. Randy Travis crooned between the radio static, softly filling the space created by their silence. What began as a few sniffles, erupted into wracking, uncontrollable sobs.

Ted Masterson pulled off at the next exit into a deserted gas station. He turned off the ignition and pulled Betty Buchannon into his arms.

"Shh. Bett, Bett. It's all right baby, go head, let it out." He held her close, rocking her.

"I love you Betty. You know that don't you?" Ted drawled.

She shook her head

"Then you know everything's going to be all right. You're safe now. He'll never hurt you again. Shh, hush baby. Hush now." He stroked her hair and kissed her head.

"What about the boys?" she stammered.

"Betty your sons are grown." He lifted her face in his hands.

"You stayed there and took all that abuse for years to protect them. You did all you could for them. You were a good mother to your boys and you were a good wife to Buc. You should have no regrets. You gave those boys a good foundation. You set them on a path that will lead them right to us and our new lives together. We'll see them again soon. It's time for you to be happy. I'll do anything to make you happy."

He gently kissed her. He lifted her face close to his, kissing her again until he could feel her trembling fear replaced by desire. They made love in the car under the autumn moonlight in a gas station off I-95.

Afterwards, they shared a Marlboro. He reminisced on their past. He'd loved her since that first day in grade school when he saw her golden plaits bouncing on her head as she played hopscotch. All the boys liked her. She was so pretty he was too scared to approach her. He watched with a pained heart as she chose the persistent Bucky Buchannon. They married when she was fresh out of high school. Betty remained faithful to Buc for thirty years.

Ted had married and divorced twice, but his love for Betty Kingsley Buchannon remained constant. Tonight was the first time they'd made love.

Even though he didn't approve, he always respected her marriage to Buc. He knew she would eventually find the courage to leave him. Ted Masterson's patience was immeasurable. He knew it would it was just a matter of time. He watched Buc Buchannon fall into the corrupt side of his profession and eventually, fall apart.

Ted started "seeing" Betty three years ago. She was approaching fifty but she looked closer to sixty. Her skin was tough and creased from years of tears and vicious beatings. But underneath, he could still see the golden haired beauty who he had fallen for all those years before.

He talked her into saving whatever money she could get from Buc. Betty never asked him why she needed the money. He told her that her life was going to change and she had to be ready. She trusted him and did what he said.

It began to be like a game, trying to see how much money she could get from Buc. She'd manufacture reasons that she needed things for the boys or for the house. She'd find the best deals and bargain the prices down further, bringing home exactly what she said she needed. She'd take the money she saved and hide it away.

Ted told her that he would someday take her to Canaan. She was ready to take that journey. With her nest egg and the money Ted had accumulated from various jobs he'd done for Buchannon and others, they had more than one hundred thousand dollars. A plumber by trade, he'd open a business after they found a nice home and settled in. He'd make sure that it was filled with love. He wasn't worried in the least about Buchannon. The coward would never confront him if he found out about him and Betty. If he did, Ted Masterson would kill him.

Chapter Thirty-Nine

Jules smashed the ball into the wall with the paddle over and over again. It had been weeks since he'd been to the racket ball court. It was Thursday and the club was packed with desk jockeys trying to make up for a sedentary week. It was the reason Jules had to wait so long to get a singles room. It was worth it though. He didn't feel the need for company. Alone he could be as aggressive as he wanted without listening to the inane chatter of one his associates. With every invigorating whack of the ball, he felt his stress reserves deplete.

The biggest case of his career was now history. He'd thrown himself into the flood of new cases that deluged him in the wake of his new celebrity. It was a lot of work but not a lot of challenge. He'd hired two paralegal assistants and his receptionist was now working full time. The small office did not accommodate his growing staff. He'd soon have to make a decision on buying more office space or moving all together.

His staff was adept and professional, handling the workload with ease. Things could scarcely have been more perfect. Except that he was still thinking about Audrey Wilson.

She hadn't called him that day after they went to the Spice Rack. He wanted to call her a dozen times, but he didn't want to push it. If anything was going to happen between them, she would have to initiate it.

Cindy had left him several messages recently. She was back stateside and wanted to see him. Though he believed in burning love's bridges, he considered giving her a call.

She'd eventually have to collect her things that he still had in bags cluttering his bedroom. He no longer felt anything for her, but a little time spent with her might deflect the growing feelings he had for Audrey. Using Cindy as a diversion would be tacky and he knew that ultimately, it would do him more harm than good. It's like craving something sinful to eat and nibbling on everything else to try to satisfy the urge. It just doesn't work.

He pounded the ball once more before walking off the court toward the locker room. He showered, dressed, and ate the bland dining room fare offered by the club and headed for home. Exhaustion pressed down on him as he turned the key and entered his apartment. Though it was only a little after seven, he pulled off his clothes, left them in a pile on the floor and slid underneath the covers. He couldn't remember the last time he'd felt so alone, or in so much pain.

*　*　*

"All right, you been sitting here moping into that Irish Coffee long enough. You gonna tell me what's wrong or not?"

Audrey met Renita at the Spice Rack on Thursday night for dinner and drinks. When she arrived, her appetite was a no show, leaving her to opt for only liquor instead.

"I gotta tell you something but you gotta promise not to hit me or call me bad names."

"I don't believe in making promises I can't keep, but I'll try. Go for it."

"I've been seeing Jerry." She mumbled, hoping the words would be lost in the sounds of clinking glasses, conversation, and laughter from nearly tables.

"Jerry who?" Renita asked distractedly.

"Jerry Hollingsworth, fool."

"I'm the fool? Who's seeing Jerry Hollingsworth, me or you? Have you lost your mind or what?" Renita moved the glass from her sister's reach.

"I know what he did to me was wrong, but he called me a couple of weeks ago and I guess I was kind of curious. I hadn't seen him since he moved away to New York and…"

"You're not kidding? You've been seeing Jerry Hollingsworth."

"Renita listen. I still had some unresolved issues. I just didn't want this thing to hold any unnecessary power over me."

"Oh, no. Here we go with that ole moon in the seventh house bull-shit." Renita flagged the waitress down and ordered a basket of spicy chicken tenders and a second gin and tonic for the two of them.

"It's not bull. When I trust my intuition, I'm never led astray."

"Should I light some candles and do a few incantations?" Renita snorted.

"I refuse to talk to you until you stop making fun of me."

"Okay. Don't get yourself all in a knot, Ali Baba." Audrey shot her sister a contemptuous glare before continuing.

"We met a couple of times for dinner. Nothing more. I never felt that our relationship had reached full closure and I needed to end things my way. Jerry had other ideas."

Renita lifted her arm, checked a nonexistent watch, yawned, and cast her sister a weary gaze.

"He wants to get married."

"You're lying!" Renita's sat wide-eyed. Her full attention now on Audrey.

"Nope."

"You cussed his ass out, didn't you?"

"No. I didn't cuss him out. I told him no thank you and that was the end of that."

"Wow! I wonder what drove him to that?"

"Who knows? I met Jerry and his brother Rob at Freddy's. He asked me right there in front of Rob. I couldn't tell him no then. I called him later that night."

"I'll be damned. How's ole fine Rob doing? He married yet?"

"He's doing fine, and no, he's not married. You know he was lead detective on the Daniels case. His partner was killed and he's still depressed about that. Otherwise, he seems real good."

"Maybe the two of ya'll should hook up."

"What? That's nasty."

"How's that nasty? He's single, you're single. Plus it would serve that bastard Jerry right if you ended up with his brother."

"Ren, there's no way I'd get with Jerry's brother or the brother of anyone else I've dated. That's incest or something."

"It wouldn't be dating, and it wouldn't be incest, it would be fucking. Everybody needs love. Ain't no sense lettin' all that go to waste."

"The only thing that's wasted is your filthy mind."

The waitress brought the basket of chicken and fries, then sat their drinks before them. The women munched on the greasy food for a minute before Audrey broached what was really on her mind.

"You remember Jules, don't you?" She sampled the spicy chicken. Her fingers were sticky with sauce.

"Yeah. The scraggly white boy you brought in here the other night." Renita sucked sauce from her fingers.

"I think I kind of like him." She looked up to gage Renita's response.

"So."

"I mean like, like. I really enjoy his company and when we're not together he's on my mind."

"You don't like him." Renita tossed a greasy napkin on the table. "You're just playin' that ole tired get back at the ex game."

"What the hell are you talking about?"

"You caught Jerry screwing a white girl. You've never gotten over it. Now all of a sudden, Jerry's back in you life and you've got a white guy so you can give him a dose of his own medicine."

"That's ridiculous!"

"Is it? You've never dated any white guys before and you criticized me and anybody else you saw dating somebody of a different race."

"That's not true." Audrey looked away. She felt like a hypocrite.

"It is. But be that as it may, what's the problem?"

"He wants to pursue a relationship, but I don't think I trust him."

"You think he's just trying to get some black drawers?" Renita sucked at sauce and munched on another piece of chicken.

"They're all after the panties. I guess I am kind of nervous about dealing with a white guy. We ain't all like you."

"What's that supposed to mean?"

"It means you've always preferred white men."

"It's not that, it's just that when I toured, I met all kinds of people. If there was an attraction, we just went with it. This society has us so brainwashed that we try to turn everything into some kind of race issue. We're constantly focusing on things that are unimportant. If Jules were black, you wouldn't be sitting here in this dive with me. You'd be at his house hoping he'd fall asleep first so he wouldn't hear you snore."

"But what if it turns out to be a serious thing? I don't know if I'm ready for that."

"Were you ready for all of those miserable brothers that's been rollin' up on you your whole life?"

"But I like black men."

"Audrey, why don't you be real. You're afraid of what people will say or think of you. You've had so many surface relationships that you wouldn't know something real if it bit you in the ass." She grabbed another napkin, wiped her mouth, then took a sip of water. "If you really want to see this guy, that doesn't make you any less black. Just go with it. If something deeper develops, good for you. It sure beats coming in here getting juiced up and going home alone. Or worse, going home to Emory Kimborough."

They both said amen and touched glasses to that.

*　　　*　　　*

Perspiration beaded his brow as he struggled to open his lids. RINGGG! There it was again. He had not been dreaming. It was the phone. The clock on the night stand said eleven o'clock. He had gone to bed so early that it seemed much later. He snatched the instrument from it's cradle, answering in a voice he hoped told the caller exactly how he felt about having his sleep disturbed.

"Jules, it's Audrey. I know it's late, but I was out and I took a chance that you hadn't had dinner."

"I'm at the Spice Rack and I'm having the chef here cook up a pile of food. I thought if you're up to it, I'd stop by and we'd have dinner."

Jules rubbed his face. He had to be dreaming. He looked at the clock again to see if time had changed since the last time he'd checked.

"So do you want dinner?" He hadn't responded and could hear her breathing on the other end. Waiting.

"Huh? Uh, yeah. That would be great." What the hell? He never would have expected her to call him at home. He ran his fingers through his hair and pulled the top sheet over his nudity.

"Are you still there?"

"Yeah. Let me give you directions."

—

Everything that she had on was white and to Jules, Audrey looked like an angel.

"I brought wine, cheese, crackers, roast chicken and potatoes, deep dish apple pie and ice cream. I hope you've got coffee. The real thing, not that instant crap."

She complimented him on the tastefully furnished apartment. The entertainment area, a wall filled with books, movies and CD's was incredible. The music collection was too overwhelming to make a selection. She picked up a disc that had been left on the end table.

"Do you mind?" She held up Sarah McLachlan's *Surfacing*. He shook his head. Audrey popped the CD into the box and smiled as the folksy guitar melody of *Building A Mystery* filled the room. She went to work unpacking the bags she'd brought, moving at lightening speed, and talking just as quickly. Jules tried to grab some of the bags to assist but she shooed him away. He spread a linen table cloth and place settings before them and watched in wonder as she bustled about, unwrapping packages and setting them on the coffee table.

They sat on the floor with their legs folded beneath them, eating the food as Audrey chatted about most everything that came to mind. She talked about the paintings and sculpture he displayed, the masculine color scheme of the room, she talked about Renita and the Spice Rack. She talked about the weather, and the promise of snow in the air. She talked about a couple of new clients that she courted. Jules contributed little. If his tacit demeanor bothered her, she didn't let on. She seemed to have no problem carrying the conversation. When their stomachs were so full that only gluttonous groans could escape her lips, Jules turned to her with serious eyes.

"Audrey, this was a very nice gesture. I've enjoyed myself more than I have in a while. I just have one question. What are you doing here?"

"I'm here having dinner with you."

"Why? You could have eaten at the Rack." *Surfacing* was going around for the second or third time. *Witness* beat behind them, the drums giving him courage to act on his passion.

He moved closer to her, so close he could smell the wine on her breath. Her chest moved up and down as if she were telling herself to breathe. She opened her mouth to speak but couldn't. He would deny himself no longer. His mouth was on hers. He could feel her beating heart. Her lips were soft and sweet. He spoke tender words of love, words of longing. She responded in kind.

His hands moved over her purposefully. He could feel her desperately trying to suppress the moan that escaped when his hand touched her bare skin. He undressed her quickly, looking at her deep brown skin, kissing her everywhere until she pulled him inside of her.

The sweetness became passion as they kissed, bit, licked hungrily, answering all of the questions time had posed since their first meeting. They laughed softly and murmured love poetry, rocking together until they exploded. Lying spent, chests heaving, locked in love's embrace, Jules smiled down at her. He held her face and kissed her a dozen times.

"Stay with me, Audrey." He brushed her hair away from her face and kissed her again.

"I don't want you to ever leave. I'm in love with you."

She looked into his eyes. Her response was interrupted by the sound of the key turning the lock. The door opened and the room suddenly flooded with light.

"What the fuck?"

Jules looked up at Cindy and felt his heart drop. She was looking down on them, naked on the living room rug. Expletives spewed hard and sharp as the Cindy grabbed anything she could lift and threw it at him. Jules pushed her toward the back of the apartment yelling at her to calm down. They went into the bedroom and the door slammed.

Chapter Forty

"What kind of shit are you trying to pull, Buchannon? Whatever problems you're having with your hired guns is just that, your problem. If this is some weak attempt to shake me down you can take it somewhere else. I don't play games."

Buc Buchannon had decided to have a showdown with A.J. Daniels. With his wife gone and his sons grown, he had little to lose. He'd grown weary of his relationship with Daniels. For a few coins, he'd become a puppet dancing a macabre dance as Daniels fiddled a grim tune. Their partnership spanned twenty years. In that time, Buchannon assisted in more firings, threats, and instances of extortion and murder than he could count. He knew that it was only a matter of time before he'd reap the harvest of the seed he'd sown.

A face-off with Daniels was inevitable. Coming here like this was forcing his hand. But he didn't care anymore. Everything that mattered to him was gone.

Buc's face poured sweat five minutes into the meeting. His neck was deep pink and wet as he stuck his finger in the collar of his shirt. It tightened around his throat like a noose.

He'd become the worse kind of boot licking lackey. He had long ago relinquished his self respect to the DA. For a time he could suck a drop of self respect from a bottle, but even the liquor stopped lying to him. His only out was to get out. He had to end this now.

"I don't know what to do about this guy, A.J. He has threatened to expose the whole thing. We've been dealing with Masterson from the start and he knows everything. We used him to get rid of Chief Kenneth Tyree and you know what would happen if that got out. Masterson has so much shit on us we would never see the light of day."

"Masterson doesn't have shit on me. I've never even met the man. I believe he's someone you conjured up to extort money from me. Whatever it is you're trying to sell I'm not buying. This meeting is over."

"I need your help A.J. Ever since the job on Hurley this guy has been putting heat on my ass."

Buchannon detected the glint of suspicion in Daniels' eyes. If he couldn't get him to implicate himself, he was doomed. A.J. Daniels didn't get to where he was by being stupid. He turned an icy gaze on the sweaty cop.

"This meeting is over." The words were almost inaudible. Daniels turned to face the view of the city. Buc nodded to the man's back, fumbled the door open and made his exit. With labored breath he made his way to the car. He sat for several minutes before he felt composed enough to drive.

He drove through several communities until he reached his old neighborhood and an alleyway near a street where he played as a boy. This section of town was still just as poor as when he was a child. The kids who ran and played in the street now were black. But when he looked at their faces, he saw the same look that him and his friends wore many years ago. The smiles were happy, reflecting days of laughter and innocence. Their eyes held hope, promise and the idealistic dreams that filled their hearts and heads.

Looking at his face in the rearview mirror, he found it increasingly difficult to accept the coward who looked back at him and the boy who'd always wanted to be a cop were one and the same. When had this intruder stepped in and taken the soul of little Bucky Buchannon?

He exited the car and retrieved a box from the trunk before heading for a run down apartment building. He maintained this cheap apartment for conducting some of the seedier aspects of his business affairs.

The apartment was complete with all the latest in office technology. He reached inside the pocket of his sport jacket and pulled out the voice activated recorder and listened to what transpired between himself and A.J. Daniels. He'd placed one of the miniature devices in each pocket before meeting with the DA. He had everything he needed to duplicate the tapes.

He considered making enough copies to send to all of the news stations, the radio, and newspapers, but he had no way of knowing which of the outlets wasn't in the pocket of Daniels. He didn't know if this would yield the results he wanted, but he had to take the chance that someone out there would be interested in the truth.

It took him several hours to make the duplications. He typed a letter giving names, dates, and details of every bloody assignment he'd done for Daniels over the years. He created labels, prepared the envelops for mailing and placed one of the documents, along with one of the tapes, into an envelope to give to Dava Storm. He wrote a brief note to his mistress with instructions on how to handle the enclosures.

Once finished, he collected his work materials and stored them in their designated places leaving the room neat and clean. He closed the door on his way out, taking the bag containing the contents of his last attempt to perform his duty as a police officer. Buchannon got in his car and headed for the home of Dava Storm.

Chapter Forty-One

The door to Redlands was open that evening, spilling the throng of waiting patrons and the aroma of the best soul food in town into the street. Jules was running behind schedule and hoped he hadn't kept Ed Dixon waiting too long. The two had developed a friendship in the wake of the trial and spoke often when they saw each other around the apartment building or at the offices on Saxon Boulevard. But this was the first time Ed wanted to meet away from their usual familiar surroundings.

There was a briskness in the evening air. The glass windows and the door steamed opaque not allowing Jules to see if his friend was inside or not. He stood patiently outside with the others. Their appetites whetted by the smell of fried chicken and peach cobbler. The aroma snaked its way through the crowd, holding them hostage in eager anticipation of sitting before heaping plates of the delicious fixings.

It took a few minutes for Jules to make his way inside the restaurant. Ed Dixon sat in the corner of the room waving to the lawyer, motioning him over. He was polishing off the last piece of cornbread from a basket that sat in the middle of the table.

"Sorry I'm late." Jules said grabbing a menu.

"Rough morning? Or is it the aftermath of a rough night?"

"You don't know the half of it. I've been off balance all day."

"The little lady keepin' you going, huh?" Ed smirked.

"Excuse me?"

"Audrey Wilson. You seein' her, ain't cha?"

"We're uh, just friends." Embarrassment colored his face.

"My ass. She won't give it up, huh?" Ed sucked at food trapped between his teeth. "Don't sweat it man, she likes you. I can tell. That's a fine woman. Real nice, and real smart."

Jules nodded, still embarrassed. He wished he could talk to Ed about last night but it was still too painful. He felt like the happiest man alive when she appeared at his door. After wishing for her and hoping that she felt the same way, they were finally together. His heart swelled and grew tender thinking of her.

He couldn't believe that Cindy had picked that moment to come over. He didn't know she still had a key. He knew how the whole thing must have looked to Audrey. When he opened the bedroom door to drag Cindy and her shit out of his apartment and his life, he wasn't surprised to find Audrey gone.

A surly waitress with straight greasy hair and soft casts on each arm, came over and wrote their orders on a small pink pad and left.

"What's up with Suzy Scissorhoands?" Jules asked when he was certain the woman was out of earshot.

Ed shrugged before gulping from the large glass of ice water until it was empty. The waitress returned with a pot of coffee.

"May I have another glass of water please?" Ed asked. The woman let out an exasperated sigh as she filled the glass without looking at him.

"Can I get you some coffee, sir?" She smiled at Jules, bending the pot in his direction.

"Yes, thank you."

She filled the cup with the steamy liquid and was turning to go when Ed called her back.

"Uh, excuse me, Miss? Can I get a cup of coffee too, please?"

Suzy pressed her lips together making a loud smacking sound before returning with the pot and pouring a cup for Ed. The two men sipped from their cups and took in the early evening crowd. Jules grimaced as

Ed slathered a dollop of butter onto another square of bread before popping it into his mouth.

"Things are going real well with the buildings." He said when he'd finished chewing. "It's been very profitable so far. The little maintenance that's required is next to nil. Thanks for all of your help getting me started."

"I really didn't do that much. Besides, my ten percent is all the thanks I need."

They both smiled, returning their attention to the hot buttered bread.

"Have you heard from Ellise?"

Ed shook his head, his expression clouded.

"Don't worry Ed, and don't give up the faith. That's got to be a major consideration for her. Not to mention what it would mean to your son. But it'll happen."

"I hope so Jules. I want nothing more than to make things right by them."

"What else is going on?" Jules changed the subject.

"Let me run something by you. Lately I've been thinking a lot about the school and my last day there. I'd played that entire day over in my mind so many times that I thought I had covered everything. But recently I remembered something. This whole thing has been such a nightmare that I'd almost convinced myself I'd dreamed it. I don't believe Mr. Franklin killed that girl. He did a lotta bad things, screwing around with students and coming down on me for things I didn't do, but I think they got the wrong person. Believe me, I know what that's like. I wouldn't wish it on a dog."

The waitress was back. She glared at Ed and sat a plate full of meat loaf, black-eyed peas, collard greens, and macaroni and cheese before him with enough force to make the peas jump. A plate of fried chicken, potato salad, corn on the cob and baked beans was placed in front of Jules. Another basket of bread was positioned between them.

The waitress refilled their water glasses before her thick, nylon clad thighs swished to another table.

"You gonna tell me what the deal is with you and that waitress or what? What'd you do Ed, promise to call her the next day and didn't do it?"

"No, worse than that." Ed worked his tongue around a mouth full of food.

"She'd been trying to get with me for the longest but every time I come in here I kind of ignore her. Lately when I come in here I get the funny business."

"Aren't you afraid she might give you the Miss Celie Special?"

"The what?"

"You saw *The Color Purple*?" Ed nodded. "Remember when the asshole stepfather came to visit and she spit in his water or maybe it was lemonade? Ole' Suzy might do you the same way."

"I think it was lemonade. I never touch the stuff." Ed continued to eat.

Jules laughed and shook his head. They dove into the plates, each eating nearly all of their food before continuing the conversation.

"So who do you think killed Jackie Daniels?" Jules sopped baked bean juice with a piece of bread.

"I just don't remember hearing anything about this when the police were questioning people. I mean, wouldn't they want to talk to everyone who visited the school that afternoon?" Ed queried.

"I would think so." Jules sat over his plate completely immersed in his friend's description of events the day of the murder. His story made perfect sense. He digested this revelation as he ingested the remainder of the meal. This development was certainly worth further investigation.

"That's very interesting. I don't think anyone even looked at that before." He swallowed the last of the beans.

"You know what we have to do don't you? First we have to order two peach cobbler a la modes, then we need to go see Rob Hollingsworth at police headquarters."

*　　　*　　　*

"Mr. Dreyfus, Mr. Dixon. What can I do for you?" Rob Hollingsworth shook hands with the visitors. He bent his lanky frame to a seated position on the corner of the desk.

"We have some information in the Daniels case." Ed Dixon offered. Rob looked completely disinterested.

"I know it's late to be coming to you with this, but I just started remembering things that happened that day that I'd totally forgotten."

"The case is closed." Rob replied. "They're not going to reopen it based on something that popped into your head. Unless you have concrete proof of something of a relevant nature." He posed the statement as a question.

"I thought the case was currently under appeal. Are you telling me Franklin's lawyer isn't appealing his conviction?" Jules was incredulous. He would never let a client of his waste away in a cell without pursuing every angle.

"I can't answer that," Rob was saying. "But from the departments point of view, it's a done deal."

"But what about the evidence that couldn't be tied to Franklin? Aren't you at least curious as to who that might belong to?"

The detective watched them both for a minute before offering them chairs. Detective Judy Manning occupied the desk that used to belong to Jake Hurley. She eyed the duo curiously, letting her new partner feel them out. She now seemed less engrossed in her paperwork. Her eyes wandered from the file on her desk to the two civilians.

"All right, what have you got?" Rob opened a drawer. "Do you mind if I tape this?"

Jules looked over at Ed who shook his head. Rob pushed the record button and Ed repeated what he'd told Jules at the restaurant.

"It was around four fifteen, maybe earlier. I was out back cleaning up the recreation field. Parking for the faculty and administration is nearby and I could see people getting into their cars and leaving for the day.

"I was power washing a section of the stairs. Them young bastards had spilled soda, urinated, put a bunch of graffiti and Lord knows what else out there. I saw Mrs. Franklin heading for the Admin. Building. I didn't think anything of it at the time, I mean, her old man is the headmaster and all. I went back to work. I remember seeing her leave about thirty minutes later."

"Can you describe her demeanor?" Rob and his partner were intrigued.

"I didn't notice anything. She just got into her car and drove away."

The detectives looked at him and then each other.

"That's what I remember. I guess it sounds trivial, but she was there. I'm sorry I didn't think of it sooner. When I did I didn't say anything for a while because I thought surely Franklin's wife would have been questioned since he admitted messing around with Miss Daniels." Now it was Ed's turn to pose a statement like a question. Rob looked away.

"Wanting to avenge her husband's infidelity is certainly motive for murder." Jules searched Rob's face for a sign of concurrence that he didn't find.

"Mr. Dixon. Mr. Dreyfus. Thank you for coming in." Rob rose and clicked off the machine.

"We appreciate the information, especially in light of everything that you went through. It must have taken a lot for you to come here today."

Ed Dixon accepted this as about as close as the police would come to apologizing to him for his unjust confinement.

"Is there anything you can do?" Jules rose, his eyes level with the detectives.

"You're the attorney Mr. Dreyfus. You know how these things go. I'll have to take this to the Chief. It'll end up on the DA's desk. I can't speculate on what will happen from there. I'll do all I can and we'll see what develops."

Chapter Forty-Two

Althea Franklin sat on the sofa thumbing through the catalog she'd picked up at a local market. She hadn't realized how much the threads of her life were interwoven with James and his position until all of the trouble began.

Once his connection with that Daniels woman was made public, Althea's life began to unravel. Her telephone calls to friends were not returned. Her name was removed from lists of organizations which she had supported for years.

She found herself being snubbed at restaurants by the help as well as by the patrons. Their heads went together, whispering surreptitiously, eyeing her all the while. It was as if overnight she'd gone from privileged to pariah, noted to notorious. Why were they treating her like this? After all, it was James who was the guilty one. He had been the transgressor, why should the penance be hers?

She even detected a hint of malevolence from the real estate agent she'd invited over to help her sell the house.

"Well," the woman looked over the tortoise shell rims of her glasses. "I'm not sure if I can help you sell this...house." She sat on the edge of the settee as if fearing the gaudy fabric would contaminate her tailored suit.

"The market is very fickle. Most respectable people shy away from properties with a history such as this one. Now there are always those who for what ever reason, are drawn to this sort of thing. You just never know."

She squinted, moving her eyes around the room registering surprise at some of the things that she saw.

"No one wants to be stuck with a worthless piece of property that they can't get rid of. Not that your home isn't lovely. I find it very…original. Very interesting. But you know how some people are."

"Yeah, bitch," Althea thought. "I know exactly how some people are."

She'd already met with representatives from the other realty companies in town. Their responses had been similar, fraught with venom and insensitivity.

She hadn't considered how she would support herself while James was in prison. Their savings accounts had been greatly diminished by the trial. The small inheritance she'd received from her parents would only go so far. She would have to sell the house and get a job.

She tossed the magazine onto the floor and cursed. This was James' fault, she thought ruefully. Their lives were ruined due to his lack of control. And due to Jackie Daniels.

"That little slut had the nerve to get up in my face." Althea thought, reflecting on that day so many months ago. The meeting was the result of the call she had gotten from Jackie the night before. She was stunned that the girl would call her. The surprise at getting the call led her to authorize the meeting before she even realized what she was doing.

As their scheduled meeting time approached, she considered not going, but something in her wouldn't let her stay away. When she entered the building she spotted Jackie going down the stairs. She followed her. They met in the small utility room in the lower level of the school.

Her face burned red hot as she remembered the haughty girl telling her that she loved her husband and he loved her. She told her all of the filthy things they did all those nights and that they had spawned a child. According to her, James was ecstatic when she'd told him the news. He'd told her his wife was barren and had never been able to give him a child.

"You're a liar! There's no way my husband would ever have said that. You'll do or say anything to have your way. I'm not going for it and I'm not about to let a harlot like you destroy my marriage."

"Please! Give me a fucking break!" Jackie snorted. "Althea dear, your marriage is a sham. James has never been faithful to you. Everybody knows it. I wanted to meet with you because I wanted to ensure the divorce and the separation of property would go as smoothly as possible. We each have a certain position in the community. There's no need in turning this into something ugly."

"Bitch you must be crazy!" Was it true? Had James been unfaithful to her all along and everyone in town knew about it? Althea couldn't believe this was happening to her. Everyone thought she was a fool. For what other reason would this woman think she could approach her and expect her to graciously step aside so she could fuck her husband in the light of day?

"I knew you'd take it like that. I'm only trying to deal with this with a level of civility so that we each come away with our dignity intact. But at this point in your life I suppose it's a bit late to acquire qualities with which one was not bred."

"How dare you, you stupid little slut." That's when Althea hit her. Jackie put her hand to her face and smiled.

"I'm having his baby. He loves me and we're getting married. There's not a damned thing you can do about it."

The truth of her statement pierced Althea's heart. How many nights had she heard the whispered conversations, him professing his love to her? The tapes were confirmation that the party on the other end was Jackie Daniels. Her husband was leaving her for this little smart mouthed trollop.

As soon as she spoke the words, Althea knew that she wanted to hurt her. She wanted someone to feel the pain that had been heaped upon her, bearing down on her chest each time her husband was late, or lied, or was mean to her.

The girl moved close to her. She was speaking but Althea didn't remember what she said. She watched her full lips. They had pleasured her husband, touching, speaking, giving him what Althea could not.

Before Althea realized what she was doing, her hands were around the woman's throat. They scuffled. Jackie fought as best she could, but Althea was not only the stronger of the two but she had gotten a hold of Jackie first, getting a position of dominance in the fight and never letting go.

Her hand burned like fire as Jackie dug her nails into it, almost causing Althea to release her grip. But she was determined not to lose this fight. Determined to make her pay. She repositioned her hands around the girls throat, pressing until she no longer struggled. Her eyes were lifeless, her body sprawled upon the floor.

Althea's breathing was audible, sweat poured from her face to her neck. She pulled a towel from those strewn around the floor during the struggle. She mopped her face and neck before wiping it over the knob and doorjamb. She pulled a heavy bucket in front of the girl and spilled a huge tub of soiled towels on top of her.

Using the towel to hold the knob, she pulled the door shut. She stuffed the towel inside her jacket, took a deep breath and headed for the school parking lot.

* * *

The doorbell rang twice before she cracked it open. Sunshine burst into the foyer, brightening the space and the face of Althea Franklin. Recognizing the visitor, she opened the door and offered Rob Hollingsworth a glorious smile and entrée into her home.

"Detective Hollingsworth. Do come in."

Her eyes darted to the woman and two uniformed officers who accompanied him. She smiled graciously, inviting them in.

"It's wonderful having unexpected company. James never liked that, but to me it's like Christmas. Please come in."

"Mrs. Franklin, we need you to come downtown for questioning."

"Questioning? About what?" She straightened the bric-a-brac on an etagere.

"The Daniels case." Rob replied. She spun around to face him.

"Oh that. I thought you people had that thing wrapped up. Do you need more testimony from me? Is my husband up for some kind of appeal or something?"

"We'll discuss it downtown. We have a warrant, or if we need to resort to force…"

"A warrant? Nonsense. I'll come with you. That's not a problem at all. I am a law abiding citizen. I'll gladly do whatever you say."

The group walked the long stone path toward the street and the waiting patrol cars. Althea talked nonstop, marveling at everything along the way.

"It sure is a beautiful day. I should be preparing the ground for my spring garden, but I've been incredibly remiss in my household duties. Of course, the landscapers do all of the heavy stuff and keep the grass neat and beautiful, but the garden is my pride and joy. Did you know I won the Blooming Daffodil Award three years running? Mrs. Taft-Davies was absolutely green! She hired a fancy landscape designer who helped her win last year. I don't think she should have qualified since she used a professional. What do you think?"

She chattered endlessly. The uniformed officers were silent as they led her to the patrol car. Her pumps clicked down the stone path to the street, crunching dried leaves along the way.

Chapter Forty-Three

"You sure you don't want some help?"

"Naw, I'm okay." Audrey scarcely looked up. She had left her door open to let in some air while she packed. This was the second time Jules had dropped by. He seemed as uncomfortable as she at seeing each other for the first time since the incident at his place. She was moving out of her office that day. The business she and Bobby were planning was finally starting to gel. They were moving into a larger, less expensive space a few blocks down on Plum Street.

She kept filling cartons as Jules shifted from one foot to the other. He seemed sincerely sorry and she knew she should be more sensitive, but she just wasn't in the mood. She really liked him. Took all this time to relax her guard and he was living with another woman all along. That's what happens when she follows her heart, or in this case, her genitalia, and not her gut.

"Audrey, can I please talk to you?" He came in and closed the door. She tried to dissuade him by casting a vicious glare in his direction, but he wouldn't be deterred. A defeated sigh escaped her lips as he raised her chin and looked into her eyes.

"Cindy and I used to live together. We broke up months ago. I left messages at her mother's house for her to pick up her things. She's been in Europe and was just now coming over to get the stuff. I didn't know she had a key. What happened was humiliating for you. You certainly didn't deserve it and I'm sorry. I don't know what I can ever do to make it up to you."

"Hey, don't worry about it. I'm trying to finish up here, so if you don't mind..."

She heard the door close. An apt metaphor, she thought. She was so tired of opening the door to love only to have it closed in her face.

She'd concentrate on her business and forget about Jules and what they'd shared. The timing for her move couldn't be better. She'd turn over a whole new leaf. One that didn't include Jules Dreyfus.

Epilogue

"I love riding the bus, Mom."

"Are you still mad at me for taking you away from your friends?"

"No, I'm not mad."

He looked out the window as rundown shacks, dilapidated barns, and frozen, early winter fields sped into view and then away. He thought about the guys that he'd considered family and what a hard time they'd given him about leaving.

"What you mean you movin' to Rosemont, Ohio?" Buster's gaze a combination of disbelief and envy.

"Eribody know das a jive punk ass town." One of the other boys said.

"And Hapeville is the crown Jewel of the South?" Jooney responded.

"Rosemont cain't be no worse than this place."

"Why you goin' there?" Another boy asked curiously.

"Cause he a jive, punk ass bitch." Buster replied, pushing Jooney's shoulder so hard he nearly fell to the ground.

"My Moms is moving." Jooney jumped up quickly, embarrassed. "I gotta go with her. What I'm 'sposed to do, let her go by herself?" Jooney tried to keep the tremble out of his voice. He wanted to sound tough, but he was afraid he sounded like the mama's boy they always said he was. That's the reason he joined the Diablos. He was tired of being bullied around for not doing the things that the other kids did. If he belonged to The Family, he'd have everyone's respect.

He gritted his teeth, daring the tears to fall as he was jumped into the gang. He knew he'd made it when they tattooed the serpent onto the back of his left hand. His initiation was complete.

It had been he who poured the gasoline and lit the match to the homeless man they found sleeping under Poplar Bridge. The act reinforced his commitment to the group. It had surprised him how easy it was to kill. Once he imagined the bum was his good for nothing daddy who'd run off leaving him to take care of his mother, the heinous act wasn't difficult at all. That night a ceremony was held. He was rewarded for his unflinching bravery by gaining his first lightening bolt. It was etched on the back of his hand near the serpent's coiled form.

Until that night, they'd picked on him, called him 'Mama's Boy." With his elevated status, the harassment stopped but the handle stuck. Jooney spent every waking hour making a conscious effort to live a life contradictory to the moniker. He was known on the streets as the baddest kid in town.

So they all stood around him in wonderment. El Diablos flanked by Ella Diablos, their girlfriends. Feeling the ensuing tension, they'd stopped their suggestive dancing to TLC's *I'm Good At Being Bad*, which blasted so loud the boom box vibrated with the strain of supporting the sound.

"You tell your Moms that you're staying here." Buster ordered.

"I cain't do that man."

"Why not Mama's Boy?" the bigger boy laughed. The other boys responded with bogus laughter, too loud to be sincere.

They were nervous. Although sixteen year old Buster, at almost two hundred pounds and nearly six feet tall was their leader, they knew Jooney never showed fear. They knew he never backed away from a challenge.

"Go on, Mama's Boy. Take your little bitch ass home to your ole bitch ass mammy."

The statement had barely left his lips before Jooney was on him. The fight was brutal. Jooney tore into the big boy. Buster's hatred for Jooney was evident as he found himself losing the fight. He'd wanted to use this as an opportunity to divert the respect the group had for the fearless younger boy. But Jooney wouldn't back down.

One of the girl's tossed Buster a gun. There was a struggle. The gun went off and Buster lay on the ground, blood soaking his shirt, forming a pool on the ground beneath him.

The older boy survived the shooting. They told the police they were playing with a gun they found and it went off. No one was charged. Buster was hospitalized. Jooney knew as soon as he was out and well enough, there would be trouble. One of them had to die. It was the only way to an acceptable conclusion in their small violent world.

His mother had been surprised when he no longer resisted when she spoke to him about leaving Hapeburg. If he stayed there, he would break her heart and she was the only person who mattered to him.

"How much longer will it take us to get there?"

"It won't be much longer."

"Mom, I'm sorry for giving you such a hard time about moving. I didn't want to leave school and my friends."

"Those boys were not your friends, Jooney. They're a gang, criminals. They're loud and rude and ill-mannered. They may treat you nice and fulfill some need you should be getting at home. But they don't care a thing about you."

"I know it's been hard on you being raised without a father. But you've handled it well. You've been very mature in a lot of ways. But you're not a man, you're a boy. It was wrong of me to put that kind of responsibility on you. You handled it well, though." She put her arm around his shoulder and squeezed him to her. "I'm very proud of you and always have been. But I couldn't stay there and let the streets take you away from me. I want to give you every opportunity to be the best that you can be. I'll do whatever I can to raise you in a clean and decent way."

He looked away from her, ashamed of the things he had done and relieved they were leaving before she found out about them. What would she do if she discovered her son was just like them, a thug, a murderer?

"So you really didn't want to leave Hapeburg either, did you Ma?"

"Hapeburg is my home, Jooney. I've been there all my life. It's hard leaving your home. I can't complain about my life. It hasn't been bad. But some people haven't been so lucky. I've seen this town ruin people. Good people. I've seen many lives destroyed. I won't let that happen to you."

"What if Dad doesn't want me?"

"He wants you Jooney. He wants us both. He's the only man who ever has. I never told you that. I was just too stubborn and pride-filled to let him in. He hurt me once a long time ago. My pride wouldn't let me forgive him. Every time I looked at him I felt so hurt. The pain of what he did would flood in and I couldn't think straight. I wouldn't allow myself to forgive him."

"He tried to get in touch with you over the years, but I always blocked him. I didn't want you to know him and I wanted him to suffer for hurting me so bad. I was wrong for that Jooney. You deserved to have a father all these years and the reason you didn't was because of me." A pained, ragged breath escaped her lips. She cleared her throat and continued. "Good people make mistakes. What we have to try to do is learn from our errors and grow from the experience. I'm trying to make things right by you Jooney. And by your Daddy. Can you forgive me for using you to hurt him?"

Jooney couldn't answer. He grabbed his mother's hand and held it tight. He shook his head and looked outside. His breathing steamed the window, masking his reflection and the tears that rolled down his face.

* * *

"Hey Ed! Why don't you take a break man? I got sandwiches up here." Jules small blond head popped out of the seventh floor window. His voice boomed out on the otherwise quiet street.

"There's something coming on the news I think you might want to see."

"Ah ight, I'll be there in a few."

Ed gathered the paint cans, brushes, and rags. Wiping his hands as he opened the door, he deposited his work materials inside the closet at the foot of the stairs. He walked over to the elevator and rode it upstairs to Jules' office.

"That call was right on time man. What's going on at Audrey's?"

"She's moving today."

"Oh, that's right." He noticed his friend's hang dog look and didn't know whether to pry, but then thought, "What the hell?"

"What's going on with you two?"

"Nothing man. Nothing at all. We finally got together the other night and my ex barged in on us. She showed up to get her things. I don't want to go into details, but it was a bad situation Ed."

"You love Audrey, don't you?"

"Yeah." Jules looked at Ed, then away.

"Don't give up then. Buy her flowers everyday. Call her. See her. Do whatever it takes to make her realize you're for real."

Jules looked unsure.

"Maybe you're right. At this point, what do I have to lose?"

He touched the mute button on the remote so they could listen to the news while they ate. They had reported new developments during the break and he wanted Ed to hear the latest developments in the Daniels case.

"In a startling turn of events, Althea Franklin, wife of James Franklin, former Headmaster at the Academy was indicted today in the murder of Jackie Daniels. The case exploded into the news again recently when DNA proved that some of the evidence found at the scene of the crime matched samples taken from Mrs. Franklin.

"This case has been baffling from the start with roller coaster-like twists and turns unfolding since the body of Academy teacher and daughter of District Attorney A.J. Daniels, Jacqueline, was found over a year ago.

"For those who have been following this case from the start, you will remember that the school janitor, Ed Dixon was accused of the crime by the school's Headmaster, James Franklin. In the early stages of the initial investigation, one of the chief investigators in the case, Jake Hurley was killed in a hit and run accident. It was later discovered that he and DA Daniels wife were having an adulterous affair. Mrs. Daniels took her own life, leaving a note professing her love to the slain detective. The note also said some damaging things about A.J. Daniels, implying Hurley's death was not an accident and that Daniels was involved."

"Meanwhile, telephone records led the police to suspect Academy Headmaster, James Franklin of having an intimate relationship with Jackie Daniels. He was brought in for questioning and Dixon was released. Evidence showed Franklin was the father of Miss Daniels unborn child. Franklin was tried and convicted based largely on speculation and testimony about alleged misconduct at the school.

"The case took another turn when Police Chief Buc Buchannon took his own life and left behind damaging information implementing District Attorney Daniels in crimes ranging from money laundering to murder. An investigation is currently underway checking the validity of the allegations.

"There will be a press conference at noon by acting police chief Robert Hollingsworth who is expected to confirm a reported twenty count indictment of Mrs. Franklin. Stay tuned to Action Two News for the latest in…"

"Wow! Can you imagine Franklin's wife killing that teacher?" Jules wiped mayonnaise from his mouth with a paper napkin.

"What about all that other stuff? All those alleged murders that the DA contracted, the theft and everything. What makes people do those kinds of things?" Ed shook his head in wonder.

"I think it's disgusting." Jules replied. His disgust didn't keep him from taking a huge bite of ham and Swiss.

"It's amazing what some people would do for money and power. I think poor Mrs. Franklin just snapped. I remember seeing her from time to time at the school." Ed said. "I never would have thought her capable of killing somebody."

"She's not exactly a spring chicken. It's difficult for a woman of a certain age, all by herself. She stood to lose a lot when her husband left her." Jules surmised.

"She could have found somebody new. She's a good looking woman. Look at how she's posing for the cameras like she's at a George Hurrell portrait shooting instead of going off to jail."

"Or Nora Desmond ready for her close-up. She looks pretty good though." Jules said. "And she's dressed to kill."

Ed balled up the waxed paper from his lunch and threw it at Jules. They volleyed the make shift ball back and forth making a game of it. Their recreation was interrupted by a knock at the door. Jules batted the paper into the wastebasket as he moved to answer it.

"May I help you?" The woman was brown and petite. The boy standing behind her was lanky, the spitting image of his dad.

"I'm looking for Ed Dixon."

Jules stepped aside, letting the callers into the room.

Through tears, Ed saw the familiar face lined by more than ten years of pain and worry. But lovely still. He looked into the eyes, dark encircled from sleepless nights. But still bright. The tiny frame, more roundness on the hips. But still beautiful. He saw in her eyes, distance and closeness, trust and not. Still Ellise.

He ran to her, lifting her as he sobbed like a dying man just given a second chance at life. He grabbed Jooney and the three of them cried together until they laughed.

Ed Dixon let out a relieved sigh. More than a decade of longing, the deep pain of wanting and not having. He'd go through that hell a thousand times more for the glimpse of heaven he saw in their eyes.

*   *   *

Audrey felt his warm gaze even before she looked up. The hopeful gleam in his eyes was so pitiful she couldn't help but smile.

"Don't you ever quit?"

"No, I never do." Jules walked over and started putting books into an open carton.

"I hear they're going to knock out some walls so you can have the whole floor. Things must be really looking up for you."

"Yeah, it's going okay. I'm expanding the staff and considering bringing in a law student."

A couple of minutes passed. He looked around for ways to busy himself. She knew she shouldn't make it so hard on him, but a side of her enjoyed watching his discomfort. When he looked at her and spoke again, he almost caught her smiling.

"Did Ed ever mention Ellise and his son to you?"

"Yeah, they're in Alabama or Mississippi or somewhere."

"Not anymore they're not. They're in my office. It looks like they'll finally be reconciling."

"Oh, that's great! I'm so happy for Ed. He's a great guy."

"He's amazing. He never gave up." Jules touched her hand. "Neither will I, Audrey."

She looked up from the box she was loading. She liked his determination. But did he have enough resolve for the two of them? Audrey didn't know, but she knew she would enjoy finding out.

Printed in the United States
1272200003B/282